To my beloved Golden Retriever, Pickles, my constant companion for every book I wrote. He listened patiently to me reading my manuscript aloud and would nudge my arm when it was time to take a break. Thank you for all the fun, mischief and love.

NEXT
GIRL
MISSING

BOOKS BY L.A. LARKIN

L.A. LARKIN

NEXT
GIRL
MISSING

bookouture

Published by Bookouture in 2023

An imprint of Storyfire Ltd.
Carmelite House
50 Victoria Embankment
London EC4Y 0DZ

www.bookouture.com

ISBN: 978-1-80314-622-5
eBook ISBN: 978-1-80314-621-8

ONE

It looked just like a genuine Franklin Police Department poster. He had mirrored the style perfectly: the word MISSING was at the top in red caps on a black background, Anna's photo was on the right, and her physical description was on the left.

If you have information about Anna Moorehouse, call Franklin Police Dept.

He'd even included the Franklin PD phone number.

In the photo, Anna looked younger than her twelve years, and it was her innocence that had drawn him to her. Her brown eyes looked shyly at the camera, her black hair neatly braided, her lips parted in a nervous smile revealing crooked teeth that would need braces. It was a school photo—so easy to get hold of without anyone knowing. He had then listed her height, weight, build, eye and hair color, and race—African American—as well as the date and time she'd gone missing.

To be exact, the date and time Anna *would* go missing.

His eyes lingered on the last line—the location: Fifth and

Park Street—then he ran a gloved palm over the poster he had just taped to the glass of the bus shelter.

It was late afternoon and already dark. A biting wind whipped past the shelter, and the chilling rain had started turning to sleet. People didn't dawdle; they had their heads down as they raced to a warmer destination. Parents had collected their kids from school a while ago, and it was too early for office workers to be heading home. A mom clutching a little boy's hand hurried past him, moaning that she had forgotten to buy milk. A student loped toward the bus shelter, eyes focused on his cell phone, earbuds blocking out any other sound.

The man glanced behind him into Pioneer Park, which was all shadows, save for the path winding up the hill. Only dog owners were crazy enough to walk there in such freezing temperatures, and they didn't hang around for long.

A streetlight bathed one end of the three-sided glass bus shelter in a weak yellow glow. He doubted that his poster would be noticed until daylight, by which time he would be long gone, and he was confident that nobody was paying him any attention. He was, after all, in a winter jacket, the hood pulled up to hide his face, and there were no security cameras in this mostly residential area. He looked up and down the street, which was the main access route to downtown from the hilly suburbs of Pioneer and Lennox. The traffic zipped by, windows fogged, mushy ice splashing beneath the tires.

The 443 bus was due in five minutes. It was time to return to his car and wait.

Why was it, Anna wondered, that everyone believed Caroline's lies? Was it because she was pretty and white, and Anna was plain and black? Caroline's blue eyes had looked so guiltless when she'd told the teacher, Mrs. Roberts, that she hadn't stolen

Anna's lunch and she didn't know why Anna would say such a mean thing. Then Caroline had looked at Anna, then at her Walmart daypack—which she'd kicked around the playground earlier—with such pity in her eyes that Anna had begun to doubt her own memory.

"Why do you say such cruel things?" Caroline asked, sniffing back a tear.

She could even fake tears. Anna's were for real.

"I'm not cruel!" Anna retorted. "She's cruel. She always takes my lunch."

"You dropped it, silly."

"Anna Moorehouse," Mrs. Roberts said, "I've spoken to a number of girls about this, and they all say you dropped your lunch and then tried to blame Caroline. I'm very disappointed in you."

For the rest of the afternoon, Anna managed to avoid Caroline by hiding in the washroom. She almost made it out of the school gates without incident, except her legs and arms were so long and clumsy that she tripped over her own feet. Caroline and her gang laughed and laughed, calling out *dummy* and *lying bitch*. Stupidly, Anna cried, which made them laugh even more. So instead of taking the school bus, Anna started walking home: she couldn't bear the thought of Caroline's snide remarks.

It was freezing cold, and sleet blew in her face. Anna's hair was soaked, and her shoes were sodden because the slushy ice was deep. She had another block to walk before she arrived at the apartment complex where she lived with her mom and dad. Her dad, a firefighter, wouldn't be home tonight; he was working nights. Her mom usually arrived home at seven.

Anna's stomach rumbled—she hadn't eaten since breakfast. When she got home, she'd chew on some cookies to stave off the pangs until her mom cooked dinner.

Ahead was the bus stop where she would have got off the

bus if she'd taken it. She guessed that Caroline was home by now, probably watching videos on her phone, pretending to do homework that Anna knew that she had already bullied Stacy Green into doing for her. Everyone was afraid of Caroline.

Anna glanced into the park, which she found creepy at night. A week ago, a woman had been mugged there. That had freaked out Anna's mom, Mary, who had told her never to go there at night.

As she walked toward the bus shelter, she noticed a missing-person poster. She drew closer, curious, but car headlamps turned the shelter's glass into mirrors, reflecting searing light and blinding her momentarily. The car pulled up and the engine ticked over. It was a weird place for a car to stop, but it wasn't her business, and she was cold and wanted to get home. She kept walking.

"Anna, it's me," a man called out. "Your mom's had an accident."

Anna whirled around. Disoriented by the glare of the head-lamps, she wasn't sure where the voice had come from. Was it the car?

"Anna! Over here! Mary asked me to find you."

The car's passenger window was down, but she couldn't see who was inside, and the rear windows must've been tinted because they appeared solid black. Her mom had drilled into her to never take a ride with a stranger. If she was ever afraid, her mom said, go to a house or a shop, and ask them to call 911. Anna didn't have a cell phone. Her parents said it was too much money. So Anna stayed close to the bus shelter's side wall and peered nervously at the car window.

"Who are you?" she called, her teeth chattering with the cold.

"I'm a friend of your mom's. She wants me to drive you to the hospital. Her injuries are real bad."

A rush of panic had Anna wringing the ends of her woolen

scarf until it became a tight spiral. She couldn't see the man's face, but his voice sounded kindly.

"What happened to her?" Anna asked, taking a step closer.

"She hit her head. Hurry. Get in. I'll take you to the hospital."

Her mom worked at the shipyard. She was a personal assistant. She wasn't supposed to go anywhere dangerous.

"I... I don't know you."

"Sure you do!"

He held something close to the gap in the window. She stepped forward to look at it.

"I've never seen you before. Where's my dad?"

"He's with her. Why don't you call him? Here." A hand clutching a phone reached toward the open window.

Anna wanted to cry. She didn't know what to do. She fidgeted from foot to foot and felt hot tears on her cold cheeks.

"Anna, please hurry. Your mom needs you. You can phone your dad on the way."

Anna shuffled closer to the car and reached out to take the phone. She could see the car's dashboard with its blinking lights and just make out the man she was talking to.

As her finger brushed against the phone, he pulled it back. "Hop in. You can call him while I drive."

The door clicked open. Should she run to Auntie Ruby's house? Should she go with this guy? Why wasn't Dad here?

The man's phone rang. The ringtone was a funny sound, like a merry-go-round.

"Hello, yes. Geoff. How is Mary doing?"

The man was talking to her dad. He beckoned for her to get in the car. Wafting on the warm car air was the smell of furniture polish, like the wax her mom used on the antique table she'd inherited from Grandma.

"Dad!" Anna called, pushing her head through the open window.

"She's gotten worse?" the driver said to her dad. "I'm with Anna now. We'll be there in twenty."

Anna pulled her head out then slid into the leather passenger seat. "Please can I talk to my dad?"

"There's no time." He pocketed his cell.

The window began closing, and there was a clunk as the doors locked. The car sped off and into the late afternoon traffic.

"Mister, you're taking me to the hospital, right?"

"It's okay, Anna—you've nothing to fear. It will be over soon."

A weight like a heavy stone hit her stomach. The man was creepy. "I want to get out." She tugged at her door handle. The door stayed locked.

"Child locks," he said. "For your own safety."

"I want my mommy," Anna wailed, tears welling in her eyes.

He smiled at her. "Did you like my poster?"

TWO

MAY 6, 2015

The apartment complex where Anna Moorehouse's mother lived had been hailed by Mayor Xavier McAllister as a shining example of the new low-income homes the city was building in the outer suburbs. Since then, Franklin's infamous rain and snow had dulled the ten-story building's shiny exterior paintwork, the elevators were frequently broken, and Mary Moorehouse's living-room wall was blistering with damp. Forty-five-year-old Sally Fairburn had done her best to persuade the property managers to fix the problems. When she'd worked as a victim support advocate with the district attorney's office, Sally had held some sway in these situations. But, burned out, she'd taken early retirement and, therefore, the property manager wasn't interested in her complaints. In his view, Sally was an interfering do-gooder who should mind her own damn business.

Sally sat on a sagging sofa opposite Mary: a broken woman who was afraid to step outside her apartment. Before Mary's daughter was taken by the Poster Killer, her brown skin had been flawless, her smile radiant, and she'd loved her job as a personal assistant. These days, Mary had gone prematurely gray, and she suffered from eczema around her hairline and elbows in particular, which stemmed from her anxiety disorder.

In Sally's three years as a cop and twenty-two years as a victim's advocate, the unsolved Poster Killer investigation was the one case she couldn't let go. Six girls were taken, only one body was found, and the serial killer had not been caught.

Sally hadn't been involved in the manhunt. Her skill lay in comforting the victims' families, and even though she was officially retired now, she still met regularly with the victims' families, all of whose lives had changed irrevocably as a result of the ordeal. Sally felt they were her family too; she grieved with them and did her best to help them move on because she understood their loss all too well. Every time she visited a parent or sibling of the missing girls, it was a painful reminder that she, too, had lost a child. In the midst of the Poster Killer abductions, which spanned 2010 and 2011, Zelda, Sally's thirteen-year-old, had taken her own life, and the question of why she did it reverberated in Sally's head day and night.

Sally had left her job because she too was broken, and she couldn't heal. As her shrink put it, all the time Sally had been giving support to others, she'd ignored her own mental and emotional wellbeing, which was in tatters. So Sally had taken a reduced early retirement pension and moved to the forest suburb of Pioneer Heights, some twenty miles from the city center.

Moving house was part of the healing process. When Sally was up to it, she'd look around for a part-time role that involved less stress than her previous occupation. Her fourteen-year-old son, Paul, was her hope and joy, even though he spent most of his time in his room, and when he did come out, he blamed her for pretty much everything. But Sally would always make time for Mary, and the other parents whose lives had been torn apart by their daughters' abductions.

"What you doing in those running pants, hon?" Mary

asked. "Your legs look like two pieces of licorice. And that vest! It's freezing out there!"

"When I run I get pretty hot." And Mary's apartment was always overheated, perhaps to compensate for the damp walls. "Sorry about the gear. I got delayed and didn't have time to change."

Sally jogged every weekday morning, accompanied by her friend Margie Clay, whom she'd known since elementary school.

"You heard from that reprobate husband of yours?"

"Ex-husband and no."

"Maybe it's a good thing. He was no good."

Sally didn't want to talk about Scott. It brought back too many painful memories. "We ran a different route this morning. By the river. And you won't believe what we saw?"

"I don't know. Why don't you tell me?"

"A stag. He was crossing the river. Beautiful animal."

"Well, bless me, how wonderful."

"Hey, how about I drive you there? We can park real close. Maybe the stag's still around."

Mary shook her head. "You know I can't do that. What if Anna calls and I'm not here?"

It was highly unlikely that Anna was alive, but Sally had no intention of taking away the one thing that Mary had left—her hope.

"How about I get you a cell phone and we divert the land-line calls to your cell. That way, Anna can always reach you, even if she dials your home number."

Sally had suggested this idea many times, and each time Mary rejected it.

"It's okay, hon. I'm happy to wait here for her call."

Mary had been waiting five years for her daughter to contact her.

She looked down at her cup of tea, which she hadn't

touched. "I don't know why you keep coming to see me, Sally. There's a new girl who visits." She was talking about Sally's replacement. "She's not much older than Anna. What would she know about life?"

Mary's gaze lifted and connected with Sally's. There was a second or two of brightness in the grieving mother's eyes. "Anna's eighteen today. It's her birthday. My little girl's all grown up."

"I know it's her birthday," Sally said, tears welling up in her eyes. Birthdays and Christmases were the worst. On special occasions like these, Sally behaved exactly as she would if Zelda were alive. She always bought her daughter a present, which she wrapped and took to her daughter's graveside. In the same way, Sally honored Anna's birthday. "I made a cake." On the floor was a hemp shopping bag. Sally took out the plastic cake carrier and handed it to Mary. "And brought candles."

Mary peered through the transparent lid at the chocolate cake that had Anna's name on it in white frosting. "Oh my, that's perfect. Anna loves chocolate."

"Shall I light the candles?"

"I'll keep it for later on. Anna might come home, then we can have it together."

Sally left the cake on the kitchen counter, knowing it would sit there for a week, uneaten, and Sally would have to throw it in the trash on her next visit. This happened every year.

On her way back into Mary's living room, Sally studied a row of framed photos of Anna on the sideboard, taken at various stages of the girl's short life. Happy, treasured memories. Anna's father had died fighting a warehouse fire only months after Anna's disappearance.

"Such lovely photos," Sally said.

Mary had the TV on and was channel-hopping. "Oh look, it's a *The Bold and the Beautiful* repeat."

Sally had no interest in the series, but she watched the

episode with Mary, just so Mary had company. About halfway through, Sally's cell rang, a landline number she didn't recognize. She answered.

"Is that Sally Fairburn?" Gravelly, spoken like an accusation.

"Yes, who is this?"

"You haven't changed your number. Good. I want you to come and see me."

Sally tried to place the voice and couldn't. "Who are you?" she asked with growing unease.

The man snorted. "How many people do you know in Walla Walla?"

The state penitentiary. Walla Walla held some of the state's worst male offenders—serial killers, rapists, pedophiles, crime lords. Sally's body spasmed with fear, and her hand knocked the tea mug off the chair's arm. It rolled across the dusty carpet, spilling its contents. The clatter caused Mary to look away from the TV.

Why would a maximum-security prisoner call her? Sure, in her career she had crossed paths with a number of Walla Walla inmates. Usually, it had been during court cases, when Sally sat with the victims' families. On the odd occasion, she and a victim had met with the perpetrator of the crime at Walla Walla, as part of a program in which the assailant apologized for what they had done. One such inmate was a man who'd murdered his wife's lover. One was a rapist. The last one, a vile man who'd been locked up for child prostitution and sex trafficking, had used the situation to further torment his victim. His name was Theo Durrant, and Sally would never forget how he'd gloated at the anguish he'd caused in that meeting.

It couldn't be him, could it?

It was like a dark cloud had blocked out the sun, and she felt gooseflesh rise all over her skin. Durrant was serving a life sentence but had escaped prosecution for the one crime that

Franklin PD's homicide detectives were convinced he was guilty of—the abduction, rape, and murder of the six girls attributed to the Poster Killer.

"Theo Durrant?" Her voice quaked.

Mary wriggled out of her armchair, crossed to the sofa where Sally sat, and gave her a questioning frown. Mary knew the name. He had been the prime suspect.

"The one and only," said Durrant. "Now listen, you're going to visit me tomorrow. I've put your name down on the list. It's approved."

Sally didn't doubt that Durrant had the power to control the prison visitors' list. The word was that not only did he control some of the prison guards, he also ran his criminal cartel from his cell, with the help of his son, Christos, who so far had avoided arrest.

"You've got the wrong person."

"Don't question me. Just do as I say."

"I... I don't understand. Why?"

"This ain't an official visit. It's you and me having a chat, like old friends."

The thought of being Durrant's friend made her nauseous.

"I... really can't." Desperation gripped her by the throat, and her voice became a whisper.

"Listen to me," said Durrant. "I know who the Poster Killer is. You want the families to know the truth? Come here at ten-fifteen tomorrow. Don't be late."

"I... I can't help you."

Another snort, or perhaps it was a laugh? "Yes you can, and you will. I tell you what you want to know, you give me something in return."

Theo Durrant had means, opportunity, and motive for the abduction of the six missing girls. He was even caught on CCTV purchasing cigarettes at a corner store near the middle school Stacy Green had attended, just ten minutes before her abduction.

"Detective Clarke, he's the one you should be talking to. Please." Sally sounded shrill. She felt like a fish on the end of Durrant's line, and she was struggling helplessly to free herself.

Mary took Sally's hand and mouthed, "What's he saying?"

"No police, you hear me?" Durrant said. "Just you. Tomorrow at ten-fifteen. Be there." Then he was gone.

A choking sound. Had she made that noise? She couldn't breathe. She drew a trembling hand to her throat.

"What did he say?" Mary repeated.

Sally couldn't catch enough breath. This couldn't be happening. She wasn't a cop. "How did he get my number?"

"Sally, you're scaring me, honey."

Durrant was pure evil. Only one fifteen-year-old girl had managed to escape Durrant's brothel where she'd been imprisoned. She had gone into witness protection, but someone in the police department had revealed the girl's location and she had been clubbed to death: a slow and agonizing death meant as a warning.

Mary squeezed Sally's hand so tightly, her fingernails dug into Sally's palms. "He's got my baby, hasn't he?" Mary said. "Where is she?"

"He said he knows who took the girls. He didn't say he knew where they were."

"Of course he does. He took them!" Mary screeched. "Tell me where Anna is!"

"He didn't say. He wants me to see him tomorrow. At Walla Walla."

Mary's distressed face morphed into a hopeful smile. "Oh, praise the Lord."

Sally rose awkwardly, feeling lightheaded. Why was this happening to her? "Mary, I can't do it. I can't face him. I'll tell the cops. They'll talk to him."

Mary stood. "He called *you*. He wants to see *you*, not those useless cops. You have to go. You have to!"

Sally grabbed her purse from the sofa. "I'll talk to Clarke. It's the right thing to do."

"No! Please, Sally! You can save my baby girl!" Mary clawed at Sally's arm.

Sally threw open Mary's apartment door and ran down the fire stairs.

THREE

From where Sally stood on the street, the Franklin PD head office looked much like every other high-rise downtown, apart from the three patrol cars out front. Sally had left her car in the underground parking garage a block away.

She entered Franklin PD's headquarters and announced herself to the officer at the front desk, who she knew from way back. The cop made a call to Detective Clarke, then he asked her to wait. It was almost comforting to be back in a building she knew so well. The smell of the place—a bit like sun-heated plastic and worn leather—brought forth a rush of memories. Uniformed and plainclothes cops acknowledged her with a nod and a smile, but she was too preoccupied with Durrant's phone call to strike up a conversation.

In fact, Sally couldn't sit still with nerves, and in the end, she got up and pretended to look out the window. She was still in her head-to-toe black running gear, and her walnut-brown hair, flecked with a touch of gray these days, was tied back in a short ponytail. When she had bolted from Mary's apartment, she'd headed straight here. She wanted to tell Clarke in person —it was all too easy to dismiss a phone call.

"Fifth floor, Sally. You know the way," said the desk cop.

She thanked him but dawdled, torn between seeking Clarke's help and her fear of Durrant. He had made it clear that he didn't want her to contact the police, and here she was, about to meet with the lead detective on the Poster Killer case. How far did Durrant's network of spies and thugs extend? There had been rumors that he bribed and blackmailed police officers too. But they were just rumors. Telling Clarke about Durrant's phone call was the right thing to do, and besides, she was too afraid of Durrant to meet him. Once he had his claws into her, he'd never let her go. No, she concluded, she had to inform Clarke.

Adrenaline still coursing around her body, she took the elevator to the fifth floor. When the elevator doors opened, Clarke stood there waiting, his brow as deeply furrowed as usual and his suit as neat as it always was. Even his tie was positioned perfectly. How he managed to look impeccable given the long hours he worked, she couldn't fathom. It must stem from his military background.

"You okay, Sally?" he asked, studying her face. "You're looking a little peaky."

Sally had a peaches-and-cream complexion which tended to give her a ruddy, healthy glow, but right now, all color was gone from her face.

"I'll be okay," she said.

Clarke threw open the department door, and Sally was instantly engulfed in a cacophony of voices, ringing phones, and an energetic buzz that helped her to cling to her positivity. He led her past busy detectives, messy desks, whiteboards with head-and-shoulder shots and names scrawled beneath them, to his office at the other end of the room.

"What's this about, Sally?" Clarke asked. He had a head of thick blonde hair that gave him a Scandinavian look. "We got a woman stabbed to death, a guy shot dead at work, and an unidentified body in a barrel."

Some things never change, Sally thought. She had never known Homicide not to be overwhelmed with cases.

"It's about the Poster Killer."

In January 2011, at just thirty-eight years of age, Detective Clarke had been appointed the lead detective on the Poster Killer case, taking over the reins from Detective Foster. After three abductions and no leads, Foster was moved sideways and then shortly thereafter he retired. Foster had been old school: he relied on gut instinct, his network of informants, and intimidation tactics that Sally found questionable. Clarke, in contrast, was a by-the-book detective.

"I have some new information," Sally continued, taking the chair Clarke offered.

He shut the office door then sat behind his desk. "Shoot."

"Theo Durrant rang me out of the blue. Claims he knows who the Poster Killer is. Told me to visit him at ten-fifteen tomorrow. I think he wants a deal."

"He's tried this before, Sally. He's yanking our chain. Attention seeking."

"This time it's me he contacted. To be honest, he's really spooked me. He told me not to involve the police, and I wasn't sure if I should even tell you."

"He's toying with you," Clarke said, arms folded across his white shirt. "He took those girls. We just couldn't nail the son of a bitch."

She straightened her spine. In her head, she heard her father telling her not to slouch. *Nobody wants to marry a slouching, useless girl like you*, he would say, shaking his head at her across the dinner table. Her mom never contradicted him, but under the table she would gently pat her daughter's hand.

Sally glanced down at her left wrist, where the exposed skin was still marked with semi-circular indents. That was where

Mary had dug her nails in to stop Sally from bolting from her apartment.

"Maybe he wants to confess?"

Clarke smirked. "Like hell he does! We could take him to Guantanamo and waterboard him and he still wouldn't confess. Look, Sally, I want to solve that case as much as anyone. More, because I'm the guy who failed to arrest the scum who took those girls. But why now?"

"I don't know. Guilt? Something's changed in his life?" Sally moved to the edge of her seat. "It's got to be worth a conversation, right?"

"Sally, listen to me. Don't go near that man. He wants something from you."

"I was hoping one of your team would go see him. I just think, what if he knows something useful? The victims' families need closure."

Clarke sighed and rubbed a hand across his forehead. "I'll send someone. But not tomorrow. Maybe next week. Durrant is a narcissist. We're not going to come running when he wants."

"Then he'll blame me. He's killed people for less," she pleaded. "Please, I'm afraid. Not just for me. For my son."

Durrant had done horrific things to the people who betrayed or disobeyed him. He particularly liked throwing gasoline over them and setting them on fire.

"Sally, I get you're afraid of him. But he'll spend the rest of his days in jail."

Did Clarke think her an idiot? A rush of anger spurred her on. "He can still get to me. Why aren't you taking this seriously?"

"Okay, okay. I'll send Lin. She'll take the appointment."

"Lin?"

"Detective Esme Lin. A transfer from Seattle PD and keen to prove herself."

Clarke opened his door and yelled out for Lin. A petite

Asian American woman in a pantsuit and heavy-duty biker boots came over.

"Yes, boss."

"This is Sally Fairburn. Used to work in victim advocacy. She knows all the families of the Poster Killer's victims. There's been a development and I want you to handle it."

"Okay."

"You're going to Walla Walla tomorrow morning. Theo Durrant claims he knows the identity of the Poster Killer. I think he's dicking us around, but it's worth a trip. He contacted Sally," he said, nodding at her. "You're going in her place."

"Boss, I'm in court in the morning."

Clarke swore under his breath. "Contact Walla Walla. Sally's on the visitors' list. Cancel tomorrow and make it another day and take Sally's name off the list. She ain't going."

"Why now?" Lin asked, flicking a glance at Sally. "And why contact Sally?"

"I can answer that," Sally said. "He joined the restorative justice program and met with one of his victims."

"And how did that go?" Clarke asked, with a curl of his lip. He had no faith in restorative justice.

"Not well. But my point is that he's met me once before. Maybe he thinks you're more likely to listen to me if I plead his case."

"Well, he'd be wrong." He turned to Lin. "Watch yourself with him. He's slippery."

Clarke left Sally alone with Lin, who asked questions and jotted down notes. Then Sally took the fire stairs down to the lobby, keen to avoid meeting anyone who knew Scott, her ex-husband. Scott had been a popular patrol officer, and Sally was still embarrassed about him walking out on her and moving to Chicago. After he'd gone, people she had thought of as friends started to avoid her. Including cops.

Coming up the fire stairs was a dark-haired young cop Sally knew and liked. He recognized her and smiled.

"Hey, Sally," Aiden Foster said. He was the twenty-five-year-old son of retired Detective Richard Foster. "How's life treating you?"

Aiden was tall like his father, with a winning smile, and had plenty of female cops vying for his attention. Aiden had joined Franklin PD just six months before Sally left the DA's office, and their paths had crossed a few times. What she'd seen of the enthusiastic young cop had impressed her: he was a bright kid who handled victims and their families with compassion, but he could hold his own on the streets.

"I'm really good," Sally replied. "Keeping busy, you know. How's your dad?"

She didn't want to go into why she was there.

"He's okay. Misses the job. He would come back in a heart-beat if he could."

"It was his heart, right?"

"Yeah, the doc gave him no choice. Said if he didn't retire, he'd be dead."

Aiden glanced up the stairs. Two cops were coming down. They nodded at Aiden and kept going. "So what are you doing here?"

"Catching up with old friends. I shouldn't keep you. Good to see you, Aiden. Please say hi to your father for me."

Sally took off down the stairs once more, the feeling that she might just have made a terrible mistake defying Durrant chasing her from the building.

FOUR

Sally hurried away from the Franklin PD building. She stopped on the street corner, glanced behind her to check that no police officers she knew were heading her way, then took a small bottle of water and a blister pack of Valium from her purse and swallowed two pills. She was shaking, her mind racing, terrible thoughts of Durrant's retribution filling her head.

Sally hated her dependency on Valium, but she had used them for too long to stop now, just like she was dependent on sleeping pills at night. Scott had gotten her on to both, just one of the subtle but effective ways he had kept her under his control, fueling her self-doubts and ensuring she became reliant on him. After their divorce, it had taken her two years of therapy to even admit to herself that her marriage to Scott had been poisonous.

Just taking the Valium made her feel better even though it hadn't had time to have an impact. It was a five-minute walk to the underground garage where her Honda Civic was parked. It was a sunny day and the streets were busy with shoppers, office workers, and tourists heading for the Natural History Museum at the top of the hill. Maybe Sally was being paranoid? Durrant had bigger fish to fry than her.

Across the road, a black Ford Fusion pulled out from the curb. The windshield caught the sun for a moment, the glare making Sally squint. It moved slowly, as if the driver was elderly or uncertain which way to go. Sally turned the corner and walked up the steep hill. The Ford Fusion had pulled over on the opposite side of the street and the engine was idling. Was the driver watching her? The car's tinted windows made it impossible to know. It gave her the creeps.

Sally increased her pace. *It can't be Durrant's mob. How could they have got here so fast? Stop panicking*, she told herself.

She flicked a look at the idling car then started to run, dodging pedestrians. She was thankful she was still in her running shoes.

She turned the corner—the entrance to the underground parking station was about halfway down the street. The pavement was less busy now so she sped up.

She peeked behind her as she ran. The Ford Fusion had turned the corner and was driving down the same street, this time on the same side of the road as Sally. Her heart almost missed a beat, and adrenaline surged through her body, combating the effect of the Valium she'd taken moments before. This was weird. Definitely weird.

A few more yards to go.

Her cell rang. Not missing a stride, she felt in her purse, found the phone, and checked the caller ID. It was her son. She frowned. It was late morning—he should be in class.

"Paul, what's up?"

"Not feeling too good. Can you come and collect me?"

Ahead, the same car had stopped further down the road. She could only just see it because a white van was parked between her and the Fusion.

"Yes, I'll come now."

"Mom, why are you panting?"

"Long story. Tell you later. Tell your teacher I'm on my way, okay?"

"Yeah."

She shoved the phone back in her bag and turned down the narrow passage between the entrance and exit lanes that led to the elevators and the fire stairs. Across the four lanes were boom gates—the Fusion's driver would have to take a ticket to enter the parking lot. Sally didn't plan to hang around to find out if they did indeed do that.

She ran past the payment machines. She would normally pay now so she didn't have to pay at the gate on departure, but she felt exposed and desperately wanted to be in the relative security of her vehicle. At least there she could lock the doors. So she stabbed her finger on the elevator button. Her car was on the lowest level—six—because all 1,500 spaces were almost taken.

The indicators above the elevator told her it was on level three and it wasn't moving. Sally hated the fire stairs because they usually smelled of urine.

A car's headlights lit up her face. It halted at the automatic barrier, and her mouth went dry. It was the same car that seemed to be following her. Sally stared up at the indicator for the elevator, which told her it was on level four. Too slow.

Sally reached for the entrance to the stairs and pushed past the heavy door. On the floor, some fast-food wrappers and a drink carton lay decaying on the concrete. At least the space didn't stink of urine.

She ran down the first set of concrete stairs to level two. The fire door on that level had a large number two painted on it. Sally kept going, sweat breaking out all over her body.

Level three. She was fast and was sure she could reach her car before any vehicle could, given the labyrinthine route they had to take through the lot. And anyway, her pursuers didn't know what level her car was parked on.

Level four. Hand in her purse, she felt for the car key. Her fingers touched it. She pulled it out, and the door to level four flew open. Sally gasped as she almost collided with two young men in suits. They also looked startled as she bumped an arm with her elbow. She squealed and kept running, then realized her key wasn't in her hand anymore. Halting abruptly, she looked up the flight of stairs. It lay on the floor near the door to level four.

One of the men picked it up. "Is this yours?"

Sally didn't want to approach the men. "Yes, thank you. Please just leave it on the ground."

The guy with her key glanced at his colleague, then did as she asked. "Sorry if we spooked you."

The men began to climb up the stairs.

Sally used her sleeve to wipe the sweat from her forehead. She felt bad she'd been so rude.

When their footsteps had receded, she raced up to collect her key then turned around and ran down to level six.

She stopped at the door. What if her pursuers were on the other side of the door?

She pushed the handle down slowly and then pulled the fire door open a crack. The bottom level of the parking lot smelled damp, and the lighting was poor. There were plenty of vehicles, but she couldn't see or hear anyone walking about.

She pulled the door open wide enough for her to sneak through then closed it slowly behind her so it wouldn't slam. All she could hear was the churning of an air-conditioning unit and the drip-drip-drip of water. No car engine idling. No voices.

With a terrible sinking feeling, Sally realized she couldn't recall where she'd parked her car. She'd been too distracted by her imminent meeting with Clarke. She tried to retrace her steps. She remembered she'd had a long walk to the elevator.

And a silver Mercedes or perhaps a BMW next to her car. She looked around for a sign. She saw one that said EXIT, but that was no help.

Sally started walking. The ground beneath her running shoes was wet in places, and her shoes splashed through the shallow puddles. She glanced behind her, then around the parking bays. Where was her car?

Somewhere on an upper level she heard car wheels screeching, and began running again, desperately scanning the space above her for a sign to the elevator. At last she found one. She was going in the wrong direction.

She sprinted past the rows of cars, clicking her key fob. If she got close enough the key fob would unlock her car and the lights would flash. But nothing happened.

"Come on," she muttered.

Running past the elevator and a payment machine, she clicked her key fob repeatedly. Ahead, a whole row of cars sat in semi-darkness—the lighting above it wasn't working. She saw the Mercedes first then her Honda Civic and slowed. Had it been this dark when she'd left her car here?

Sally looked behind her. The sound of screeching tires was drawing closer. She felt inside her purse for her cell, so she could call for help if she needed it. But there was no reception down there.

She heard a noise behind her and whirled around. The elevator door opened and a woman with two kids ambled through, all licking ice creams. At least Sally had company now.

She clicked her key fob frantically, and this time there was a click as her car unlocked. Sally ran to it and got in, centrally locking the doors. She then dropped her purse and phone onto the passenger seat and stabbed the key into the ignition.

A wave of relief swept through her as the engine roared into life. She sped out of her parking bay, headlights on, and drove like a maniac until she reached the exit.

Before she opened her car window to slot her ticket into the machine, she looked all around to see if anyone was watching and waiting for her. Sally paid with her credit card, then accelerated out into the street.

The Ford Fusion was nowhere to be seen.

FIVE

APRIL 15, 1990

Sally was twenty years old when she graduated from the police academy and assigned to Franklin PD's city division. It was her first day and the police sergeant's welcome speech was interrupted by a phone call. The sergeant wandered off. The other rookie cop, Diedre Kelly, seated to Sally's right, suppressed a yawn. Her eyes wandered around the department, then she leaned close to Sally.

"He's a bit yummy," Diedre whispered.

Sally followed Diedre's line of sight to a broad man with muscular shoulders who was laughing at, she guessed, his colleague's joke. Diedre ran a tongue up and down her bottom lip. "I'd buddy up with him any day."

Diedre was right. The uniformed cop was good-looking, although he really should ditch the 1980s mustache. However, Sally wasn't interested in dating. She wanted to give this job her all, not just to prove to her judgmental father that she would make a fine police officer but because she got a kick out of helping people. It had been a toss-up between a career as a paramedic, a firefighter, or a job with the police. She liked the idea of working with a community, building relationships and trust over time, and so she'd opted for the police because she felt the other two roles didn't really allow for that sort of daily interaction.

"You won't last a week," her dad had said. "What's a shy girl like you going to do when you have to face a killer, huh?"

The sergeant returned to his desk.

"I've assigned you both experienced cops who'll show you the drill. Diedre, you're with Officer Esposito." The sergeant yelled across the floor to a tubby cop with patch of thinning hair on his balding head.

"Oh great," muttered Diedre, who then headed out on patrol with Esposito.

"Scott," the sergeant yelled.

The officer Diedre had been eyeing up came over and smiled warmly at Sally.

"Scott Fairburn." He shook her hand. "Good to meet you, Sally."

He looked at her as if she were the only person in the room. She blushed like a bashful schoolgirl and hated herself for being so silly.

"Follow me, kid," Scott said as he led her to the parking garage where the squad cars were kept. Sally found it weird that he'd called her kid—she reckoned he wasn't much older than her, but she let it pass.

Two weeks later, he asked her to dinner. Not only that, but he had somehow discovered her favorite restaurant. She was impressed. So here they were, seated at a table for two in a cozy Italian restaurant and he was asking her to talk about *herself*. She couldn't believe it. Sally had only dated one guy she'd met at school, who was only interested in himself and doing what he wanted to do.

"Why did you become a cop?" Scott asked, after ordering for both of them.

"It sounds clichéd, but I guess I like to help people," Sally said.

"Me too," Scott replied, topping up his glass with red wine. Sally was drinking Coca-Cola. "It makes me feel good, you know. There's so much violence out there. If I can prevent someone getting hurt, I'll do it. That's why I like being a patrol cop. I'm the first respondent."

"I hear you talked down a suicide a few weeks back. He had a gun, didn't he?"

"Yeah, the poor guy lost his job, then his wife." He shrugged. "He kept waving this damn gun about, so I talked to him, tried to connect with him, you know. It took a while, but he eventually put it down. No big deal."

"No big deal? Are you serious? He's alive because of you."

Scott smiled. "Hey, you did pretty good today. It's not every rookie who can cope with so much blood."

Scott was referring to the body they'd found in an abandoned house. The man had been shot at close range by a sawed-off shotgun. There wasn't much left of his face and there was blood spatter everywhere. Sally had had difficulty keeping her breakfast in her stomach, but somehow she'd managed it.

She blushed. "Thanks."

It was rare that she received compliments. Her parents believed that praise would make her conceited.

"Does it get easier?" she asked.

Their pizza arrived. Scott had wanted one with pepperoni and she had liked the idea of shrimps, chili, tomatoes, and cheese. She had expected them to order two smaller pizzas. But he'd suggested they share a large one and make it what Sally liked. He certainly was a gentleman.

They both took a slice and bit into the hot and spicy pizza.

When Scott had finished his mouthful, he said, "Good choice. This is gonna be my new favorite. Anyway, back to your question. You get used to the blood and brutality. You have to find a coping mechanism. Still care, but just not too much. Otherwise, it breaks you."

Sally stopped chewing.

He must have assumed she was worried. "You're doing just fine, Sally. Really. And I have your back, okay?" He reached across the table and held her hand. "I'll look after you."

This was the first time he had held her hand and his grip was gentle but not soppy. It felt good to be touched by him, although she was a little irked that he assumed she needed looking after.

"I've got your back too."

Scott chuckled and picked up another slice.

Sally was uncertain what to make of his response. Was there a hint of sexism? She was a woman of few words, but she was fit and knew how to look after herself. And she was as tall as Scott—five feet eight inches—which gave her a commanding presence. After living twenty years with a father who believed women should stay in the kitchen, maybe she was being oversensitive. Right now, she was more worried about his public display of affection.

Sally said, "Do you think it's okay to hold hands in public? I mean, what if someone from work sees us?"

"Cops don't come here, but you're right. We should keep this under wraps until... until we know where we're heading."

Wow! This was moving fast. Maybe a little too fast. They'd met just two weeks ago. The pizza churned in her stomach. Dating another cop wouldn't be easy, especially one who was her mentor. *This is a bad idea*, she told herself.

"You know, I think we're so much alike," he said. "It's kind of uncanny. We were both only children. We like movies and trekking. What music do you like?"

"I'm into jazz and blues."

"Me too. I like all the original jazz artists like Duke Ellington, but I'm really into Pat Metheny and his jazz fusion band."

"So am I," Sally said. "It's not often I meet a guy who likes the same things as me."

It was as if a shadow crossed his face. His eyes lost their brightness. "Have you dated many guys?"

It must have come out wrong. "Me, no. I had a boyfriend at school. That's all. And you?"

The gossip at Franklin PD was that Scott had been in several short relationships with girls much like her: quiet, empathetic, self-reflective.

"I'm twenty-five so I've had a few relationships," Scott said. "Have no plans to settle down yet, but when I saw you, I was drawn to you. Call it fate, who knows?"

It felt as if her heart swelled inside her chest. He was such a nice guy. So thoughtful, and she was certainly attracted to him. But she didn't think she was as keen on him as he was on her.

"I'm having a really nice time, Scott, but can we take it slowly? I have a new job and, well, I never expected to be dating my partner. This could make things difficult at work."

"But you want to date, right?"

"Um, well, yes."

"Great." He squeezed her hand fondly. "I've booked tickets for a jazz club Saturday night. Just you and me. I checked the work roster and we're not on that night. I'll pick you up at seven."

"Saturday? I'm having dinner with a girlfriend. I'm so sorry. Can we go another time?"

Scott withdrew his hand and looked hurt. "Is this your way of saying you don't want to be my girlfriend?"

"No, not at all. The jazz club sounds perfect. It's just I've promised to have dinner with Margie."

"It's just dinner with her, right?"

"Well, yes, but—"

"And she's a good friend?"

"My best friend."

"Then she won't have a problem with you taking a rain check."

Sally hesitated. She knew she was being manipulated, but he was doing it because he wanted to take her somewhere special. That had never happened to her before. On the other hand, she didn't want to be one of those people who dropped their best friend when a potential boyfriend arrived on the scene.

"I'll talk to her," Sally said.

SIX

MAY 6, 2015

Sally's son, Paul, stared at her as she drove home. "You're all sweaty."

"I was late for a meeting. I had to run."

Sally wasn't going to tell Paul about her worrying morning. He had a pinched look about him, and he was paler than usual. When she'd picked him up from school, the teacher had said he'd been vomiting. Perhaps he had a stomach flu, or had he been smoking pot again? He'd done it before and had been sick as a dog afterward. And to think he was only fourteen. When Sally was that age she thought a pot was a utensil for cooking.

"You don't do meetings, Mom. You don't work anymore," Paul said, resuming his sullen staring out the windshield.

"Well, I had a meeting today. How are you feeling? Do you have stomach cramps?"

"Nah. I puked, that's all."

"Did you eat anything that might've caused it?"

"No, Mom." He sighed heavily.

Paul was big for his age. Broad, with a wide neck, like his father. He'd been picked for the high-school football team in a linebacker position. He was fast and strong, and he'd helped his team make it to the state championships. But he had a big chip on his shoulder about his dad, and a tendency to lash out, which could get him into big trouble. She didn't blame him for being angry. Scott had been a cruel father. Playing football helped Paul burn off some of his anger.

"I won't be upset with you," Sally said. "Just tell me if you smoked a bong with Reilly."

Reilly Doyle was a bad influence on Paul. At some point she would need to tackle Reilly's parents again. The problem was that they regarded smoking pot as a rite of passage for a teenager, and the last time she'd spoken to the Doyles about it, they'd said that both boys would grow out of it. Sally had a different view. She used to volunteer at the Pine Creek YMCA, sometimes for the teen nights and sometimes for the tween nights. It was a safe place for the kids to hang, or at least it used to be. More recently, drug dealers had started hanging around the YMCA, targeting kids. Sally suspected this was how Reilly got hold of the marijuana.

Paul heaved his shoulders up, then down, and sighed. "No, Mom." He then turned his head. "And don't sniff me, okay?"

Sally could usually detect the distinctive sweet smell on his breath and the filthy water stink on his hands. This time, she couldn't.

She drove the rest of the journey in silence, her thoughts returning to the underground parking lot and the car that had seemed to be tailing her. Had she imagined the whole thing?

As she gripped the steering wheel, she used her thumb to rub the ridge of hard skin where her wedding and engagement rings used to sit. It was a nervous tic. The wedding band had been too tight, and over the years, a ridge of hardened skin had formed beneath it. When the divorce papers came through, Sally had to have the rings cut away by a jeweler. She'd kept the damaged rings for some strange reason that she still couldn't fathom.

Perhaps it was because even now, after two years of therapy, she couldn't understand how she had believed their marriage was fine. When her shrink first told her that she'd been gaslighted by her husband, she had vehemently denied it. At that time, Sally had been so in his thrall that she no longer knew her own mind.

Paul glanced her way and saw what she was doing. "What's up?"

"Nothing." She stopped doing it and smiled, then reached out to rest the back of her hand on his forehead. "I'll take your temperature when we get home."

Paul pushed her hand away and said nothing.

They turned into Pioneer Drive. After the divorce, Sally and Paul had moved to the suburb of Pioneer Heights to start anew. Their old house in Memorial Park was full of tragedy and heartache, so after selling the family home and splitting the proceeds fifty-fifty with Scott, she'd bought the two-bed townhouse at 9256 Pioneer Drive, which was bordered by miles of national park and great running and walking trails. It was a relatively newly developed area, designed to feel like a small country town, with a pedestrian-friendly town center instead of strip malls. Sally had chosen the location because it was where her friend Margie lived, and the high school had a good track record for the number of graduates who went on to college, as well as one of the best football teams in the area. The townhouse was small, but the mountain and forest views from its roof terrace were magnificent. She hoped it would be their healing place.

Sally pulled into an on-street parking bay just as her cell began to ring. It was Mary, who had already left several messages. Sally let it go to voicemail, got out of the car, and unlocked the front door. Paul walked into the living room—there was no hallway—and dropped his school bag on the floor, heading for the kitchen. Sally realized she'd left her purse in the car so she went out to get it. After she'd retrieved it and locked the car, she dialed Mary.

"Why didn't you call me back?" Mary said peevishly.

"I was with Detective Clarke. He's sending Detective Lin to meet with Durrant."

"That won't work!" Mary said. "They couldn't get him to confess last time and they ain't going to now. They're useless!"

"I am the wrong person, Mary. I'm not trained to question suspects in the way detectives do. Lin is highly competent. She's much more likely to extract information from Durrant than I am."

"He won't tell a cop anything. Listen to me, Sally, I've been thinking. I'll come with you to the jail. We'll see him together. I'll beg him."

That was a big call for someone who hadn't set foot outside her front door for years. But begging Durrant for information would only feed his sadistic, narcissistic ego.

"I was never any good at investigating crime," Sally began.

"That's baloney. Your wretched husband told you that, didn't he?"

Mary was right about that. Sally wanted their conversation to end.

"Leave it with me. I'll keep in touch with Lin."

She swiveled to face the house and found a man standing in her way. Sally yelped with shock. Where had he come from?

He was in his late sixties or early seventies with white hair and a trimmed white beard with a hint of copper through it. He wore corduroy pants and a dark blue blazer and he blocked her path to the front door.

"Call you later," she said to Mary and hung up.

"Can I help you?" Sally asked, taking a step back from the stranger.

It passed through her mind that a new couple had purchased the townhouse two doors down, but there was an intensity to the man's stare that hinted his wasn't a cordial visit.

"Sally Fairburn?"

"I don't know you. Can you tell me who you are?"

"Bryan Topham. I want to ask for your help with a project. May I come in?"

Well, he was certainly forward. But Sally knew better than to invite strangers into her home, even if they had an educated, polite voice.

"Now's not a good time. What's the project about?"

He took a step closer to her, which made her deeply uncomfortable.

"I'm writing a book about the unsolved Poster Killer case."

"Woah!" Sally said. Why was Durrant and now Topham coming to her about the case? What was going on? "I don't know anything. Please can you leave."

"Sally, let me explain."

"Tell me how you know where I live."

"Oh, that's easy. I got your address from the DA's office."

Now Sally was freaked out. Her former workplace would never have revealed that kind of information.

"I'd like you to leave me alone please."

Sally tried to walk around him, but he put out his hand and touched her arm.

"Please—hear me out."

"Let go of my arm!" Sally sounded angry, but she was shaking like a leaf. Was this man associated with Durrant?

"Hey!" shouted Paul from the doorway. "Let go of my mom."

Topham turned to look at Paul. "It's all right, son—we're just talking."

Paul stepped onto the path. At six feet, he was taller than Topham. "Mom wants you to go. So get!"

"Okay, son, there's no need to be like that. This project

means a lot to me, and I thought Sally might be able to help."
From his blazer pocket he pulled out a business card with his
name, cell, and email details, and handed it to Sally. She hesitated, then reluctantly took it.

"Call me," Topham said.

"Mom doesn't want to call you, okay!" said Paul.

Paul's dark eyebrows were furrowed, his mouth an angry
slit. Any moment now he might headbutt or punch Topham.

Sally recognized the signs and stepped between them. "Mr.
Topham, please go!"

The man walked down the street and got into a flashy,
cobalt-blue Audi. He drove past them, and Paul gave him the
finger. Sally tried to slap his hand down, but Topham had seen
Paul's insulting gesture.

"Don't antagonize him," Sally said.

Sally had already upset Durrant and Mary, and now this
Topham too.

Hurrying into the house, she locked the door behind them.

"Thank you for coming to my aid," she said to Paul.

"Who was that creep?" he asked, shuffling past her and into
the kitchen, where he headed straight for the refrigerator.

Sally didn't want to talk about Durrant's call or the car she
swore had been following her. Paul might look like an adult, but
he was just a kid and she wasn't going to tell him how frightened she was.

SEVEN

NOVEMBER 23, 1990

It was November 23, 1990, and Sally had been a cop for seven months. Her athletic build and height gave her a commanding presence and, by watching Scott Fairburn in action, she'd learned quickly how to handle aggressive people and to defuse potentially dangerous situations. She had coped with discovering her first dead body and also with coming under fire. She and Scott were partners at work and also in their personal lives, which made life complicated, especially because Scott had insisted they keep it a secret.

More than once she'd had doubts about Scott. She was a shy person and, like her mom, someone who wanted to please others. And to please others she avoided arguments and seldom questioned anyone's opinion. In the early days, it had seemed as if she and Scott were two peas in a pod. They had much in common, or so Scott said. Over time though, his interest in the activities she liked had waned, and she'd found herself doing what he wanted to do more and more. Instead of going to romantic dinners, they went to a bar with his friends from the police department. Instead of enjoying jazz and blues bands, he took her to rock concerts. He would correct her when they were on patrol together, which was fair enough given he was her mentor. But he did it when they weren't at work too. There were times when Sally knew that she was right and he was wrong, but somehow he always managed to convince her that she was mistaken or forgetful.

Sally was driving a Ford Police Interceptor and Scott was in the passenger seat. They were chasing a suspect.

"Don't let him get away," Scott said, pointing at the car ahead of them, swerving wildly to overtake a truck.

Sally gulped. A car was heading their way—Sally didn't have enough time to overtake the truck.

"What are you doing?" Scott demanded.

"I won't make it."

"Sure you will!"

No, I can't. Scott shook his head as she waited until the car coming the other way had passed.

"He's turning right. Faster!"

She turned the steering wheel hard right, the wheels squealing, the siren on the car roof blaring, their emergency lights flashing.

They were chasing Mathias Jensen, who had stabbed his wife to death at their house then gone on the run. In the distance, other patrol car sirens wailed. Backup was on the way, but they were the only cops tailing him. Jensen's silver sedan swerved onto the other side of the road to overtake a slow driver, narrowly missing a car coming the other way.

"Jeez! That was close."

"Do the same," Scott directed.

She calculated she had just enough time and pulled out. A bus was coming in their direction. She took her foot off the accelerator.

"Do it, Sally!" Scott shouted.

She stamped the pedal to the floor and only just made it past the car before the bus whizzed by them.

"What if he kills someone because we're chasing him?" Sally asked, her grip on the steering wheel so tight it was giving her a headache.

"We're taking this guy in. Nobody else. You and me, got it? This is our arrest."

They were in a 25mph street, and Jensen was doing over 40mph, forcing them to match his speed. Only one in ten pedestrians survived being hit by a car doing 40mph, and Sally knew that however good her reaction time might be, at this speed she might kill someone. "Shouldn't we ask the supervisor what to do?"

The pursuit supervisor, back at base, had given them the go-ahead to pursue the suspect, although it was assumed they wouldn't take unnecessary risks. If the chase became too dangerous to the public or to them, they could withdraw. The webcam in their vehicle was recording the view through the windshield and clocking the speed they were travelling. It was her neck on the line if someone got hurt. She chewed her lower lip, uncertain what to do. He must have noticed.

"You're new," Scott said. "This is a normal pursuit. Trust me."

Ahead, Jensen jumped a red light. Sally took her foot off the accelerator. It was a busy intersection, two lanes either side.

"No!" yelled Scott. "Do it!"

Sally's instincts told her to stop. But she couldn't let Scott down. He had wanted to drive that morning, but he'd let her do it because she'd pressed him into it.

Sally accelerated again. Her breath caught in her throat. Scott pressed a button and changed the normal siren wail into a repeated, ear-splitting burst to draw maximum attention to their presence. Vehicles had begun to cross the intersection. It was like playing Russian roulette—would the traffic stop in time?

"I can't," she croaked.

"Do it!" said Scott, in a tone that didn't invite any argument.

Sally stared straight ahead, too afraid to look to her left. A brown van was just entering the junction. She swerved to avoid it. Tires screeched. A sports car veered off the road and narrowly missed a fire hydrant before hitting a shop wall.

"Keep going. We're going to catch this scum. You and me, Sally."

On more than one occasion, Sally had noticed that Scott's ego often won out over common sense.

"But the collision."

"I'll call it in. Don't take your eyes off Jensen."

Scott contacted Renee, the supervisor. Told her about the accident. Insisted they keep going.

"There's no shame in standing down," Renee said.

"I know that, ma'am, but we can do this," Scott said.

"He's turning onto the freeway," Sally said.

"Ma'am, get traffic off the freeway."

"Wait for backup. We need him surrounded," Renee said.

"Copy that."

Sally took the slip road onto the freeway and accelerated to 60mph—the speed limit. But Jensen was doing over 80mph, forcing Sally to replicate his speed.

Jensen overtook numerous vehicles, swerving around slower ones. Ahead, a slow driver was overtaking an even slower vehicle. In the farthest lane, a tow truck was sticking to the speed limit. Jensen was stuck behind a wall of vehicles.

"Get real close. Maybe we can get him to pull over."

Sally wanted to say that their supervisor had told them to wait for other police cars to catch up, but she didn't want to contradict such an experienced and well-respected cop, so she said nothing.

She closed the gap between their vehicle and the suspect's. All of a sudden, Jensen swerved to the right and tried to overtake the slow-moving vehicles by using the shoulder. Sally couldn't see the road ahead because of the vehicles that formed a wall up ahead.

There was a sound like an explosion and a burst of flame. Sally slammed on the brakes and took the breakdown lane. She saw carnage and fire. Jensen's car was wrapped around a stationary pickup truck.

Their Interceptor came to a halt behind Jensen's burning car. A body lay several feet away, covered in blood and glass. Jensen hadn't been wearing a seat belt so he'd been thrown through the windshield, hit the rear of the stationary truck, and died instantly.

Later, Sally discovered the webcam in their car had been switched off. She swore she remembered Scott telling her that he'd turned the camera on. Both Sally and Scott had to put in a report. Shaken by the incident, she went to make a cup of sugary tea. Scott followed her into the tiny kitchen and closed the door.

"We need to get our story straight, okay? We pursued him onto the freeway, and we kept up the pursuit because he fired at us. That's when he crashed. He wasn't looking where he was going."

"He didn't fire at us, Scott."

He stepped forward and put his hands on her shoulders. "Sally, you have to trust me. I'm only trying to protect you. The man you were pursuing died, and you failed to switch on the patrol-car camera. It looks suspicious. You see that, don't you?"

She stared at him, puzzled. "You told me the webcam was on."

"I didn't. It was the other way around. You told me it was on."

That wasn't how she remembered it. "We can't lie. There's no evidence he fired at us on the freeway."

"Forensics will find a bullet fired from his pistol on the free-way. You understand?"

Sally understood perfectly—he wanted her to fabricate her report.

Scott's buddy Walter Jackson and another cop had arrived on the scene a few minutes after Sally and Scott. Had Walt, as he was known, helped Scott fire the bullet from Jensen's gun?

Sally didn't want to do what Scott asked, but in the end, she caved. She went home soon after she'd written her fabricated statement, claiming she felt unwell.

That evening, Sally didn't let Scott into her apartment when he knocked on the door. She was disgusted by her own weakness, but how could she contradict an experienced officer like Scott?

She vowed to call off their relationship in the morning. It might cause problems at work, but it was better to end it now, before she made a mistake and married the wrong man.

But in the morning Scott turned up with a bunch of red roses and an apology, claiming he'd done it to protect her and promising it wouldn't happen again.

EIGHT

MAY 7, 2015

It was early Thursday morning when Sally and her running partner, Margie, left the Falls Trail and ran across Pioneer Park. Paul was asleep. Whatever had ailed him yesterday had gone by the evening. His friend Reilly had come around to use the PlayStation and they had been as raucous as usual. It was a crisp May morning, but the sun lifted Sally's spirits after what had been a sleepless night.

"Durrant will know by now. I'm beginning to think I've done the wrong thing," Sally said, her strides measured, her breathing rhythmic.

All night, Sally had fretted. Was it too late to change her mind?

"No, you were right," Margie said next to her. "It's about time the police did their jobs." She turned her head. "You need to focus on *you*. You're doing so well. Don't let scum like Durrant stall your progress."

Sally glanced at Margie, at her jazzy pink-and-black running pants and vibrant fuchsia singlet, and smiled. Margie was a bundle of energy and brightness. Born in Jamaica, she had migrated to America with her parents when she was a toddler.

"I don't know what I'd do without you," Sally said. "I'm so grateful you stood by me all through my marriage. He pushed almost everyone I loved away."

"Yeah, well, I'm as stubborn as a mule."

"I wish I was more like you."

"No, you don't. I scare people!"

Sally laughed.

Margie continued, "People were fooled by him, just as you were. I was too, at the beginning when he was charm itself. But I've come across enough covert passive-aggressive narcissists to recognize them for what they are."

Margie was director of a mental wellness charity and had introduced Sally to her therapist, Karine O'Malley.

"I still can't believe I let him control me."

"Honey, there are millions of people in the world who are gaslighted by someone they love. Some never realize what is happening and live their whole lives abused this way. You're doing great."

"You really think so?"

"Sure I do. But to heal fully you need to focus on you. Scott still has a hold over you and you need to keep fighting it. I'm concerned that if you get dragged into Durrant's evil world, he'll take over your life, just as Scott did. He sounds like he's the ultimate manipulator, and you only just escaped from Scott."

There was much about her life with Scott that Sally still didn't understand, like how she could have believed she'd had a loving marriage when the very last words Scott had said to her was that he hated being married to her.

"I'm more worried about Paul. He's so angry, and I don't mean typical teenage testosterone anger."

"He still blaming you for Zelda's suicide?"

Sally turned her head away so her friend couldn't see her watery eyes. Suddenly, all Sally could picture in her mind's eye was Zelda curled up in her bed, her long fair hair fanning out over the pillow, her eyes closed. Deathly still.

"Yes. He's right though. I should have noticed the signs. I should have done more."

Margie stopped running. "Wait up!"

Sally stopped too.

Margie said, "I know all about guilt, remember? My baby died."

Sally did remember— it had been cot death that had taken Margie's little one.

"For years I blamed myself. It very nearly destroyed me and my marriage. So you have to stop blaming yourself for what Zelda did. We all know why she did it. We know she was being bullied at school. We know you did what you could to help her. But there are some things you just can't prevent happening."

Sally wanted to change the subject because she knew she would never stop blaming herself. "There's a new Thai restaurant on Fourth. I've heard good things about it. Would you like to try it some time?"

Margie took the hint. "Sure. I love Thai food."

They recommenced running, and when they reached the bottom of the hill, they headed for the gate on Fifth Street. Not far from the exit was the bus shelter where Anna Moorehouse had been abducted five years ago. Every time Sally jogged past it, she felt icy fingers run up her spine.

A flash of red and black caught Sally's eye, and with it came a flashback that caused her to stumble. She put out a hand to stop herself falling. Margie ran on for a little, then doubled back.

"What's wrong?" she asked.

Sally looked over her shoulder. There was a poster stuck to the bus-shelter wall. It could be any old poster, but even from this angle, the layout was terrifyingly familiar. "Come with me."

Her feet didn't want to move, just like her mind didn't want to believe what her eyes had seen was real.

"You're shaking," Margie said.

Sally crept a few paces, then she gasped.

All the Poster Killer posters had a distinctive style. There was no doubt that what she was looking at was his work. The word MISSING was in big red letters on a black rectangular banner across the top, and the face of the girl looked out from the page. Only this time it was Sally's face—and her name. Slowly, Sally raised a finger and pointed.

"Oh my God!" Margie said. She looked at Sally then back at the poster. Then she shook her head. "Is that somebody's idea of a sick joke?"

"That's me," Sally whispered, grappling to understand what was happening.

The past and present were colliding.

Sally looked at Margie. "It's Durrant. It has to be." All of a sudden, she was icy cold.

"What if it is? It doesn't mean anything. The Poster Killer is long gone, and besides, he kidnapped young girls."

That was true. Eleven- to thirteen-year-olds.

Sally peered closer at the poster, and her hand shot up to her mouth. "My running top. The one I wore yesterday." She tugged at the neck of the top, which was designed to wick sweat away from the skin. "Look! In the background. The lookout where we always pause for breath."

Both women looked around them. Was he watching them now? An old man, clutching a shopping bag, sat on one of the uncomfortably small plastic seats inside the shelter. In the park, another man walked his dog, and a couple of joggers they knew by sight were running up the hill. The street was busy with early commuter and delivery-truck traffic. There was nothing out of the ordinary except a poster that told the world Sally Fairburn was a missing person.

"We have to get away," Sally said, panic rising inside her. "He takes his victim once the poster appears."

"But Durrant's in jail."

"His thugs aren't. Come on—let's go." Sally readied herself to jog away.

"I'll take a photo," Margie said, removing her cell from a belt that also held her house key and credit card.

"Hurry!" Sally squeaked, staring madly around.

Margie took a photo. "We have to report this."

"Everyone will see it! I don't want this." Sally's panic was strangling her—she could barely breathe.

"Not if I do this." Margie picked at the edge of the tape with a long fingernail.

"You can't do that," Sally gasped. "You'll contaminate the scene."

"Watch me."

Margie pulled the top piece of tape away from the glass and the poster came away easily. She did the same with the lower piece.

"Okay, let's go!" Margie said, rolling the poster up.

She gave Sally a shove, and they both set off at a sprint, Sally gulping in breath, her fear driving her onward.

They didn't stop until they reached Sally's townhouse. Only when the door was locked behind them and they were sitting down did Sally make the call to Clarke. She'd already forwarded to him the photos Margie had taken and shared with her.

"Yep?" Clarke said brusquely.

There was loud music and the sound of a car's horn in the background. He was probably driving to work.

"The Poster Killer, he's... back," Sally blurted out, then coughed—a honking dry cough. Her throat was ragged from the sprint home.

"What did you say?"

"The Poster Killer is back. He's after me."

"Jesus, Sally, slow down. What do you mean after you?"

"Check your text messages."

"I'm driving."

Sally felt like throwing her phone across the room. Why wasn't he listening? "He's put up a poster. And I'm the missing person."

NINE

Sally checked her watch—it was 10:18 a.m. She was late. At least she was at Walla Walla State Penitentiary just as Durrant had asked her to be, waiting for him to be escorted from the "at risk" wing. It seemed that even the most hardened criminals drew the line at child rape and child prostitution, so he was kept away from the general prison population. Detective Lin had removed Sally's name from the visitors' list, but when she'd pleaded with the guard on duty to check with Durrant, her name had been put back on.

Clarke and Lin would be annoyed about her seeing Durrant, but her life—and perhaps her son's too—was in danger, and she wasn't going to risk enraging the man she believed was the Poster Killer. If the bus-shelter poster had been Durrant's warning, she was heeding it. So while detectives and forensic experts cordoned off the bus stop and examined the poster, Sally got in her car and drove to the jail. On the way, she called Paul's school and asked them to keep an eye on him. She didn't tell them about the poster. She simply said that she may have to collect him, for family reasons. More than anything, she needed to know he was safe.

To say that Clarke was upset with Margie for removing the poster was an understatement. But she was a member of the public, and he had to bite his tongue. She had meant well, but by removing the poster, Margie had contaminated the crime scene.

Durrant, sixty-eight, entered the room at a leisurely pace and sat on a plastic chair facing Sally. Between them was a Perspex wall which was reinforced at waist-height by steel plates. Drilled into the Perspex in a circular pattern were holes about the circumference of a dime through which they could confer.

Durrant, in an orange boiler suit, his hands cuffed, leaned back into the seat, his eyes sparkling with mirth. At first glance he appeared to be a perfectly ordinary grandpa: thinning silver hair, round affable face, a Santa belly.

"You're late. I detest lateness."

Those grandpa eyes were suddenly ice-cold. Sally wanted to run away, but her limbs felt useless, and she was powerless to move. *Say something. Don't show him you're afraid.*

"Mr. Durrant—"

"Speak up or sit closer," he ordered.

Sally raised her voice. "There was a poster on a bus shelter today, the exact same style as the ones used by the Poster Killer. Did you tell someone to put it there, so I'd have to come and see you?"

Durrant was a predator. He sensed her fear and leaned closer. "Who's in the poster? Pretty, is she?"

Sally paused. He knew who, surely? He had ordered one of his thugs to put it on the bus shelter for her to see, hadn't he?

"Me."

Durrant laughed uproariously, his shoulders bobbing. "Maybe the killer's got a taste for older ladies these days."

Sally felt the sting of his mockery. She knew her neck and face had gone red.

He saw it. "Ain't seen a lady blush in many years. No offence meant, Sally. I'd have you, any day."

He looked her up and down. She'd dressed simply: jeans and a white shirt. Under his scrutiny, she felt like she was being undressed. She instinctively raised an arm and pulled the shirt collar together where the top two buttons were undone. He noticed and smirked.

"Mr. Durrant, please tell me why you put my face on a Poster Killer poster."

"I didn't. You disappoint me, Sally. I thought you were cleverer than this. Your brain turn to mush or something?" He sat with his elbows on his thighs. "I'll spell it out for you. I never put up any posters. That's not how I operate. If I ever took girls off the street—and I'm denying I ever did—I sure as hell wouldn't advertise it on a poster."

"If you're not him, then tell me who is."

He crossed a leg. "Did you listen to a word I said? I told you not to call the cops. And what do you do? You call the fucking cops!"

Sally jumped in her seat. The affable expression had twisted into an angry snarl. Just as quickly, the snarl was gone.

"I... I..." Sally had lost the ability to speak.

In the next-door cubicle, a woman with a baby in her arms was shouting at the prisoner she'd come to see, demanding to know how she and her daughter were supposed to survive without his child support. The prisoner, a large man with visible tattoos on his neck and hands, looked away and said nothing, which only made the mother angrier.

"Hey!" Durrant raised his voice at the tattooed man, just a few feet away. "Tell your woman to shut her mouth."

The inmate retorted with a barrage of expletives, and a prison guard in a black uniform intervened, warning both men that if there was any trouble, their visits were over.

Durrant turned his head slowly back to Sally. "Young guys.

They got no respect. And you, you've caused me trouble. Trouble I now gotta deal with. So you owe me."

"Here's what you're going to do. You tell that dick-brain Clarke that I can name the Poster Killer, but before I do that, I get a pardon and go into witness protection."

"I can pass on your request. Will you leave me alone if I do?"

"You make it happen, Sally. You leave here, you tell Clarke that I have to be moved out of here today. No delays, you hear me. Then I'll tell him who he or she is."

He or she? Was he playing games with her? The killer had to be male. The only girl's body found, Francesca Molinari, had been raped before she was strangled.

"You think a woman did it?"

"I'll tell Clarke when I'm out of this place. If he doesn't take my offer seriously, you'll go to the media, tell them Clarke is doing nothing to solve the case and I know who did it. You hear me?"

"I can't do that—"

"You will. Because I'm telling you to."

Sally almost peed her pants. People who defied him had a nasty habit of dying horribly.

"And you know the right people in the DA's office."

He was overestimating her influence there.

"The victims' families deserve the truth. Just tell me, for their sakes."

Durrant's upper lip curled. "All marshmallow and sweetness, aren't you, missy? Maybe I chose the wrong person."

He looked over his shoulder then leaned close to the Perspex. "It has to happen today."

"Why?"

He drew even closer. "There's a hit out on me."

For the briefest of moments, Sally saw fear in his eyes. This was her chance. He needed her more than she needed him.

The thought shocked her. How could she be so ruthless? Then, in her mind's eye she saw Mary, desperate to know what had happened to Anna. Sally couldn't fail her, so she pushed on.

"Give me something. Clarke will need more than my word. Tell me one thing about the killer that the cops don't know."

Durrant stood stiffly. The prison guard came over. "Keep me updated. This meeting's over," Durrant said.

She shot up so suddenly the metal legs of her chair screeched across the concrete floor. "Wait! You have to give me a clue!" she called.

He remained where he was, and with a jerk of his head, the guard walked away. Then Durrant stepped close to the Perspex and lowered his voice. "It's not one person. It's two."

"Two!"

"You heard me. They work as a team. Now get me out of here."

"Earlier, you said he or she. Did you mean he *and* she?"

"Stop your fishing."

"I need more," Sally said, emboldened by Durrant's clear desperation to leave Walla Walla.

He gave her a cold stare. "Get me out of here, or you'll be sorry."

TEN

Sally's stomach heaved. She raced from the state penitentiary's meeting area and dived into the visitors' bathroom, where she promptly spewed up her breakfast. Wiping away the residue with toilet paper, she flushed, washed her hands, and then stared at her reflection in a mirror that had a crack in one corner.

Who was this woman staring back at her? Where had her courage to challenge Durrant come from? Was this how she used to be before Scott had come into her life?

She leaned against the edge of the basin, unsure if her legs would support her. Durrant had made it quite clear that if she failed to get him out of Walla Walla, she would regret it. If he was telling the truth and he hadn't been responsible for the missing-person poster, then it had to be the Poster Killer warning her to back off. Did this mean that the killer—or killers, as Durrant would have her believe—feared Durrant would reveal their identities?

"What have I got myself into?" she murmured.

The bathroom door swung open, and the woman with the baby whose partner Durrant had yelled at earlier came in and headed for the baby-changing table. She looked to be late teens or early twenties with long hair that frayed and thinned at the tips. She paused and glared at Sally.

"Your boyfriend's a cunt," she said, then continued to the baby-change table.

That was about as much as Sally could take. She left the bathroom in a hurry, collected her belongings from the prison guard, and didn't stop until she was out in the open air, the huge parking lot stretching out before her, mountains and forests in the distance. She paused to breathe in deeply, hoping to cleanse herself from the evil she'd just faced. But all she could smell was the sourness of her vomit.

Taking a tissue from her purse, she blew her nose hard. Then she dialed Clarke, who didn't pick up. Her message told him she'd visited Durrant and had important information for him. She was kind of relieved she didn't have to tell Clarke directly about her disobedience and hear his angry response. Perhaps by the time she drove to Franklin PD to see him, he would have calmed down.

Durrant's threat echoed through her head. She was under no illusion that her life was in danger if she didn't do what he said. She would have to take special care to keep herself and Paul safe. Her priority was to pick up her son from school. Perhaps her imagination was running wild, but she wasn't going to give Durrant's thugs the opportunity to kidnap her son.

The prison's parking lot was eerily quiet. Her visit had been shorter than the allocated time, and she guessed the other visitors were still inside talking to their loved ones. She'd left her car two rows from where she stood, and she set off at a fast pace, suddenly aware of how alone she was. Sure, there were CCTV cameras all over the prison, but as far as she could recall, there was only one at the entrance to the visitors' building and one other as you drove in and out of the lot. Sally was in a blind spot.

Her mind flashed back to the car that had followed her into the underground parking garage in the city. She looked left, then right. No cars were on the move, but she sped up anyway, jogging past the first row of vehicles.

She saw her car and pulled out her key, unlocking it remotely. Again, she swiveled her head from side to side, searching for anything unusual. She was a few paces from her Civic when a flash of blue caught her eye to the right. It was a blue Audi and the opening of the door had caught the sunlight.

Sally froze. Bryan Topham got out of his car, which was only three bays away from hers. Had he followed her here? She ran for her Civic, bile in her throat.

"Sally, wait!" Topham called.

She kept running.

The rusty sedan next to hers had parked too close. She could open the door just enough to squeeze into the driver's seat, but she had to twist her body to do so. She knocked her right knee off the base of the steering wheel, slamming the door behind her. She had only just centrally locked it when Topham's face loomed outside the window.

"Go away!" she shouted.

Sally stabbed the key at the ignition but missed.

"Sally, we have to talk," Topham said.

His nose was just inches from the window, so close she could see the white hair in his nostrils.

"Stop following me!"

"Has Durrant confessed? Please, Sally, I have to know."

He didn't sound like a man researching a book. He also didn't sound like one of Durrant's thugs. He was desperate.

She glanced at him. "Why? Why do you have to know any of this?"

He drew in his chin, taken aback. "My book."

That was a lie, she was sure of it. Sally jabbed the key into the ignition and started the car.

"I can't help you," she said.

She'd already told one man this today, and here she was saying it again.

She reversed the car. Topham stepped back. When her car was out of the bay, she pressed the accelerator and drove past him. He waved at her.

"I have information," he shouted.

Sally had already been given enough information to last her a lifetime. She didn't need any more, especially from a stalker like Bryan Topham.

ELEVEN

Paul slouched in his seat in Franklin PD's city station while he and his mom waited to see Clarke. He flicked a look at her. She sat on the edge of the chair, leaning forward, tearing at a fingernail with her teeth. She hadn't done that for a while. She was freaking out about something, but she wouldn't tell him what, and now he was really pissed. Why did she treat him like a baby?

She'd been acting weird when she'd come back from her morning run. Then they'd had a fight because he didn't want to go to school. He'd pretended he was sick, just like he'd done yesterday, but she hadn't fallen for it this time. Whatever was bugging her, it was enough for her to forget that this week he had exams: math, American history, geography, and English. He hadn't studied for them. There was no point. He was going to be a professional football player. All he had to do was play the game hard and get noticed by a talent scout.

"Tell me what's going on, Mom."

She looked askance at him, lowering the fingernail she'd been gnawing. "Do you remember when you were about nine or ten there was a criminal the police wanted to catch called the Poster Killer?"

"Yeah, I'm not stupid. You and Dad talked about him all the time, and school went into scare-mode. We had to do lockdown practice."

So that's it, Paul thought. He was missing today's math exam because his mom was freaking out. He silently thanked the dude everyone called the Poster Killer.

"You heard us? I didn't know that," Sally said, then shook her head.

"Is that why we're here?"

"Okay, I guess you should know. I went to see a prisoner this morning who claims he knows who the killer is. That's why we're here. I have to update the detective in charge of the cold case." She spoke slowly, as if she were choosing her words carefully. That meant there was something she wasn't telling him.

"Okay, so why take me out of school?"

"He used to use posters to announce his intended victim." She paused.

"So?"

"All right. This morning I found a poster. It was of me. We don't know who put it there, and it could be a sick joke—"

Paul interrupted. "You mean a killer is after you?" He said it loudly, and a woman seated near them turned her head and stared.

"No, not necessarily. I mean, um, nobody knows. I wanted to be sure you were safe, should the threat prove to be real. But I'm sure it's nothing."

"Then why are you acting scared?" Paul asked.

She shifted her butt in the seat. His mom did that when she was asked a tricky question.

"Because if it is the Poster Killer, we have to be careful. I want you with me."

"No school?"

"Until we know what's happening."

Paul punched the air. "Yes!"

"They said you can do the exams at home."

His elation was short-lived. "No way!"

"You thought I'd forgotten?"

Clarke beckoned them from the elevator, holding the doors open with one hand. Paul didn't remember the cop, but he remembered this building.

"Maybe you should stay here," his mom said.

"No way," Paul said. "I'm fourteen, Mom. I want to know what's going on."

She hesitated but allowed him to follow her into the elevator. The doors closed.

"Paul, how ya doing?" Clarke said, patting him on the back. Then to Sally he gave a taut nod. "Sally."

Paul got the feeling Clarke wasn't happy with his mom. Was Clarke one of his dad's friends? When he'd walked out, Sally had lost a bunch of friends who were cops, which she'd been upset about at the time.

When they reached the fifth floor, they entered Homicide. There were cops everywhere, their focus drawn briefly to him and his mom. Paul thought he recognized some faces from the birthday parties, barbeques, and picnics they'd been to when he was younger, always with police families. And at the center of it all had been his dad.

"I hear the Pioneer Panthers could win the state trophy," Clarke said. That was the team Paul played for.

"We're *going* to win it," Paul said, standing tall, although he was already taller than Clarke.

"Good for you."

Once they were seated in Clarke's office, Clarke said to Sally, "You sure Paul should hear this?"

She glanced at Paul, who was going to argue the point if she asked him to leave the room. "I'm sure."

Paul sat up straighter. He was being treated like an adult and he was going to behave like one. And besides, for once his mom was talking about something interesting. He couldn't wait to tell Reilly about it.

Clarke said, "I get the poster is a real shock for you. But meeting Durrant was a bad idea."

His mom didn't reply—she just shifted in her seat. Paul stared at her. She was doing that thing she used to do with his dad—working out what to say to keep the peace. Acting all weak.

Seconds ticked by.

"Mom?"

She stopped behaving like a zombie and spoke. "The poster terrified me. I thought Durrant had done it because I'd told you about his request to see him. I wanted to stop him hurting me—or Paul." She gave her son a weak smile.

Clarke nodded. "Did he identify the Poster Killer?"

"He gave me a clue. Two clues." She cleared her throat. "He said that the Poster Killer is two people."

Paul gawped at his mom. Two killers. Okay, this was getting serious.

Clarke said, "It's one man and it's Durrant."

"Forgive me, Detective, but I don't think so," Sally said, sounding more confident. Paul was secretly cheering her on. "Durrant made a good point. His business relies on operating beneath the radar. Why would he put up posters about girls he'd taken off the street? He wouldn't."

"Because it's a game to him, Sally. And he likes toying with us, making us look bad."

You're doing that all on your own, buddy, Paul thought. Clarke was like his dad, always blaming everyone else for his mistakes.

"But it could be two people, right?" Sally said. Paul was impressed at how she was persisting. Her therapy was working.

"One puts up the poster, the other lures the girl into the car. And Durrant said something else. He said he or she, like he wasn't ruling out a woman being involved."

She glanced at Paul then. "Paul, honey, there are things I need to say that you may find upsetting. Maybe it would be best if—"

"No," Paul said. "Don't shut me out."

Clarke and Sally exchanged looks.

"Okay," his mom said. "But if you want to leave at any time, just say."

"I'm staying," Paul said, folding his arms.

Clarke spoke. "We considered the idea of two abductors working together and the idea of a man and a woman. There was no evidence to support it."

"There have been male and female serial killers, Detective. And think about it, who is a girl going to trust more, a strange man in a car or a friendly woman in a car?"

Clarke rubbed his hand across his mouth. "All right. Let's run with that idea. Why now? If he knew who the killers were, why wait so long to offer it as a bargaining chip?"

"He said there's a hit out on him and he has to get out of Walla Walla today. He seemed afraid."

Clarke smiled. Paul was pretty certain the detective liked the idea of the hit. This conversation was turning way more interesting than he had imagined it would be. He'd have heaps to tell Reilly as soon as they got out of there.

"Does he think I can wave a magic wand and he goes free?" Clarke asked.

"He wants to go into witness protection."

"Jeez." Clarke shook his head. "Have you any idea how impossible it is to get someone like Durrant out of a maximum-security jail? And why should I? This is all bullshit."

"What if he's telling the truth?" Sally asked. "If he dies tonight, you could lose the first real lead you've had for years."

"We're better off focusing on the poster. Forensics are working on it."

Paul could feel anger swelling inside him. People never listened to his mom. It was because she was quiet. It wasn't fair. Dad used to talk over her all the time, like what she said didn't matter.

"I know people in the DA's office. I can help you," Sally said. "Can't you at least arrange for Durrant's transfer to another jail?"

"I'll look into it."

"When? The clock's ticking, and Durrant could be murdered any minute." Her voice was raised, and her cheeks had turned red. "I have to tell him what's going on."

Atta girl, Mom!

"I'll inform the warden Durrant must be in twenty-four-hour lockdown."

"That's not good enough. And what do I tell him? He wants to be kept informed."

"You tell him we're working on it."

Paul couldn't hold back. "You're not going to do anything, right? You're just jerking Mom along."

"Paul!" Sally said, sounding shocked.

Paul continued, "Maybe this Durrant guy trusts Mom. She's handed you clues. And you're treating her like she's stupid."

"Son, you don't understand what's going on here."

"Yeah, I understand. You're going to ignore Mom." Paul stood. "Just like Dad did."

TWELVE

Sally could feel the heat of Paul's fury, but at least it wasn't aimed at her.

"Thank you," Sally said, smiling at her son. "It meant a lot to me, the way you stood up for me in there."

"I thought you were pissed at me."

"Not at all. It's just I've never seen anyone argue with Clarke like that." Sally glanced at the female officer standing by the door. "Will you be okay?"

Paul shrugged then pulled out his phone.

She closed the interview-room door behind her. The female cop would stay with Paul, and he could occupy himself with games on his phone, but he was under strict instructions from Clarke not to share anything about what he and Sally had discussed and especially not to use social media. Paul had begrudgingly promised, and Sally felt confident he would honor that promise, but the cop had still been ordered to watch how Paul used his phone.

Sally followed Clarke to another interview room where her cell phone was hooked up to a voice recorder and they were all given headphones. She and Paul had been kept waiting two hours while Clarke brokered the necessary arrangements with the prison warden to move Durrant in an armored vehicle to Franklin PD's cells. It wasn't what Durrant wanted, but at least it temporarily got him out of the state penitentiary and gave them time for him to tell them the Poster Killer's identity—or identities.

Sally sat opposite Clarke. Lin sat next to him.

"The warden's given permission for the call to go straight through to a phone which will be handed to Durrant," Clarke said. "Are you clear what you're going to say?"

"I think so. It's true, right? You are going to bring him here for questioning?"

"Yes."

"Okay." She took in a deep breath. The exhalation was ragged with fear. She dialed the number she'd been instructed to call.

A male answered.

"I'm Sally Fairburn and I need to speak to Theo Durrant urgently."

Sally glanced up at Lin, who gave her a reassuring smile.

"Wait a moment," the prison guard said.

There was the sound of footsteps on a metal surface, men's voices rumbling in the background. "Durrant. For you," Sally heard the guard say.

"Yes," Durrant said. He sounded loud, but perhaps it was because she was hearing his voice through headphones, just as Clarke and Lin were too.

"It's Sally Fairburn. I've been working hard on your behalf and I have some good news. An armored police vehicle will transport you to Franklin PD's cells. You'll be interviewed and you'll stay the night here under twenty-four-hour supervision."

"Not good enough," Durrant said. "Too many bent cops. I'll be dead in that cell before morning. I have to get out of this place pronto and into witness protection. I have to disappear, you hear me?"

Sally looked at Clarke across the Formica tabletop for guidance. There was a circular coffee stain right near her trembling hand, which must have happened during a previous interview.

Clarke mouthed, "Working on it."

Was he working on it or was she about to lie to a man who had already threatened her?

"Detective Clarke is working on that. It takes time to set up."

"Did they tell you to say that?" Durrant asked.

Again, she looked at Clarke. He nodded.

"Yes."

"He there with you?"

Clarke nodded.

"Yes."

"Who else?"

Lin nodded.

"Detective Lin. That's all."

"Then I guess they're listening. Clarke, don't fuck with me. I need witness protection right now, or I'm a dead man and you'll never catch the killers."

There it was again. The plural.

Clarke spoke. "Witness protection for a lifer isn't easy to get done, Durrant. You need to give me more than what you gave Sally. Two killers, you say. I want names. Then you get witness protection."

Clarke was off-script. Was he making this up? Sally felt icy fingers of dread creep up her back. She shivered. Durrant would blame her. He'd send his thugs after her. And what about Paul? Would he hurt her child? Sally opened her mouth to plead with Clarke, but a sharp shake of the detective's head stopped her.

"Oh no you don't," Durrant replied. "I give you names and you leave me to die. But I will tell you one more thing."

He paused. Sally heard her heartbeat thudding as she waited. Clarke stared straight ahead and waited.

"Sally knows who they are."

Her eyes widened. Clarke and Lin stared at her. She shook her head vehemently and mouthed a no.

"Stop dicking around. I need names," Clarke demanded.

"Witness protection or nothing."

"Listen to me, Durrant. In an hour, you will be picked up and brought here. Get ready to leave, because a cell here is our best offer."

Clarke reached across to her phone and ended the call.

"What did you do that for?" Sally shrieked. How could he put the phone down on Durrant?

Clarke leaned back against the chair. "Why does he think you know the *killers*?" he asked, making air-quote signs with his fingers.

"I have no idea."

Both Lin and Clarke stayed silent.

"I really don't know what he's talking about."

Did they seriously believe him?

Lin piped up. "You may not think you know who he is. I'm still of the opinion it's one guy. But maybe you do know this person and you don't know it yet. Can you think of anyone it might be? Think back to when the first girl was taken—Anna Moorehouse. You consoled her parents. You were present during their interviews. Did anything jar?"

"You're not seriously thinking Anna's parents did it?"

"Everyone was, and still is, a suspect. What I mean is, was there anything that didn't sit right with anything you heard or saw? Victims' relatives. Friends they knew. People at the school."

"Nobody springs to mind. Can I have time to think about

it?" Sally looked at the door. "I must get Paul home. I don't want my son here any longer. I'll call you if I think of anyone."

Clarke hesitated, then nodded.

Sally left the room as fast as she could. The thought that she might know the killer or killers made her feel nauseous. She collected her son, and they made their way down to the first floor in the elevator.

"What happened?" Paul asked.

"Let's talk in the car. Not here."

"I hate this place," Paul grumbled. "Whenever Dad was supposed to pick me up from school and drive me home, he always brought me here. Set me up at a desk and left me alone while he talked and laughed with his buddies."

"I didn't know. I'm sorry." She was discovering there was a lot about Scott she didn't know.

"Did you know he took me to a bar once? Made me sit in a corner while he drank. I was, like, seven or eight."

"I'm so sorry, Paul. He told me he frequently had to work late and you were happily drawing."

"He lied. You were like a zombie when he was around."

"I know. That's why I see a shrink." Sally put out an arm to draw him to her.

"Don't," he said, pulling away.

"I tried," said Sally. "He was so dominating. But I always did my best for you and Zelda."

"Yeah, right."

The elevator doors opened, and they crossed the foyer in silence. She felt the sting of his rebuke. There were things Sally was ashamed of, but she had always done everything she could for her children.

When they were on the street, Sally said, "You remember the time he wanted to send you to summer camp and you didn't want to go. You were eight."

"He called me a crybaby and said it would toughen me up."

"I cancelled your place and took time off work. We had fun. I taught you to kayak. Scott wouldn't speak to me for a whole week."

Paul shrugged. "Whatever."

He walked away. She caught up with him.

"I love you. I will always do whatever it takes to keep you safe. Your happiness means everything to me. You know that, right?"

Some of the tension in his shoulders subsided, and he gave her a twitch of a smile. "Yes, Mom."

She embraced him, and he didn't try to pull away.

"Always remember I love you," Sally said.

THIRTEEN

Sally deadlocked the front door then walked through the house to the back to make sure everything was how she had left it. The backyard was fenced, and the gate had a bolt. An intruder would have to jump the fence to get into the yard, and given that it was overlooked by neighbors on either side, it was likely they would be spotted. *We're safe. Nobody can get in.*

Paul helped himself to some milk from the fridge, drinking directly from the carton. She would normally ask him not to do that, but not after the day they'd had so far.

"If you want to talk more about what's happening, I'm here," Sally said.

"I'm good," he said, putting the carton back in the fridge.

Paul headed for the stairs but turned around before he began climbing them. "You stood up to Clarke. Proud of you, Mom."

Sally blinked rapidly in surprise, then a big smile broke out on her face.

"Thank you." This was the first time he'd complimented her like this. Her shrink had told her she was making good progress and now her son had suggested the same. She'd been told to acknowledge her victories, those tiny steps to believing in herself again. "It felt good doing it."

"It was really cool." He paused, looked down, then swung his shoe over the stone floor. "I'm glad Dad's gone."

"Me too."

Paul went to his room to play video games. She brought him some of her homemade pea-and-ham soup with lots of slices of buttered toast, which he proceeded to eat without taking his eye off the game. Sally ate hers in the kitchen, or perhaps it would be better to say she played with her soup for a while. Her stomach churned with nervous acid. She couldn't stop thinking about her conversations with Durrant and Clarke. What did it all mean for her and Paul? And why had Durrant claimed that she knew the killers? Her skin prickled at the horrid thought.

She was under no illusion that Clarke and Lin wanted her to think carefully about possible suspects, when in truth, she was mentally drained, and she would dearly love to forget that the last two days had ever happened. Even though Paul seemed chilled about their situation, she worried he might be putting on an act for her sake.

Sally looked up at the time on the oven's control panel. Durrant should have been picked up by the armored police vehicle by now and be on his way to Franklin PD. In another hour, perhaps the ordeal would be over. Durrant would have identified the killers and the named suspects would be taken in for questioning.

She gave up trying to eat her lunch. She threw the toast in the bin and put Saran Wrap over the bowl so that she could perhaps eat it later. Then she went upstairs, passing Paul's bedroom. The door was ajar, but the noisy video game was a silent world to Sally because Paul wore headphones. She stepped into her bedroom and shut the door.

Storage space in her townhouse was limited: she had no attic because the roof was flat, and no parking garage either. Her closet was full, mostly with boxes of family photos and Zelda's belongings: special things Sally couldn't bring herself to let go. Under her bed were four plastic storage boxes with lids.

She kneeled down and pulled out a box with a blue lid. It contained her work notebooks, going all the way back to 1993, when she'd started her career in victim support. The style of her notebooks had changed over time, but for the last five years they had been hardcover with a ribbon to mark the page, each one a different color and labelled with the year.

She found six notebooks spanning 2010 to 2011, the period the Poster Killer had been active, and laid them on the bed in chronological order. Each book contained her personal notes on the six victims and their families, and each one had a different color jacket—Moorehouse (pink), Blake (blue), Green (green), Ibrahim (purple), Kapoor (yellow), Molinari (orange); girls aged from eleven to thirteen, all from different ethnic backgrounds.

Detectives had searched for a common denominator: they lived within ten miles of each other, and four of the six went to the same school as Zelda—Ronald Reagan Middle School. The remaining two victims, Francesca Molinari and Tazeen Ibrahim, had been eleven years old at the time and attended Pioneer Elementary School. They all attended clubs at the Pine Creek YMCA.

Both Detective Foster and then his successor, Clarke, had focused on the YMCA and the schools, convinced that the abductor had selected his victims on the basis that they all took public transportation home, namely the bus. Sally had volunteered at the YMCA and knew all the missing girls. Sometimes, at night, she drove some of them home because she didn't like them taking a bus. Sally recalled the endless interviews: teachers and parents, club coaches, bus drivers, and regular users of the bus routes the girls took. CCTV and cell-phone footage had been scrutinized, but the killer had chosen his locations well because there were no cameras pointing at the bus stops where the girls had been snatched, and there was no common make and model of car seen at all six locations.

Sally pulled the pink notebook toward her and ran her fingers across the shiny cover, then felt the edge of the white sticky label upon which she'd written in bold letters *February 12, 2010: Anna Moorehouse*. She was almost afraid to read it; it would bring back such harrowing memories.

She sat cross-legged on the floor and steeled herself. When she was ready, she opened it, the spine of the book tight from having been shut for several years. She read her handwritten record of her first meeting with Mary and Geoff Moorehouse, Anna's parents. It brought back their horror, their disbelief such a thing was truly happening, their fear, and, much later on, their despair at the police's failure to find their daughter. It was ridiculous of her to even imagine the parents were responsible, or any of the relatives who had also been interviewed.

For the first time, Sally paid attention to the women. She hated to admit it to herself but there were plenty of examples of serial-killer couples. Karla Homolka and Paul Bernardo, AKA the Ken and Barbie Killers, had raped and killed three women, including Homolka's younger sister. The infamous British child killers, Myra Hindley and Ian Brady, known as the Moors Murderers, had abducted and killed five kids.

Sally paused in her reading and thought of Geoff, who had been questioned but had been at work at the time of the abductions. Ruby, Mary's sister, had no apparent reason to kill her niece, who she genuinely seemed to adore, and had witnesses who'd confirmed she'd been working in her flower shop. Sally checked for mentions of female teachers or parents who'd behaved oddly toward Anna, but nothing stood out.

Placing the notebook down on the floor, Sally straightened out the cricks in her back. She had been slouching as she read and now her lower spine was sore. She moved to sit on the bed instead, building a wall of pillows between herself and the headboard for some support.

She opened the second notebook, which was labelled *June 7, 2010—Caroline Blake*.

Thirteen-year-old Caroline had been the youngest of five daughters. Her parents were devout Catholics and popular members of the local church. Tiffany, the eldest, was described as the "black sheep." All the daughters were tall and blonde, but Tiffany had all the potential to be a catwalk model, and her parents had been horrified when Tiffany had defied them and taken a modelling contract in LA. Mr. and Mrs. Blake had refused to speak to her after that and behaved as if she were dead. Only when Tiffany had returned to Franklin and married Chase Feinstein, a garage mechanic, had the rift between her and her parents begun to heal. Then, two weeks after Caroline had been abducted, Tiffany had murdered her baby, Madison. It was an unbelievably distressing time for the family: their youngest daughter was missing and their eldest was standing trial for manslaughter, then, later, convicted.

Tiffany had been suffering from postpartum psychosis when she'd killed her child and claimed she didn't remember doing it. Was she also capable of abducting and possibly murdering her sister? Could she have been working with someone else? Had her husband, Chase, been involved?

Sally's head was spinning with questions, and so far, she had nothing useful to give Clarke.

Sally moved on to the next notebook titled *October 25, 2010—Stacy Green*. Sally remembered her well: she had been one of Zelda's best friends. A sweet girl and very bright, but incredibly shy. When Stacy was taken, Zelda had been inconsolable. She'd begged her father to find Stacy, venting her fear and fury at him in violent rages. There wasn't a cop in the city who didn't want to put a stop to the abductions but their efforts came to naught.

"Did this tip you over the edge, Zelda?" Sally muttered. "You two were so close."

Stacy's mom was single, and Stacy had been a latch-key kid. Ms. Green had no boyfriend or partner. Stacy's grandfather lived locally, and on the afternoon she'd disappeared, he was supposed to have picked her up from school. He'd been delayed in a work meeting and turned up at the school too late, so he had an alibi for the time she'd disappeared. Apart from Stacy's friends and an old lady next door who kept an eye on Stacy when Ms. Green was at work, their social circle had been small.

Needing a break, Sally poked her head into Paul's room to check he was okay—but he hadn't moved and was still playing the same video game.

She went downstairs for a glass of water then took out the trash. A solitary magpie perched on her fence, then flew to the small patch of grass in her backyard and watched her. Sally's neighbor fed the magpie and it had become so tame it would approach people expecting food. It bobbed its head at her.

One for sorrow, Sally thought, remembering a rhyme she'd learned as a kid about the significance of magpies. Was the bird a sign of bad things to come?

Going over her old notes had brought up lots of distressing memories, and Sally felt a sadness envelop her. Where were those girls? Were any of them alive? The discovery of the body of the last victim had dampened Sally's hope for the others.

She went inside and made a coffee, then headed upstairs once more and began to skim through the fourth notebook: *March 24, 2011—Tazeen Ibrahim*. Her parents were Lebanese migrants and they'd brought up Tazeen and her brother, Farez, to be proud Americans. They made a point of not speaking Lebanese at home, only English. Her father was an associate professor of Applied Mathematics and a practicing Muslim. Farez walked his sister to and from school every day, although latterly he'd put his sister on a bus because he'd wanted to walk with a girl he was smitten with. Their parents didn't know about this. The day of the abduction, Tazeen had disembarked at the bus stop nearest her house and then vanished.

Sally checked her notes on the girl who Farez had been secretly dating. She was Christian and they'd both said in their statements that they'd feared their parents would disapprove of their relationship.

Sally considered this situation for a while. What if Tazeen had threatened to tell her father about them? Was that motive enough for the brother to commit murder?

Sally shook her head. It was a ridiculous theory because it didn't explain why five other girls had been abducted too.

The fifth notebook was labelled *May 4, 2011—Vinesh Kapoor*. It was depressing reading. She was a talented tennis player. At the time she'd been abducted, she should have been in a tennis lesson, but she had excused herself because she felt unwell. Her mom and dad had been working, so they'd asked the coach to put Vinesh in a cab for which they would reimburse him later. Vinesh had gotten into the cab and then hopped out as soon as it turned a corner. Her parents had had her on a strict high-protein and no-carbs diet and she'd longed for donuts, so she'd bought some, ate them, then walked the rest of the way home. She was last seen walking down the street where the missing-person poster of her was later discovered on the bus-shelter wall.

Sally reached out for the orange notebook labelled *September 27, 2011—Francesca Molinari*. She was reluctant to read it. Eleven-year-old Francesca's bloated corpse had been discovered floating in the harbor near the hull of a cargo ship, her long black hair tangled in the anchor chain. She had been in the water too long to discover the killer's DNA, but it was clear from the bruising that she had been raped and then strangled. A huge search of the container port and the shoreline had ensued, but no other bodies had been found. After her, the abductions suddenly stopped.

The missing-person poster for Francesca had a spelling error in it, indicating it had been prepared in a rush. The other five posters did not. Was that significant?

Francesca was described by a number of teachers as "a disruptive influence" and she'd failed to turn up to school more often than she'd attended it. The day she'd gone missing, she'd skipped school and spent the afternoon smoking in the park with her best friend, Emma Manning. In her statement, Emma had said they'd bought the cigarettes from Lou Thompson, who owned the corner store. Thompson had been a suspect at one point. The Molinaris had blamed Emma for their daughter's disappearance, claiming that she'd led Francesca astray. From Sally's point of view, no one in the Molinari family stood out as a suspect for her murder.

Sally closed the last of the six notebooks. She felt heavy—weighed down by the traumatic accounts. She tried to ignore her emotions and look at the big picture from a practical point of view. The only possible couple who might commit such terrible crimes were Tiffany and Chase.

Sally checked the date of Tiffany's arrest and incarceration. She had been behind bars by the time Tazeen, Vinesh, and Francesca were abducted, although that didn't mean that Chase couldn't have continued with the abductions. He was a big, scary-looking guy and had a gruff way of speaking, but she remembered his tears over Madison's death. Underneath all that muscle and tattoos, she'd thought he had a good heart.

Sally ran her fingers through her hair. This was going to be much harder to solve than she'd hoped.

The image of Bryan Topham blocking her path to her house door popped into her head. She had meant to mention him to Clarke and forgotten. Who was he really? She doubted the line he'd spun about writing a book. Why had he appeared in her life the same day Durrant had claimed he knew who the Poster Killer was? Could there be a connection between the two men, and if so, why had Topham been so desperate to know what Durrant had told her?

Sally leaned against the bedhead and stared out of the window. Beyond the roofs and street trees, the mountains touched the pale blue sky. Could she do it? Could she draw on those short years as a cop to help solve the case? Her therapist always encouraged her to follow her instinct.

She looked at her cell phone, which was sitting beside her on the bed. She should tell the detectives her ideas, but doubt became a needling voice in her head. That voice told her she was useless, that she had no idea what she was doing. *What would you know about suspects?* it sneered.

Once upon a time, Sally had been a confident police officer.

It seemed so long ago.

FOURTEEN

JUNE 22, 1992

By June 1992, Sally had been a cop for two years, and she and Scott were engaged. When she'd first joined Franklin PD, Scott had been appointed her mentor and that was how their relationship had begun. Their boss decided to assign them new partners when they announced their wedding plans so that their personal relationship didn't interfere with their performance at work, thus Sally was now partnered with Anders Haugen, an older cop who was focused on staying alive long enough to draw his pension, and Scott was partnered with Walt Jackson, who would become his best friend.

Sally and Haugen were called out to a possible domestic in a wealthy neighborhood. A neighbor had heard screams and gunfire. They were the first on the scene. Haugen tried the front door, and Sally took the back—the sliding door was open. She radioed her partner, who joined her round the back. Inside, they heard a man's voice and a woman's pleas.

"Please don't hurt her," the woman wailed. "She's just a child."

Haugen called in backup, then followed Sally inside.

The voices came from a room at the front. A man in his thirties, shot in the chest, lay dead on the hall floor.

"You've got it. Don't lie to me!" the man in the front room shouted. "He stole it. It's mine."

"I don't know what you're talking about," a woman said. "Search the house—just don't kill us."

"You go find it. I'll take the girl."

A child screamed.

Sally peeked around the living-room door. The mother was crying, hands raised, begging the intruder not to hurt Bella. Bella, who looked to be six or seven, was held tightly by a man in his twenties who had a revolver pointed at her head. He kneeled behind her, and only his head was visible. His face was sweaty, his hair greasy, his movements jittery. He was on something. Sally suspected the intruder was after a stash of drugs. The living room had been trashed, cushions turned over, drawers emptied. Whatever his drug of choice, he wasn't likely to behave rationally.

"Find it, you stupid bitch, or you want her head blown off?"

"Okay, okay, I'll find it."

"Don't even think about making a call. I'll kill her."

As the mother left the living room, Haugen covered her mouth with his hand and dragged her away, whispering to her that they were cops. If she had screamed, the killer would have known he had company.

"You got twenty seconds," the killer yelled, "then bang!"

The mother struggled, trying to free herself from Haugen's grip.

Then the intruder started counting down from twenty.

"I can take the shot," Sally whispered to Haugen.

The mother's eyes bulged with terror. She struggled.

Haugen shook his head and mouthed, "Wait for backup."

"Fifteen, fourteen..." the man yelled. "Get back here now!"

Sally had been ranked top of her shooting class at the academy. She had a steady hand and the knack of slowing her breath so she could hold the pistol very still. The little girl's head was in the way of the man's throat and mouth. But his nose and forehead were visible. She was sure she could take him out without hurting the kid, although it was a highly risky shot.

"Wait!" hissed Haugen to Sally.

"Ten, nine, eight..."

The man had already shot and killed one person. Sally wasn't going to let him kill a little girl. She focused entirely on her aim. She didn't hear anything but her slowing breaths. She knew he must be close to counting the number one. The little girl was weeping. *Just don't move your head*, Sally thought. She aimed at the center of his forehead, held her breath, and pulled the trigger.

The man's head jerked back. Then he collapsed backward onto the floor. The little girl stood rooted to the spot, a trickle of urine on the floor, staring straight ahead, tears streaming. Sally rushed forward, aiming her gun at the killer, then kicked his revolver away. The mother picked up the little girl and ran from the house. But they were safe. The intruder was dead.

From that day forward, until she left Franklin PD the following year, she was known as *One-Shot*. Scott hated the nickname. He put the successful outcome down to luck.

Whether it was luck or her shooting skill, she had dared to do what she thought was right.

FIFTEEN

Sally heard the familiar rattling of Margie's Subaru Forester. It was like a small pebble shaken inside an empty can. Sally peered out of the bedroom window and watched Margie, in a cream skirt suit, slam her car door shut and hurry to Sally's house.

"Sally, I was worried about you," Margie said when Sally unlocked the door. "I had to come by and see how you were."

Sally looked nervously up and down the street. "Come in —quickly."

Margie strode inside in high-heeled dress shoes. Sally dead-locked the door behind her.

"You're worn out," Margie said, titling her head to one side and then the other as her eyes roamed Sally's face.

Sally flicked a look at the stairs and lowered her voice. "Paul's in his bedroom playing video games." He was wearing headphones, but if he decided to take them off, Sally didn't want him overhearing their conversation. He'd been through enough already. "Come into the kitchen. We can talk there."

Once she was through the door, Sally headed straight for the kettle. "Herbal tea?" she offered. There was no point offering Margie anything with caffeine in it. She'd stopped drinking tea and coffee years ago.

While Sally prepared the raspberry tea with a dash of honey, she updated her best friend with her news. Margie listened patiently, shaking her head every now and again and dropping the occasional exclamation.

"Damn! That's one hell of a day you've had so far." Margie smiled. "Look at you, my friend. So fearless. Is the Sally Fairburn I once knew emerging at last? I believe she is."

Sally kept her voice low. "I'm really frightened, Margie. The cops don't know if the poster is genuine or a copycat, but somebody put it there to spook me and it's worked. And Durrant threatened me. If Clarke doesn't put him into witness protection, I'm afraid he'll take it out on me, and maybe Paul."

"You took Paul out of school?"

"Yeah, but I can't hide him away forever."

"I hate to say this but once the media gets its grubby hands on the story, they'll hound you," Margie said.

"Thank goodness you took down the poster, otherwise I'd have reporters hammering on my door already."

Sally's cell rang. It was Clarke. Was her ordeal over?

She answered. "Is it good news?"

"Some good, some not so good."

Margie mouthed, "Who is it?"

She mouthed back, "Clarke," but must have made a sound.

"You with someone?" he asked.

She winced. "Yes, Margie Clay."

"This is a confidential conversation. Can you please ensure it stays that way?"

Sally left the kitchen and sat on the sofa. "I'm alone."

"Okay, first up, the poster. It's not the genuine article. Different paper stock, slight changes in the layout, and unlike the other six posters, this one is covered in fingerprints. Unfortunately, none of them are in our database."

"So it's a copycat?"

"Looks like it."

"That's good, right?"

"We don't know. We need to find the copycat. In the mean-time, stay vigilant."

"Okay, is that the good news?"

"Yes, I'm sorry to tell you that Durrant didn't make it out of Walla Walla. Somebody got to him."

Sally couldn't speak. She heard Durrant's voice in her head, telling her that he had to get out of there.

Clarke waited a few seconds and then said, "Sally? You there?"

"Yes, um. He's... dead. Is that what you mean?"

"Stabbed. Hell knows how it happened. He was locked in his cell."

Sally shook her head as if to dislodge fallen leaves from her hair. "You know how it happened," Sally said, an edge to her voice. "A guard was paid to do it."

"Don't leap to conclusions. There'll be a thorough investigation. The problem is he died before he could tell us more."

Sally made a noise like she had excruciating stomach pain. She covered her mouth with her palm, but the sound kept coming. She'd seen his fear, and she had understood it.

"Why didn't you listen to me earlier?" Sally demanded, her voice bitter. "The threat was real. Now we'll never know who the Poster Killer is."

"Don't you blame me for this. It's your interference that cost Durrant his life."

Sally saw red. If Clarke had been with her, she might well have slapped him. "No way! You made a mistake. A big one. *You've* lost a potential witness. What you can't abide is that I gathered more clues than you have in years!" She ended the call.

She was shaking with fury. "Fuck you!" she screamed at her phone.

"Sally?"

When she looked behind her, Margie was hovering in the doorway, her hand on her chest, her mouth hanging open. She had probably never heard Sally swear like that. Sally's fury had created the word and it had just burst out.

"You okay, honey?" Margie asked, sitting next to her on the sofa.

On the stairs, the thump of feet. Paul charged into the room in his socks and slid to a halt next to the coffee table.

"I heard you screaming. What's going on?" Paul stared at Sally.

"Durrant's dead," she replied through gritted teeth. Her face was hot and flushed. "Stabbed in his cell. Never even made it into the armored vehicle."

Paul rubbed the top of his scalp. "So he never talked?"

"No."

Paul started pacing, then suddenly stopped. He sat on the coffee table facing Sally and Margie. "Clarke's crap at his job. You do it, Mom. You find the Poster Killer."

"I can't."

Paul opened his mouth to argue when Margie spoke up. "Look on the bright side. Durrant won't be wreaking revenge on Sally—he's dead. And if the poster was Durrant's idea, then the real killer isn't targeting you."

"You're right," Sally said. Her rage began to subside. "Maybe life can get back to normal."

But Paul wasn't done. "I've been thinking back to when the girls disappeared. I was at the same elementary school as Tazeen and Francesca. I remember you then. How sad you were at their disappearance. You were never home, because you were with the girls' families. I hated you for it. I wanted you to myself."

Sally reached out and squeezed his hand.

Paul continued. "You really cared about them. Even as a ten-year-old kid, I could see that. So don't give up, that's what I'm saying."

Margie said, "That's a lot for your mom to take on. And dangerous." She looked pointedly at Sally. "Although, you're more than capable of doing this, my friend. This might be a crossroads for you, a way to discover your true potential. But it's risky, Sally. My opinion, for what it's worth, is either mend bridges with Clarke and work with them on the case or walk away from it totally. That means stop seeing the victims' families. There's no halfway position on something like this. The uncertainty will drive you insane."

SIXTEEN

Sally followed aisle three at the local grocery store until she found the pasta brand she was looking for. Tonight, she would cook Paul's favorite dish—spaghetti and meatballs with loads of shaved parmesan. The cold case wasn't solved, but she felt like an important chapter in its progress had been opened and she had contributed to that. When she'd completed her grocery shop, she ducked into the liquor store and purchased a nice bottle of Pinot Noir for her to enjoy with their meal.

Even though Sally felt better knowing the poster was a fake and that Durrant couldn't hurt her, she didn't dawdle. Paul was at home. She had made him promise not to let anybody into the house, but she still didn't like leaving him alone. Ten minutes later, Sally carried her shopping bag into the house, shut the front door, and called out Paul's name.

No answer. Sally put down the bag and listened. She could hear him talking to someone. It was faint. He probably had his bedroom door shut. Was he on the phone?

She took the stairs. The nearer she got to the landing, the more she could discern. His bedroom door was shut.

"No, I'm serious," Paul said. "Mom was the only person

he'd talk to and he's the scariest, creepiest guy. Or he was until he got knifed to death." A pause. "Yeah, I know. And I was there, telling this no-good cop to do his job. You should have seen his face." Paul laughed. It was a deep, loud laugh, like his father's.

Sally didn't want to burst Paul's bubble, but he really shouldn't be telling anyone about it.

She knocked on his door. "Paul? Can I come in?"

"Give me a sec," Paul called out. Then Sally heard him say, "Gotta go. Mom's back."

A few seconds later, he opened the door. Sally tried to look past him, but he was holding the door close.

"I heard voices. Who were you talking to?"

"Nobody. Was watching a movie."

She raised an eyebrow. "Was it Reilly?"

Paul rolled his eyes. "Yeah. So what?"

"Just remember not to share details of the case, okay? There are details only we know, and the police won't want them in the public domain."

"He won't tell anyone."

"Come on, Paul, he's probably already sharing it on social media. Can you please call him back and ask him to keep it to himself?"

Paul pursed his mouth in a defiant way, but he agreed, shutting the door behind him.

Sally crossed the landing to head downstairs to put her groceries away, but as she passed her bedroom, she realized her six notebooks were still on her bed and the lidded container where she kept them was open. Sally had gotten into the habit of tidying away things as soon as she'd finished using them because Scott had always complained that she had a terrible memory and never put things away in the right place. Her poor memory had been blamed when she and Scott had remembered an event differently, as was frequently the case. It was one of the techniques he'd used to undermine her perception of reality. Had Margie's arrival distracted her from putting the notebooks away? They were too precious to leave lying around, so she headed for her bed.

She looked down at them. They were scattered messily over the bedcover, the pages open. Sally wouldn't leave them like that. She tried to think back to what she'd been doing when she'd heard Margie arrive. She'd been propped up on the bed. After reading each notebook, she'd created a little pile, one stacked on the other. She'd heard Margie's car, looked out of the window, then put the notebooks in the storage box, and slid it under the bed.

Her gut tightened like a wet towel being wrung out.

She had put the notebooks away, she was certain.

She would never leave the pages open, her secret thoughts open for Paul to see.

Had he looked at them?

She left her room and once again knocked on her son's door. He was on the phone again. "Paul, can I have just a minute? It's urgent."

She heard him say, "Reilly, I'll call you back."

He yanked open the door. "What now?"

"My case notebooks. Did you look at them while I was out?"

His lip curled. "No, why would I?"

Sally felt the floor drop out from beneath her, or so it seemed.

"You look like you've seen a ghost," Paul said. "What's up?"

"I put them away."

"Mom, I didn't touch your notebooks, okay!"

Sally spun around. "He's here."

SEVENTEEN

APRIL 14, 1997

It was Sally's birthday, and she was eleven weeks pregnant with their first child, but they hadn't told anyone she was expecting. She was now a victim advocate with the DA's office.

Whilst she was excited about the new baby, her morning sickness was beyond anything she'd read about. She wasn't just nauseous in the morning. She was nauseous throughout the whole day and during the night too. There were days when she couldn't keep her food down. At first Scott had been sympathetic, but he soon grew irritated, accusing her of exaggerating how sick she felt to get out of house chores, which he resented having to do. In the end, Sally decided just to ask for Scott's assistance with anything heavy such as carrying baskets of wet laundry to the line.

As soon as Scott led her inside The Fish House, her stomach churned. The smell of cooked fish and raw seafood was too much, and she dashed to the restrooms to spew.

She'd worn a new dress for the occasion, one that was a little looser at the waist, and she feared she might have gotten some vomit down it. She hurriedly left the cubicle and checked the dress in the mirror, but thankfully, it was untarnished.

Sally washed her mouth out with water and then reapplied her lipstick, which was smudged. How on earth was she going to get through an evening at a restaurant that reeked of fish? Scott knew there were certain smells she couldn't tolerate in her condition. In truth, she had wanted to stay home and have a simple meal she knew she could stomach. She had even made a shepherd's pie for their dinner; it was one of the few dishes she could eat without feeling nauseous. But then Scott had come home and announced he'd booked a restaurant and that they had company.

How could she say no?

Sally took some long, deep breaths. *I can do this. It's my birthday. I will have a good time.*

But as soon as Sally entered the main dining area, she felt lightheaded. The noise and the heat didn't help. All the tables were occupied, and for a minute Sally couldn't see her husband. The front-of-house host asked her if she was looking for someone and then showed her to a table for four by the window. Already seated, with their backs to the entrance, were Walt and Bettina Jackson. They stood up and hugged her—Walt a little too tightly. Sally had this vision of her vomiting over his nice jacket, but thankfully that didn't happen.

"Happy birthday!" the couple cheered.

A bottle of Riesling was already on the table in a wine cooler, and a waiter offered to pour her a glass. Sally thanked him but refused.

"Come now—it's your birthday," Bettina protested.

She was a striking African American woman with cheekbones to die for. She had on an elegant sleeveless dress in silver that hugged her amazing figure. Walt, also African American, removed his jacket, clearly relieved to be free of it.

Sally glanced at Scott, who had particularly wanted to keep the pregnancy a secret until twelve weeks had passed. But how could she explain her refusal to drink wine?

Scott grinned at her and squeezed her hand. "Sally didn't want to tell anyone until she was in her twelfth week, but I guess we can tell you guys, can't we, darling?"

Sally nodded, happy to share the news. But why had he said that *she* wanted to keep it a secret?

Bettina squeaked with joy. "Oh, that's wonderful news! Congratulations. And I completely get why you don't want to drink."

"Thanks, we're very excited. It's just the morning sickness that's difficult to cope with."

"Is it bad?" Bettina asked.

"Twenty-four hours a day. It started in week two."

"Oh, you poor dear. I hope I don't go through that. We're trying for a baby too."

"So, what do you think of this place, huh? Special, isn't it?" Scott interrupted. "What a view! Look out there."

The seafood restaurant overlooked the water, and through the glass Sally could see the faraway mountains, their snowy tips tinged pink in the rays of the setting sun.

"It's beautiful," Bettina said.

"You'll put me to shame," Walt said, smiling at his wife. "Bett's always saying that I should be more romantic. Maybe I should take a leaf out of your book, my friend."

"Took some doing, I can tell you," said Scott. "They told me they were booked out, but I told them how much Sally had always wanted to come here and how it was a really special birthday, and they found me a table. A bit of charm can sure go a long way."

Sally didn't recall ever saying that she wanted to eat here, but maybe a friend had mentioned it and she'd told Scott. She couldn't remember details like that. She was already suffering from baby brain. Scott was constantly reminding her of things she'd said she would do and had forgotten.

The waiter approached their table and asked them if they'd like to order.

"Give us a moment," Scott said.

Sally opened the menu, which was like a booklet, and searched for a dish she could eat and hopefully keep down. Her finger ran down the list of starters: oysters, clams, chowder, baby octopus... Bile rose up her throat. She quickly drank some water.

"It's a special night so how about we order two dozen oysters?" Scott suggested.

Sally stared at his side profile. Scott knew that pregnant women couldn't eat raw oysters. He must have forgotten.

"I'll skip the starters," she said.

"Oh, come on, Sally," Scott said. "This is for you. What would you like?"

She selected a kale Caesar without the anchovies. She would ask for the dressing on the side. As an entree, she selected the crab cakes—she could eat cooked shellfish.

They ordered their meals. Walt and Scott talked about work; Bettina and Sally talked about babies.

"Wouldn't it be just perfect if we had kids the same age? We could be moms together," said Bettina. She nudged Walt to get his attention. "Hey, hon. We need to get a move on and get me pregnant!" Bettina laughed.

Walt grinned. "I'm working on it, honey."

When the oysters arrived, Sally excused herself to the restrooms, where she spewed again. If that wasn't bad enough, when her crab cakes arrived, they weren't cooked through—Sally had to call over the waiter.

"I'm so sorry but I can't eat these because they're raw in the middle and I'm pregnant. Would it be possible to have them cooked through?"

The waiter took them away.

"Why didn't you tell the waiter when you ordered, my love?" Scott asked, throwing back yet another glass of wine.

"I assumed they would be cooked through."

"Never mind," Bettina said, "they'll have them back to you in no time. Now, how is your new job going?"

"Good, I love it." Sally talked about her role for a while.

"I always said you were better suited to victim support," said Scott. "Being a cop was never your thing."

Sally went red in the face. "I thought you said I was a good cop."

"Of course you were, sweetie. You're just better at what you do now."

When the crab cakes were returned, Sally managed to eat a quarter of them. Any more and she would have to run for the restrooms again.

Walt and Bettina gave her a birthday present: a pretty top from store that would exchange the item if she didn't like it. They had included a gift receipt.

"I love it," Sally said. "It's so pretty."

On the way home, Scott was silent. Sally drove because, Scott had reasoned, she hadn't drunk and he had. Sally tried to break the ice with, "Thank you for such a lovely night."

Scott didn't reply—he just stared sullenly out of the passenger window.

"What's up?" she asked.

He whipped his head around and stared at her. "Isn't it obvious? You were a total pain tonight." He put on a woman's voice, imitating her. "I can't eat this and I can't eat that. I can't drink wine, and aren't I such a saint to be drinking water all night, oh and, waiter, send these crab cakes back—they're not cooked properly." Then he dropped the impersonation. "I went to a lot of trouble to organize tonight and you spoiled it for everyone."

For the rest of the car journey, he ignored her apologies.

For the remainder of the week, he wouldn't speak to her.

EIGHTEEN

MAY 7, 2015

Sally and Paul were locked in Sally's Honda when a patrol car arrived. The moment Sally realized an intruder had taken her notebooks out of the storage box, she and Paul had fled. For Sally, the safest place was her car. The police arrived in five minutes: young officers—Sally didn't know them. She explained her involvement in the Poster Killer cold case, and her fear that someone had been in her house. But they searched her home and found nothing out of the ordinary.

"No sign of forced entry. Who else has your house key?" the young female cop—Gustason—asked.

"No one. Just me and Paul."

"Are you sure you didn't forget about the notebooks?"

Sally leaned against the side of her car, ignoring the audience of neighbors that had gathered on the sidewalk, no doubt wondering why a police car with swirling blue lights was outside Sally's house. Gustason's question rankled Sally. It was the kind of question Scott would have asked.

"I'm positive. I'm tidy. I always put things away."

"She's a neat-freak," Paul said, grinning goofily at Gustason, a fair-haired, pretty woman who looked to be no more than twenty.

"You say your son was home all the time you were out?" Gustason asked.

Sally looked at Paul. "That's right, isn't it?"

"Yeah. My door was shut and I was talking to Reilly. Jeez, to think a killer could've walked past my door." Paul said it with a kind of ghoulish excitement. The thought made Sally feel dizzy, and she put her hand out to grab the side mirror.

"There's nobody there now, ma'am. It's safe to go inside. You have a good night." The cops walked away.

Paul watched them leave. "She's cute."

Sally rolled her eyes then warily went back into the house; her home didn't feel safe anymore. On the floor was the grocery bag, just where she'd left it earlier. She picked it up and started unloading the food into the refrigerator as it was still cold. She was privately seething at Clarke and Lin. She'd phoned them and left messages, but they hadn't been in touch. Surely the intruder handling her notebooks had to be related to the weird events of the last two days.

Paul helped himself to a can of Coke and loitered in the kitchen, his back to the countertop. "You still think he was here, don't you?"

"Someone was, and I'm guessing they wanted to see my notes. I can only think of two people who might find them useful. The Poster Killer. And Bryan Topham." Sally closed the refrigerator door and in her hand was the bottle of wine.

"The old guy?"

Sally stared longingly at the bottle of Pinot Noir. It was almost 6 p.m. A bit early to have a drink, but after the day she'd just had—what the hell!

Sally poured a glass, then sat at the table and took a big sip. The wine felt warm and comforting as it trickled down her throat.

She patted the seat next to her. "Come and sit down."

For once, Paul did as he was asked.

"I'm so sorry you've been dragged into all this."

"Not your fault," Paul said. "Besides, it's kind of cool."

"Oh, my darling. I wish none of this were happening. The thought that a killer might have been in our house while you were alone terrifies me. Anything could have happened. What if you'd left your room and seen him? I can't bear to think about what might have happened." Her voice cracked. She reached out and squeezed his hand. "Promise me you'll take especial care. Be vigilant."

"No need to be upset, Mom. I promise."

Sally drank some more wine. "You might as well know... I didn't tell you about this before because I didn't want you to worry about me."

Paul frowned. "Tell me what?"

"When I left the state penitentiary, Topham was there, waiting for me in the parking lot. He must have followed me."

"He's stalking you, Mom. Can't the cops stop him?"

"I haven't told them. There was just too much going on with Durrant."

"Did he say anything?"

"Same as before. He wants to talk. I'm telling you because if he follows you or turns up here, don't speak to him, okay?"

Paul crushed the empty can of Coke between his hands. "I'll punch him if he does."

"Please don't do that. Just call the cops."

"Okay." Paul fiddled with the crushed can, staring at it intently. Then he looked up at Sally. "Hey, I can help you solve this case. You know, like a PI."

The last thing she wanted was for her son to become any more involved in a serial-killer case than he already was.

"Can I stop you there? I've decided not to have anything more to do with the case. If Durrant can be murdered inside a maximum-security jail, it would be all too easy for you or me to be killed. Tomorrow I'm going to talk to Margie about volunteering for her mental wellness charity. I want to put my skills to good use."

"You can't give up now. You're the only one who can solve it."

"Thank you for your faith in me, but it's not worth the risk. My number-one priority is you, and I won't do anything more that puts you in danger."

Paul shook his head, his disappointment obvious. "I've got an idea. What about the gross guy who runs the corner store? He's got to be the Poster Killer."

"Lou Thompson? Oh, Paul, that guy was thoroughly investigated at the time. Leave the poor man alone. His backyard was dug up in the search for bodies. His whole life was torn apart. He suffered years of abuse after the cops found no evidence. People stood outside his store to block customers. Demanded he leave the area. Someone graffitied *pedophile* on his shop wall."

"No, you don't understand, I want to—"

Sally raised her voice. "Paul, stop this. Leave this case alone. I'm serious."

"Why don't you ever listen to me?" he yelled.

He stormed up the stairs and slammed his bedroom door. Sally crossed her arms on the table then rested her forehead on her arms. Why did their conversations always end in an argument?

She stayed there for a few seconds then sat up. Time to start making dinner. To keep her company while she cooked, she switched on a small TV that was mounted to the kitchen wall and flicked through the channels, searching for something fun to watch. She came across the local news. A photo of Theo Durrant, taken several years ago when his hair was darker, appeared onscreen as the news anchor reported Durrant's suspicious death in Walla Walla State Penitentiary.

"An anonymous source has confirmed that Durrant was about to name the Poster Killer. The detective in charge of the cold case, Fred Clarke, has confirmed the Poster Killer case has been reopened."

Sally's nerves jangled. How long would it be before the missing-person poster with her face on it became public knowledge? Then hordes of reporters would descend on her house. When would this ever end?

The news anchor continued, "The bus shelter on Fifth and Park Street in Pioneer Heights was the focus today of police activity. Forensic experts spent the day dusting for fingerprints. It is the same bus shelter where Anna Moorehouse was abducted on February 12, 2010. Detective Clarke refused to comment. Has the Poster Killer returned?"

She switched off the TV.

Furious, Sally phoned Clarke again. This time he answered.

"You have a leak," Sally said. "Any idea who?"

"We don't know that's the case but we're looking into it. Now, I want to talk about your notebooks. Why didn't you tell me you'd made notes?"

Her hackles were up. No apology about ignoring her call when they'd had an intruder, no reassurance about the leak. "They are personal notebooks. All my work files are with the DA's office. Feel free to look at those."

"We have. I want your notebooks. I'm sending a car round to collect them."

In the past, she might have agreed, even though she didn't like it. But her shrink had told her to only do what made her feel comfortable and happy, and to say no if she felt otherwise.

"No. There is very personal information about me and the families in there. Records of intimate conversations. It would be a betrayal to give them to you."

"You know we can get a warrant?"

"Maybe. Maybe not. Get a warrant if you must. Good night, Detective."

Right then, Sally made up her mind. She would keep investigating the case and do it without Clarke's knowledge. However—and this was the line she drew in the imaginary sand —if her actions brought any further threat to her son, she would stop immediately.

NINETEEN

MAY 8, 2015

Sally had never wanted to see the inside of another jail, but here she was on a cloudy Friday morning in a line outside the Franklin Corrections Center for Women. Every visitor had to go through security checks and hand over their phones and bags. Ahead of Sally were seven people, including a man accompanied by a sulky daughter who complained that she didn't want to be there. Sally didn't blame her. When she'd told Paul about her decision to keep looking into the Poster Killer case, he'd whooped with delight. However, very quickly his happy mood had turned into a sulk when she'd told him that he couldn't come with her to the women's jail, no matter how much he whined about it. He'd stormed into his bedroom and slammed the door.

The line shifted forward, and soon Sally was checked off the visitors' list, her purse and phone taken by the guards, and she was told to follow the yellow line on the floor. Another guard would then direct her to table twenty-three.

The visitation area had a different setup from the men's prison: square tables and two chairs per table in an open room, laid out like an exam room in a school, the four rows of tables equidistant. An upper-level walkway ran along one side of the room, where armed guards patrolled. On ground level, guards watched the tables like hawks. The inmates filed in some minutes later, all dressed in beige pants and top, although some chose to wear white T-shirts beneath the obligatory top.

The last time Sally had laid eyes on Tiffany Feinstein had been during her trial. She had been eye-catchingly beautiful: blonde hair tied in a ponytail that bounced as she walked, unblemished skin, wide-set blue eyes, six feet tall, slim. The kind of woman who could wear skinny jeans with no hint of fat rolling over the waistband, even when she sat down. In her late teens and early twenties, Tiffany had done some modelling for swimwear and lingerie catalogs and some popular clothing brands. When she'd moved to LA with a modelling contract and started taking acting classes, everyone had said she would end up a movie star. But like so many people who traveled to the City of Angels to pursue their dreams, the bubble had burst and Tiffany returned to Franklin, her modelling and acting career over. That's when she'd trained to be a teacher and married Chase Feinstein.

The thirty-year-old woman who sat opposite Sally was barely recognizable. There was a pronounced kink in Tiffany's nose from a brawl in the prison bathroom that had resulted in a broken nose and arm, and her sallow skin had a greasy shine. She slouched, which gave her a pigeon-chested appearance, and her hair, once thick and lush, now hung lank and straggly.

"Who are you?" Tiffany asked. "I don't know no Sally."

Tiffany was serving eleven years for manslaughter. She had been diagnosed with postpartum psychosis. Sleep deprived, with her husband working double-shifts and her mom too busy with her own kids to assist, Tiffany had grown delusional and believed her baby was the devil. She had suffocated Madison with a pillow.

"I'm Sally Fairburn. I know your mom and dad," Sally said.

"I worked as a victim advocate. I did what I could to help your family deal with the loss of Caroline."

Caroline's name was hard to say. It stuck in Sally's throat, because Caroline was a bully and had driven Zelda to suicide. Yet Sally's compassion prevailed. Caroline had been taken by the Poster Killer and was presumed dead, and Sally had done her best to comfort Mr. and Mrs. Blake, who'd not only lost Caroline, their youngest, but also Madison, their grandchild, and Tiffany to prison. After Tiffany's conviction, the Blake family had moved to Idaho with their remaining three daughters—the Poster Killer was still at large, and they didn't want to lose another child.

Tiffany snorted. "It's always about Caroline. But what about me? I needed help. Nobody believed me. Everyone said I should quit my whining and be grateful to have a baby. Mom said I was spoiled stupid. Nobody cared because of poor little lost Caroline."

Caroline had gone missing two weeks before Tiffany killed Madison. The detective working the case, which was Foster at the time, had questioned Tiffany about her sister's disappearance but got little sense from her. Tiffany didn't even remember killing her child, and she'd been deemed incapable of operating in the planned and organized way in which the Poster Killer executed the abductions. This supposition was borne out when more girls disappeared after Tiffany was behind bars—though Tiffany and Chase could have abducted Anna and Caroline together, and then, when Tiffany was in jail, Chase could have continued his heinous crimes on his own. And although Sally had already considered this scenario and thought it unlikely, she couldn't rule anything out at this point in her investigation.

"You're right, Tiffany. You should have had help. You were sick and you didn't receive the right treatment. The system failed you, and I'm so sorry for that."

"My parents didn't see it that way. They abandoned me."

"Your family does care about you."

Tiffany snorted. "Yeah, right. They didn't give a damn. I begged Mom to take Madison so I could get some sleep. I told her I was going crazy. I couldn't deal with the screaming. But Mom stopped taking my calls. Bitch! I asked a friend. She was too busy. I begged Chase to come home. He said we needed the money."

A fat tear trickled from an eye and zigzagged down Tiffany's broken nose. "If he'd come home, Madison might be alive now. I couldn't stop the voices. They said she was evil."

Tiffany's postpartum psychosis had led to an ongoing psychotic condition or schizophrenia for which she was receiving treatment.

"It must be very difficult for you."

Tiffany blinked, dislodging another tear. "You have no idea what it's like. They keep me so drugged up I don't know what day it is. I get passed around by the big fat bitches, and when I take a shower to get the stink of their cunts off my face, I get beaten up by the prison moms because I killed my child."

Sally gasped, but not at the language—she'd heard far worse during her career. There were meant to be systems to protect vulnerable prisoners from rape and beatings. "Have you reported this?"

"They'll kill me."

"I can report it for you. Is that how you got the broken nose?"

"I don't want you doing nothing, you hear me?" Tiffany snapped.

Fear was frequently the reason why prison rapes didn't get reported. There would be retribution from prisoners, even guards if they were involved.

Tiffany's demeanor suddenly changed and she shrugged. "Don't matter. I'm getting out tomorrow. Chase and me, we're going to have another baby."

Tiffany had that wrong—she had another seven years in jail before she was up for parole. Before the meeting, Sally had rung the prison doctor, who'd explained that Tiffany was under the delusion that she was about to be released and advised Sally not to challenge her on this because she would become violent.

"I'm pleased for you." Sally hated being party to a lie. "Can I ask you a question?"

"Sure. I got nothing else to do."

"Do you remember Tazeen Ibrahim and Francesca Molinari?"

"Yep. They're dead."

Sally felt like an electric shock had just zapped her. How could Tiffany be so flippant about them? Both girls had attended the elementary school where she'd been an apprentice teacher.

"And?" Tiffany said.

"Do you have any idea who abducted them?"

"How should I know? Francesca was a little bitch. No respect. I was secretly pleased when she got taken."

Sally balked at the comment. "Did you know the other missing girls?"

"Yeah, through Caroline. Why? You turned cop or something?"

"My face was on a missing-person poster stuck to a bus shelter yesterday. I don't understand why. I'm... well, I'm scared."

"And those asshole detectives don't give a shit, right?"

"They're looking into it," Sally continued carefully, "but I thought, well, I thought that after all this time, you might recall something that could help them find the killer. I'd really appreciate your help."

Tiffany stared at the tabletop for a while as she sucked on a strand of hair. "It's the kiddie-porn guy. He has a weird name."

"You mean Theo Durrant? Why him?"

"Kiddie porn. Kiddie prostitution. Of course it was him."

Maybe this visit is a waste of time.

"Would Chase remember anything?" Sally said.

"Dunno. I'll ask him. He's coming to collect me, you know. Promised to take me to my favorite diner to celebrate my release."

Tiffany was delusional and Sally felt for her, but she needed to get Tiffany back on track.

"Can you remember where you were when Caroline disappeared?"

"Sure. Locked in the bathroom, screaming at Madison in the next room to stop her crying."

"Any witnesses?"

"No, why?"

"And where was Chase?"

"At work. He's a car mechanic in the day and cleans the middle school at night for some extra cash."

Sally had forgotten he cleaned the school.

Tiffany continued, "Hey, why don't you come to the diner with us? Celebrate my release. I don't have no friends no more. You were always nice to me."

Sally hated to promise something that she knew wasn't real. Chase wasn't coming to take her home. There was no dinner planned. Sally felt an overwhelming sense of pity for Tiffany.

"I can't make the diner. I'm sorry. I have a question to ask, and you're not going to like it, but I have to ask, okay?"

"You think I killed Caroline."

"Did you?"

"Why would I? I liked her best."

"Would Chase kill her?"

Tiffany's face hardened. "He wouldn't hurt a fly."

"Did he show any interest in the other girls?"

Tiffany lunged across the table and grabbed Sally's hair and tugged. "Fucking bitch!"

Sally screamed—the pain in her scalp was excruciating. In seconds, two guards dragged Tiffany away, kicking and screaming.

Sally left the correctional facility with a sore head and no leads. Tiffany was delusional about Chase and defensive of him too. Could she have helped him abduct the girls? It was possible, and she might not even recall doing it. Regardless, Sally wanted to see what she could do to stop the sexual abuse that Tiffany was suffering, although if Sally reported it, against Tiffany's wishes, Tiffany might be attacked or killed by the perpetrators. She wondered if Johnathan Buss, the prison doctor, had any idea what was going on?

TWENTY

JANUARY 6, 2001

Sally was in the birthing unit of Franklin's children's hospital, and her contractions were very close together. She and Scott had already agreed their soon-to-be-born son would be called Paul Arthur Fairburn. It was Scott's father's name and he'd insisted on it. Zelda's birth had been uncomplicated, and Sally had gone for a natural birth. But Paul's birth felt different. For a start, he was a bigger baby, and she'd been in labor for eleven hours and already felt wrecked. The obstetrician had started her on oxygen and put her on a drip to improve her hydration. He'd also helped her to shift position.

"Something's wrong. I can tell," Sally told the obstetrician, who was examining her.

Sally's anxiety was through the roof, which she knew wasn't helping, but she instinctively knew the birth wasn't right. Last time, her mom, Ellen, had been there with them and her constant reassurance had eased Sally's fretting.

"Your baby is in a non-reassuring fetal status."

"What the hell does that mean?" asked Scott, who stood to one side of the bed.

"It used to be called fetal distress. Your baby's heartbeat is irregular. I would like you to consider a C-section."

Scott took Sally's hand. "Can we discuss this in private?" he asked the doctor.

"Sure, but don't leave it too long. I'll be outside."

The obstetrician left the room.

Sally felt a rush of panic as the door closed. She was feeling vulnerable and scared—scared she would lose her baby.

She pulled the oxygen mask aside. "Pass me my phone please."

Scott leaned over her and brushed some hair away from her forehead with his fingers.

"You don't need a phone. You need to listen to me. That guy is covering his ass. That's what they do. They're afraid of getting sued. I say we wait another hour. See how the baby's doing then. You don't want an ugly scar, do you?"

Sally wanted to slap his fingers away.

"Scott, I want to talk to Mom. She had a C-section."

Sally stretched out her hand to the bedside table where she'd left her cell.

"I'm here, sweetheart. You don't need your mom. I know what's best for you."

Scott moved to his right, blocking her from the bedside table.

"Please, Scott." Her breathing was getting more ragged. She felt like she was being strangled. "I want Mom. Why did you stop her coming?"

Sally pulled the mask back over her nose and mouth and sucked in some air.

"You know why, sweetie," he said soothingly. "She interfered last time. She upset you."

Scott didn't like it when anyone challenged him. And her mom had wanted to be at Zelda's birth because that was what Sally wanted. He'd never forgiven either Sally or Ellen for it.

Sally tugged at the mask, dragging it away from her mouth. "She didn't upset me. I need her. She's my mom," she yelled.

The obstetrician must have heard her because he came straight in. He glanced at the machines monitoring Sally and the baby.

"Your baby is at risk, Sally. I strongly urge you to have a C-section."

"We'll wait another hour," said Scott.

"I want my mom!" Sally wailed, tears in her eyes.

Scott rested his hand on her shoulder and pressed down hard. He was punishing her.

"Ow!" Sally cried, looking at Scott's hand.

He took it away immediately.

"The nurse can get hold of your mom," the doctor said. "But I think it's risky to wait an hour. Please, Sally, think of the baby."

"Do the C-section," Sally said, knowing that Scott would be upset with her. But her baby came first.

The obstetrician opened the door and called in a nurse.

"I'll call Ellen," Scott said to the obstetrician.

Within minutes, Sally was wheeled into surgery. Scott didn't accompany her. The last thing she said before the operating-theater doors closed behind her was, "Tell Mom I want her here."

Scott didn't make the call.

TWENTY-ONE

MAY 8, 2015

Chase Feinstein was next on her list of suspects, but before Sally riled a guy that looked like a Hell's Angel, she decided to see what she could find out from another of the Blake sisters, Sophie, first. Sophie had been the friendliest of the siblings, and she was a student at Franklin University and thus easy to track down.

Denny Hall was imposing and regal, with circular towers and manicured gardens. It housed the classics department where Sophie Blake was studying her Bachelor of Arts. Sally had phoned the faculty secretary and learned that Sophie was due at a lecture at 2 p.m. and usually went to Kaffeine for lunch beforehand.

Sally found the twenty-one-year-old eating a chicken salad with a girlfriend at a table by the window. She was chatting animatedly, and Sally watched her for a moment from a distance. Sophie was every bit as beautiful as Tiffany had been at her age, and she was also highly intelligent. Her parents had often boasted to Sally that Sophie was their brainy daughter.

Sophie looked up and saw Sally hovering near the café

entrance. She raised a hand and waved, and Sally meandered through the throng of college students to reach Sophie's table.

"Hey, Sally! It's been a while," Sophie said.

"It has. You look great. Can I join you?"

"Liz, this is Sally. Sally, this is Liz. Pull up a chair," Sophie suggested.

Liz stood and slung her backpack over a shoulder. "Nice to meet you, Sally. I gotta run. See you later."

Sally took her seat and pushed aside Liz's empty plate.

"How are you?" Sophie said. "You must be *so* terrified. I mean, you're on a poster. *His* poster. It makes me shudder just to think about it." The words tumbled out fast and loud above the din of the packed café.

Sally blinked a few times, trying to wrap her head around how Sophie knew about the poster. Margie had taken it down and Sally had handed it in to the police.

Sophie must have detected her confusion. "Your friend, the author guy, told me. It's okay, he asked me to keep it secret." She mimed zipping up her lips.

Sally swallowed. "You mean Bryan Topham?"

"That's the guy. Such a sweet old man."

Was the poster public knowledge now? Or had he been watching her and Margie when they'd found it on the bus shelter? Sally decided to play along with Sophie's assumption that she and Topham were friends.

"I'm worried. The cops don't know why my face is on the poster, or if it's really the Poster Killer doing it. Do you have any idea who it might be?" Sally said.

Sophie flicked back some platinum-blonde hair behind her shoulders. "Is that why you're here?" She frowned. "I made him promise not to tell anyone."

What was Sophie talking about? "He didn't tell me the details. Please, Sophie, I need your help."

"I don't want to talk about it. Especially not here." Her eyes danced around the café and then returned to Sally. "I wish I hadn't said anything. It's just that he was so... easy to talk to. Like he was my granddad or something."

She stood and picked up her satchel. "I have a lecture."

"Can I walk with you to Denny Hall? We can talk as we go."

"I can't. Chase is a lovely guy, and you're going to tell me that what he did was wrong. And you'd be wrong. I wanted it to happen."

Sally's mind raced to understand what Sophie was saying. What he'd done was wrong? Had they been having an affair while Tiffany was in jail?

Sophie walked out of the café, leaving her half-eaten salad on the table. Sally hesitated, then followed. She had to know how long their affair, if that's what it was, had been going on.

"Sophie, I'm not going to tell anyone. But I have to know how long you've been in a relationship with Chase."

Sally held her breath, wondering if she had blown it.

"No, you don't need to know that. Just leave me alone."

Sophie sped up; Sally kept pace. They were approaching the steps of Denny Hall. This was Sally's last chance to get the truth out of Sophie. Sophie had turned sixteen on May 1, 2010. Caroline disappeared on June 7, 2010. If Sophie's and Chase's sexual relationship had begun prior to May 1, not only would Sophie have been underage, it might have given them motive to kill Caroline if Caroline had threatened to tell their parents. Caroline had been a bully—Sally knew that. Would she also have resorted to blackmailing her sister? The girls came from a strict Catholic family, and sex before marriage was regarded a sin, let alone the illegality of sex with a minor.

Could Sophie and Chase be the Poster Killer couple?

Sally knew she was making wild speculations but it was a possibility.

"Does Tiffany know?" Sally asked.

Sophie whirled around. "She did at the time. She said she'd kill me if I kept seeing him, but Chase says she's forgotten about it. She's batshit crazy now—she thinks Chase is waiting for her. I hope Tiffany stays in jail for the rest of her life!"

Sophie set off again; Sally kept up.

"I need to ask you one more question and it has nothing to do with you or Chase. Did anyone other than Caroline bully my daughter?"

Sophie's cupid lips tightened into an angry line. "She was murdered. I'm not going to say bad things about her."

"Please, Sophie. I'm also trying to understand why Zelda took her own life. I know Caroline bullied Zelda. There had to be another bully. Why else would Zelda kill herself after Caroline was gone?"

Sophie stopped walking. "Caroline liked to throw her weight around. She made Stacy do her homework, and she took pocket money off some other girls. I think Anna was one of them. But she didn't touch Zelda, okay? She kind of liked her."

Sally watched Sophie head up the steps to Denny Hall and disappear inside, still as a statue. Had Sally heard Sophie correctly? She had to be lying—it was the only explanation. Everyone knew that Zelda had been bullied by Caroline. The school knew. Stacy knew. Nikki Jackson—Zelda's other best friend—knew. Scott knew. Nikki's father, Walt Jackson—Scott's buddy—knew.

Why would Sophie claim it never happened?

TWENTY-TWO

Paul stood outside the Pine Creek YMCA. His mom and dad had been volunteers there once, and he'd attended the tweens club whenever his parents had been supervising the next group up—the teens. When his session had finished, he'd then joined the teens group, which Zelda had attended.

The pale brick building filled a large lot with a sports hall and swimming pool, as well as a hall with a stage. He looked around the parking lot and then at the single-story building, hoping there was nobody inside who would recognize him. His mom wanted him to stay home. She didn't even think school was safe anymore. No problem there—he'd missed a biology exam today. Woohoo!

"I'm going to prove I can do it," Paul muttered, balling his fists.

His hoodie pulled up over his head and his hands in his pant pockets, he strolled through the sliding glass door. He knew where he was headed, but everything looked smaller than he remembered. Maybe when you were nine everything looked way bigger?

It was mid-morning and a game of wheelchair basketball

was happening in the sports hall. He passed the entrance to the pool—moms and babies were having a class, the moms singing to the little ones as they jiggled them in the water.

Paul kept going, but now he had butterflies in his chest. *I mean, how do you go about accusing someone of murder?*

When he reached the YMCA manager's office, he was relieved to see the name badge on the pale pine door still said BART HOWER. He peeked in through the slim glass panel and saw Bart sitting at a desk, staring at his computer. Bart also looked smaller and skinnier than Paul remembered, although he'd always been skinny, his jeans hanging like drapes over his skinny thighs. He'd cut his hair. The jerk used to wear it in a ponytail. Now it was cut so it rested on his YMCA polo-shirt collar.

Here goes nothing, Paul thought and knocked, pulling down his hoodie.

Bart looked through the glass panel and beckoned with long fingers. Paul walked in and closed the door but stayed just inside it. *Act cool*, he kept telling himself.

"Can I help you?" Bart asked, smiling.

"I'm Paul Fairburn."

Paul was ready to say more, to help the guy recall him, but Bart nodded.

"I remember you. Tweens, right? Monday late afternoons. Didn't your mom and dad volunteer here?"

"Yeah. Me and my sister usually came with them—she went to the teens club."

"Sister?"

"Zelda."

Bart's long face seemed to droop. "Zelda. Of course. I was very sorry to learn about... you know... her passing."

He means suicide. Why doesn't he just go ahead and say it?

"Yeah, thanks. Look, I, um, want to volunteer. You know, like Mom and Dad used to do."

"That's great news." Bart stood. The guy was tall. Taller than Paul's six feet. "How old are you, son?"

"Fourteen."

"We'd need consent from a parent, naturally, but what do you want to do here?"

"I, uh..."

Paul hadn't thought that far ahead. He didn't really want to volunteer—he hated younger kids. "Look, man, I'm gonna come clean with you. I need your help."

"What kind of help?" He eyed Paul suspiciously.

Jeez, this was harder than he'd expected.

"You know about the Poster Killer?"

"Who doesn't? What's your point, son?"

"All the girls came here, right? I mean, Tazeen and Francesca went to the tweens club, and the others were at the teens club."

"Where are you going with this? The police ruled out any connection to this YMCA."

Paul was sweating. A bead ran down the side of his face. "Okay, but there was a guy. He played basketball here back then. There was something not right about him."

"Okay, that's enough. As I said, the cops talked to everyone at the time. They found nothing, and I don't need you digging up dirt. This place runs on trust. We have a lot of volunteers and they're all vetted, as are the paid staff. Whatever you're doing here, just leave well alone, okay? Now, if you'll excuse me, I have a meeting."

Bart nodded at the door Paul was standing in front of. Paul moved aside; Bart opened it.

"I'll see you out," he said.

Paul wanted to yell at him to listen, but that would only get him barred from the YMCA, and then Bart would call his mom to complain. He therefore walked silently with Bart to the exit door, his face flushed with embarrassment.

Bart waved him off. "If you're serious about volunteering, call me."

Paul unlocked the security chain around his bicycle and then clipped it to the crossbar. His spine prickled, like someone was watching him. He looked all around but couldn't see anyone obvious, yet the feeling prevailed. Paul cycled out of the parking lot as fast as he could.

TWENTY-THREE

Under the pretext of needing a loaf of bread, Sally entered Lou Thompson's Corner News grocery store. She had no intention of hassling Thompson, but since Paul had mentioned him as a suspect, the idea had been like an itch she couldn't scratch. She had to be certain about him before she ruled him out.

The small store was twenty yards from the elementary school and a block from the middle school where Anna, Caroline, Stacy, Vinesh, and also her daughter, Zelda, had gone. Two teenage boys hung around outside sharing a packet of chips—they were clearly skipping class. The signage above the store advertised the lottery, and a separate backlit sign announced the store had an ATM. The windows were so full of posters and stickers it was almost impossible to see inside.

Memories flooded back. The week before Zelda had taken her own life, Sally had treated her and Paul to ice cream there. It had been October and the wrong time of year for ice cream, but both kids had been excited by the idea. Zelda had chosen a chocolate Magnum, Paul a fruit icy pop, and Sally a cookies-and-cream ice-cream bar. It had been a relief to see Zelda eating something: she'd been off her food and getting too thin.

The memory caused Sally to stop, one foot through the open door and one still outside. Her gorgeous girl. Gone forever.

I miss you so much.

Sally very nearly turned around and drove home. But Thompson, who sat behind the counter at the back, called out to her.

"Can I help you?"

Thompson had a small wall-mounted TV on low volume. Next to the TV screen was a security camera that pointed toward the door, which must be how he'd spotted her since the high shelves of grocery items would have obscured most of his view.

As Sally drew closer to the man, his shiny skin made her think of a waxwork. He must be in his forties by now, but his thinning hair made him appear older. His eyes stayed focused on her, but his head was angled up at the TV. It was wrong of her to judge him by his looks, but she found Thompson unwholesome.

Flustered, Sally asked him where she could find the bread.

"Aisle one." He nodded in that direction.

She thanked him and found the bread, berating herself for her cowardice. She had practiced her opening gambit during the drive there. Thankfully, Thompson must have recognized her because he came out from behind the counter and joined her in aisle one.

"You're Zelda's mom?"

"That's right. We came in here quite a bit after school. She passed away five years ago."

"I remember her. Nice kid, unlike some of the trouble-makers she mixed with. I'm sorry for your loss."

"Thank you. It's been hard. Still is. Um, do you have a moment? I wanted to ask you something?"

"Sure, but I should get back behind the counter."

Sally followed him, a sourdough loaf in her hand.

When Thompson was settled on his stool, she put the loaf on the countertop. "I guess you heard that Theo Durrant is dead?"

"It's headline news. Of course, I know."

"Then I guess you know the Poster Killer case is re-opened?"

He frowned. "Oh, I see. You're here to accuse me. I'm sick of it. Let me be clear." His voice grew loud. "I had nothing to do with their abduction, and I wish to God I'd never laid eyes on any of them."

"I get it, Mr. Thompson, and please don't be angry. I'm talking to lots of people, not just you. You see, I saw Durrant before he died and he gave me some information that could change everything. I know you've suffered. Can I ask you to think back to 2010 and 2011? Did anyone unusual hang around your store, or the school, who seemed to watch the girls?"

"Don't you think I've been asked that hundreds of times? I've already had a visit from a pushy detective. You're here because you think I did it. Just like the cops. They made my life hell back then. They even searched for bodies in my backyard. Just because I live alone, they assume I'm a pedophile. You want to know the truth? I hate the spoiled little princesses that use my store, but they spend money here, so I stay polite. Why would I kill my best customers?" He looked down at the loaf. "You want the bread or not?"

"Yes, how much?"

She paid using her bank card. "I'm sorry you were treated like that. Thank you for your time."

She wanted to get out of the store in a hurry.

Thompson called after her as she was about to step out the door. "I had an old guy in here yesterday asking questions."

Sally turned around.

Thompson continued, "Asked me about the six victims, if I

knew where to find their parents or brothers and sisters. I told him to get lost."

Sally walked back to the counter. "Did he give his name?"

"Didn't offer it."

"Can you describe him?"

"Yeah, looked like Colonel Sanders."

He had to be talking about Bryan Topham.

TWENTY-FOUR

Sally was in the kitchen with her cell to her ear when Paul reached home. She gave him a *where have you been?* look.

While she was talking, he unbolted the back-fence gate and wheeled his bicycle into the shed where Sally's bike was stored too. Not so long ago there had been four bicycles, back when they'd pretended they were a normal family. Sally had wanted to hang on to Zelda's bicycle, just as she'd wanted to hang on to everything that was Zelda's, but the move to a much smaller house had forced her to finally let go of most of his sister's stuff.

Sally was still on the phone and he was hungry after the ride to and from the YMCA, so he helped himself to the peanut butter, a jar of strawberry jelly, and the loaf of sliced bread. He drank from the milk carton, and she gave him a disapproving look, which he shrugged off as he began to scoop out lashings of peanut butter and spread it across the bread.

"There must be something you can do?" Sally said. "Please, Dr. Buss."

Paul made a snorting noise as he smirked at the name. Sally turned her back on him and lowered her voice.

"I understand," she said. "Yes, I know you can't. But she's being abused. Could you ask the guards to keep an eye on her?"

That caught Paul's attention.

The man's loud voice droned on, and whenever Sally attempted to interject, he just kept talking. Paul couldn't make out the words, but the doctor had one of those superior voices that got on Paul's nerves.

"That's a relief," Sally finally said. "When will you know if the transfer's happening?" A pause while she listened to Buss's answer. "That long? It's just that I fear for her safety."

Paul recognized the signs that his mom was defeated: her shoulders sagged and her voice grew even quieter.

"I see. Well, thank you for your time."

Sally put her cell on the countertop and stared out of the window. Paul bit into his sandwich as he waited for the inevitable *where have you been?* question.

Sally poured a filter coffee and was about to add milk when she said, "Please don't drink from the carton, Paul. It's germy." She used the milk anyway, then sat at the kitchen table facing him. *Here it comes*, he thought.

"Where've you been? I was worried."

Paul swallowed a mouthful of sandwich. "Don't get mad, okay?" he began. Riding home, he'd considered lying about what he'd done. *Just needed to ride my bike.* That sort of answer. But if he was going to help solve the case, he had to tell her. "I went to see Bart Hower."

"Bart? Why?"

"Because Anna, Caroline, Stacy, Tazeen, Vinesh, and Francesca all went there Monday nights. What if the killer was there too?"

"Bart has alibis for the times the girls were taken. Please tell me you didn't accuse him?"

A flash of anger. "I'm not stupid. Jeez, why do you always treat me like I'm no good?"

"I apologize if it sounded that way. What did you say to him?"

"I asked him about a guy who played basketball there. I don't know his name. But he seemed kind of weird. Always chatting to the girls."

"You did this for me?"

"I want to solve the case."

"O-kay. What did Bart say?"

"Nothing. He said he was busy. I think we should stake out the place. You know, like detectives do."

"My darling boy, this is a very dangerous case. If the Poster Killer is still around, he or they are very dangerous. I can't have you involved, Paul."

"But, Mom, I can do this."

"I know you can, but I can't risk it. I love you. I've lost Zelda. I won't lose you. I would lay down my life for you. Do you understand?"

Paul sighed. Days of boredom lay ahead. There were only so many video games he could play. "What about football practice? I can't miss it."

"That's tonight?" She'd clearly forgotten. "Okay. But as soon as it's done, we're coming straight home."

It annoyed Paul that she wanted to stop him finding the killer, but at least he would see his buddies tonight. Paul bit into his sandwich and enjoyed the squelch of the peanut butter. It wouldn't fill him though.

"Can I have an omelet?"

"Sure. It's almost lunchtime anyway."

Sally took eggs, butter, cheese, bacon, and mushrooms from the refrigerator.

"Who were you talking to just now?" Paul asked.

"Dr. Buss—he's a doctor at the Franklin Corrections Center for Women."

She broke an egg into a mixing bowl.

"Why are you talking to him?"

"I went to the women's prison and saw Tiffany Blake this morning. She looked terrible, poor thing. Someone is beating her."

Paul swallowed the last of his sandwich. "She killed her baby, right?"

"Yes, that's why she's in jail."

"Kiddie killers don't do well in jail."

Sally stared at him. "Where did you hear that?"

"Dad. He said that if they convicted the Poster Killer, he'd have a hell of a time in jail. Dad said he hoped an inmate would take him out."

"Well, I don't see it that way. Tiffany is a victim too. A victim of postpartum psychosis and schizophrenia. Most of the time she has no idea what she's doing."

"She's a killer, Mom, and she got what she deserved."

Sally continued to crack eggs into a bowl. "If I can help her, I will. Dr. Buss says he's hoping to get her transferred to a psychiatric hospital, where she'll be safe and receive better treatment."

Paul hadn't meant to slam the knife onto the table as loudly as he did. Blobs of jelly spattered the tabletop. "So you'll help a murdering bitch, but you wouldn't help Zelda. Well, fuck you!"

Sally whirled around to face him. "Don't speak to me like that! I will not have language like that in my house."

Blood raced around Paul's head. He heard his pounding pulse like drums in his ears. "She was messed up, Mom! Why didn't you get her help?"

"I tried! Everything I did, your dad sabotaged. I took her to see a shrink. Scott stopped us. I demanded action at the school. I saw Caroline's parents. They denied everything."

"It wasn't the bullying!" How many times had he tried to tell her this!

"Stop, Paul!" Sally shouted. "Don't you think I know I

failed her? I should have done more to stop it." Once again she didn't seem to have taken in what he'd said. "I thought the school was keeping an eye on her. Zelda told me it had stopped."

Paul was so shocked by his docile mother's outburst that he just stared at her. Her eyes were filling with tears. He felt bad—he always felt bad when he made her cry.

"Mom, I—"

"Why do you do this?" Sally yelled. "I can't bring her back. I know I made a terrible mistake. Your dad made a terrible mistake. We'll have to live with it for the rest of our lives."

"Dad doesn't give a shit!"

"I don't want to discuss this anymore."

She turned her back on him and whisked the eggs so ferociously they turned to froth.

Seconds passed.

"You ever wonder about the suicide note?" Paul asked quietly.

Sally stopped whisking. "How do you mean?"

"You ever wonder if it was for real?"

She didn't answer immediately—she began chopping the bacon. "What are you talking about?"

"It's kinda weird, don't you think? Why would Zelda type and print a suicide note? She used a pen to write her diaries, so why didn't she use a pen for her goodbye letter?"

"What does it matter now? We've lost her."

Sally was crying and pretending not to. He saw a tear fall on the countertop. He got up and handed her a box of tissues.

"Sorry."

Zelda and Sally were waiting to be seen by Dr. Mel Collins, a child psychiatrist. The walls were painted a bright yellow, and the wooden doors and furniture were blonde wood. Light poured in through large windows, giving the place a warm and positive ambience.

Thirteen-year-old Zelda sat in a ray of sunshine, which turned her strawberry-blonde hair into gold and made her freckled skin glow. She was tall for her age, just as Sally had been. But in the last few months her easy-going, gentle, talkative child had changed. She'd become sullen, uncommunicative. She'd gone off her food. Previously, Zelda would seek out her mom's company. Now she not only avoided both parents, she spent as much time as possible at Nikki's or Stacy's houses. It was a difficult time—the Poster Killer had abducted Anna Moorehouse and Caroline Blake, and everyone was on edge.

Ah, Caroline. The source of Zelda's depression—or so Scott insisted. The school bitch. The girl who bullied Zelda. And yet, with Caroline gone, Zelda's depression was getting worse.

Zelda's downcast eyes came to rest on Sally.

"Are you sure Dad doesn't know?" Zelda asked.

She slouched forward as if the weight of the world was on her shoulders.

"It's our little secret," Sally said.

It wasn't just Scott who'd objected to the idea of a child psychiatrist. Zelda had initially said she didn't need one, but when Sally had confided that Scott didn't know about the appointment, she'd agreed.

A door opened and a woman in glasses with long hair and a pleasant smile headed straight for them.

"Hello, Zelda," she said, "I'm Mel. Thank you so much for coming in for a chat."

"I... I have a question," Zelda said.

"Go ahead."

"Can I see you alone?" Zelda asked.

Sally tried not to look hurt.

"That very much depends on your mom. Is that okay with you, Sally?" Dr. Collins asked.

"Sure. I'll be here if you want me."

Zelda exhaled with what Sally took as relief, and Sally watched her walk away. Why was Zelda so secretive these days? Sally felt disappointed in herself. Were there things Zelda no longer felt comfortable telling her?

"Wait a minute," a male voice called from the entrance.

She didn't have to look around to know it was Scott. She went icy cold at the sight of him, in his police uniform—the picture of authority. Sally had chosen this day and time because Scott was at work. How had he found out about the appointment?

Dr. Collins turned. Zelda remained with her back to her father, shoulders hunched, head down as if Scott might not notice her if she remained still. Sally stood on shaky legs. Scott's jaw was clenched, and his eyes were furious.

"Scott, please," Sally pleaded.

The receptionist called out from behind the counter, "Can I help you, sir?"

He turned his gaze to the speaker and gave her a charming smile. "I'm here to collect my daughter, Zelda Fairburn." He stared at Zelda's back. "Zelda, honey, I'm taking you home."

Dr. Collins said, "Sir, the appointment is about to start, and your wife is happy to wait. We'll look after her."

Scott walked purposefully down the corridor, completely ignoring Sally, who tried to take his arm. It was as if she didn't exist.

"I apologize," Scott said, closing in on Zelda and Dr. Collins. He held up his Franklin PD badge. "I'm Scott, Zelda's father—it's lovely to meet you." He shook the psychiatrist's hand.

Sally remembered that dashing charm. She had fallen for it once.

"There's been a mix-up," Scott said. "My wife gets muddled. I've booked Zelda with another therapist."

Sally knew what he was doing. There was no other therapist. He'd said he didn't want Zelda to see a shrink, and he would make sure that his wishes were observed.

Sally tiptoed closer. "Scott, please let Zelda see Dr. Collins," she said. "Zelda is happy to talk to her."

"Honey, you're confusing her. She's seeing somebody else. And we're going to be late." Then Scott called out, "Zelda, we have to go."

Zelda kept her back to her father.

Dr. Collins said, "Mr. Fairburn, as Zelda is here now, could the other appointment be moved? I'd really like to talk to her."

Scott smiled broadly as if he were about to say yes. "That's just not possible."

"Darling," Sally said, "Dr. Collins comes highly recommended. I know you don't like shrinks—"

Scott cut her off. "Sweetheart, I never said that. Have you taken your medication today?"

Sally looked away with embarrassment.

Without a word, Zelda turned around. She didn't make eye contact with anyone as she walked out of the building. Scott followed.

"I'm sorry about this, Dr. Collins," Sally said. "I'm happy to pay for your time."

"No need. I hope the therapist she's seeing can help her," said Dr. Collins. Then she added, "And you." She smiled warmly.

It was as if the psychiatrist had put a spotlight on Sally's soul. She was fairly certain that Dr. Collins thought Scott's behavior too controlling. Embarrassed, Sally couldn't look the woman in the eye.

Outside in the parking lot, Scott escorted them to Sally's car and watched them get in.

He leaned in through the window. "When I say no, I mean no," he said to Sally. "Take her to school."

Zelda was pale and silent on the drive. Sally apologized. Promised she'd find a way for her to see Dr. Collins again.

Zelda just stared out of the car window, a look of resignation on her face.

TWENTY-SIX

Sally felt bruised after Paul's accusation. Of course, he'd been too young to know what her life had been like, walking on eggshells all the time. The desperate ploys she'd concocted to bypass Scott's controlling impulses to do the best she could for her kids. Paul had inherited Scott's temper, and he and Scott had clashed more times than she could recall. She knew Paul hated his father, that he blamed both of them for his sister's suicide. But this was the first time he'd raised a query about the suicide note.

After she'd made Paul's omelet, Sally went up to the rooftop terrace, desperate to be alone. Paul didn't follow her. She sat for a while, watching white clouds morph into different shapes and remembered the game she and Zelda used to play.

"It's a dog, Mommy! It's a face! Look, it's a dragon!" she would say.

On the roof terrace was an outdoor three-seater sofa and a coffee table. The glass tabletop was dusty. She ran a finger across it, then she drew a love heart and wrote Zelda's name underneath.

"I'm sorry. So, so sorry. How could I have failed you so badly?"

The sun disappeared behind a dark cloud, and the temperature dropped a few degrees. Sally went inside, down the stairs to the closet in her bedroom. On a shelf above the clothes rail was a plastic storage box with a pink lid. In it she kept precious items that Zelda had loved. Items that she hadn't been able to bring herself to give away when she'd finally cleared out Zelda's room at the old house. On her tiptoes, she felt along the shelf for the box. Her fingers touched it. She edged it toward her until she could grip it firmly and carry it to the bed.

When she removed the lid, she smelled Zelda: her fruity shampoo and her snuggly smell after a night's sleep. Lying on top of everything was the nightdress she'd worn when she died, a pink-and-white-striped cotton garment with two cute pugs inside a love heart on the front. Next to it was Zelda's personalized necklace in silver that she'd loved so much, a gift from Sally and Scott for her twelfth birthday, along with a set of acrylic paints, brushes, and canvases. Sally lifted the necklace to her lips and kissed it.

"I love you," she said, then gently put the necklace on the bedcover.

Sally picked up the nightie and hugged it, breathing in Zelda's scent. Each time she opened the box, Zelda's aroma was a little weaker. There would come a time when it would be gone, and Sally hated that thought.

"No one should have to bury their child," she muttered, tears welling up again. "I miss you so much, my beautiful girl."

For a while, Sally held Zelda's nightie to her, wishing she could turn back time.

Eventually, she laid it on the bed next to the necklace, then picked up the pink teddy bear with a red heart on its chest that said *I love you*. Sally had bought it for Zelda when she was five and having surgery to remove her tonsils and adenoids. Ever since, the pink bear had rested on Zelda's pillow.

The bear joined the nightie and necklace, then Sally spotted the beaded bracelet Zelda had bought from a charity shop with her pocket money. It consisted of tiny flat tiles that spelled out "Save Our Seas"; Zelda had loved all creatures but was especially fascinated by sea life.

The bracelet sat on top of a framed photograph of Zelda and her two best friends. The frame was decorated with pale blue glass gems, and the photo had been taken over the summer of 2010. The backdrop was of Lake Pioneer, and the girls had just returned from a kayaking adventure. Sally imagined that she could hear their joyful laughter. Zelda looked so happy in the photo.

She ran a finger over the glass, reciting the girls' names: Nikki Jackson—Walt and Bettina's daughter—Zelda in the middle, then Stacy Green, looking shyly at the camera.

It was hard to believe that two of the three girls in the photo were gone. Stacy had been abducted from a bus shelter not long after this photo was taken and never seen again. Only Nikki was alive and well.

Sally occasionally passed Nikki and her mom, Bettina, at Walmart, but since Scott had moved to Chicago, neither Bettina nor Walt had made any effort to keep up the friendship. They had been Scott's friends, and who knew what Scott had told them about his sudden transfer to Chicago so soon after Zelda's funeral? Perhaps he'd told them that Sally was to blame for the breakdown of their marriage and Zelda's death? She'd never had the courage to ask them.

Sally laid the photo frame on the bed and took out a couple of Zelda's paintings. Some she'd done as young as three years old.

Zelda's early art was of pin people with a two-dimensional house and hills in the background, depicting Scott, Sally, Paul, and Zelda. The people in them had big smiles. Later, she'd learned about light and shade and perspective, and she'd loved to sketch people's faces. Her first acrylic painting—when she was eleven—had been so good it had won a prize at school. It depicted a snow-covered forest landscape with tall pine trees and a stream that reflected the pink dawn sky. She had included a family of deer and a little girl sitting on a tree stump watching them graze. There was so much happiness and love of life in all her art.

Toward the bottom of the box was an envelope. It contained a photocopy of Zelda's suicide note. The original had been taken by the police.

Sally stared at the white envelope, too traumatized by its contents to pick it up. She had read Zelda's suicide note just the once, and it had taken all her strength to do it before she'd collapsed in tears. The words still haunted her dreams.

"You need to read it," she told herself.

Paul had put doubt into her head. Sally had never thought to question it.

Reaching into the box, she quickly slid the piece of paper from the envelope and unfolded it. At first the words were a blur.

"Look at it."

She began to read it out loud:

To my family

I'm sorry for what I'm going to do. I can't bare the pain anymore. The taunts, the bullying, the lies about me. You know who you are and what you did. You made my life hell and I hope that's where you'll go because that's where you belong. Mom, Dad, Paul, I'm sorry for what I've put you through.

I love you Mommy
I love you Dad

I love you Paul
I'm sorry.

Tears streaked down Sally's cheeks and dripped into her lap.

"Oh, my gorgeous girl, it's me who should be sorry."

For a long moment, all Sally could do was cry. Then she steeled herself to read the note again. How could there be any doubt that Zelda had taken her own life because she was bullied? The part of the note that felt out of character was the comment about wishing her bullies would go to hell where they belonged. Zelda had been like her mother in that she never wished bad things on others, however nasty they'd been. But who was Sally to judge? She'd never been driven to the brink of suicide, and if she were, she might also wish her persecutors went to hell.

Sally heard Sophie's voice telling her that Caroline hadn't bullied Zelda. She had to be wrong. Because if she were right, then why would Zelda blame the bullies in her suicide note?

Sally thought about what Paul had said. He believed it wasn't Zelda's note.

There were some parts of it that were out of character. Zelda liked to call Paul *Pauly*. But perhaps Zelda had felt that as this was a goodbye, she should use his given name? And the misspelling of "bare" was strange. Zelda had been a great speller. She would have known it should have been spelled *bear*. But she had been in a desperate state.

Why Zelda had decided to type and then print the note, Sally didn't know, although Zelda's generation had little reason to handwrite anything. They typed on their phones and computers. Although Zelda was unusual: she'd kept hand-written diaries, although they too had been taken by the police and then lost. How could they have been so careless with something so precious? Those diaries, which Sally had never read, might have helped explain why Zelda did what she did.

The doorbell chimed. She stayed put, willing the caller to go away.

Perhaps it was Margie, stopping by to make sure she was all right? Even so, Sally just wasn't in the mood for visitors.

She walked over to the window and peered out, careful to keep the drapes in front of her so she wouldn't be seen. There was an FTN News van parked outside, and a smartly dressed woman stood on her doorstep.

TWENTY-SEVEN

Standing close behind a female reporter was a scruffy man with a TV camera on his shoulder. The woman looked up and caught sight of Sally looking down at her.

"Sally Fairburn?" the woman shouted. "I'm Janine Symanski, from the FTN Network. Can we talk about the poster?"

This was all she and Paul needed, but she had been expecting it. It wouldn't be long before she had news crews camped outside her house.

Sally pulled back from the window, wishing she'd closed the drapes in every room, although the front door had five rectangular glass panels which the reporter could peer through.

She knocked on Paul's door. "Close your drapes, Paul—there are reporters outside."

She was already racing down the stairs when Paul opened his bedroom door.

Sally had a small study at the back of the house with a desk, computer, and printer. Taking some paper from a pack near the printer and some adhesive putty, Sally hurried to the living-room window, where Symanski was peering through, her face cupped by her hands so she could see better.

"Sally, I know you're on a Poster Killer poster. You must be terrified. I get that. Do you know why he chose you?"

Sally closed the drapes. "Go away. I have nothing to say!"

"Sally, any moment now a bunch of reporters will descend on your doorstep. Give me an exclusive and you can tell your story how you like. The others won't be so kind."

Paul stood at the bottom of the stairs. "Maybe you should talk to her?"

"No way."

The doorbell rang and kept ringing. Sally remembered the media frenzy when the Poster Killer had been active in 2010 and 2011. The news crews had plagued the victims' families and friends for stories. Was Sally destined to become the focus of a new frenzy?

"We have to get out of here," Sally said to Paul. "Before any more of those vultures arrive. Somewhere we can hide for a while."

The obvious choice was Margie Clay. Margie lived alone, and Sally could trust her to keep their location a secret. She phoned her friend, but it went to voicemail. Sally left a message.

There was a *thunk* in her backyard. And another. It sounded as if someone was kicking the wooden fence.

Both she and Paul raced to the kitchen. Through the window, she saw a man in his thirties climbing over her fence. He jumped down and landed on her vegetable patch, then reached back over the fence—another pair of hands on the opposite side passed him a TV camera.

Sally panicked. Her back door was solid timber, but she'd forgotten her kitchen window had no blinds or drapes.

The cameraman saw her and knocked on the window.

"Sally, I'm Josh Jones from Channel 10. I'd like to do an exclusive."

"Get out of my yard!" she shouted. "I'm calling the police."

"How do you feel about being in the sights of the Poster Killer?" Jones shouted back.

"I'll get rid of him," Paul said. He was just about to unlock the back door.

"Don't go out there. They'll make out you attacked them."

"But they have no right."

"I know. I'll call Lin."

Sally sat on the lower stairs and called Detective Lin's number. She didn't pick up.

Sally looked up and realized she couldn't see Paul. Frantic, she peeked into the kitchen. Paul held up his phone and was videoing Jones from Channel 10 on the other side of the glass.

"What are you doing?" Sally said. "Stop filming them."

He stopped then shrugged. "What's the problem? He's filming us."

He was too. The camera lens was pointed straight at them.

A man's authoritative voice cut through the ruckus outside.

"Get out of here," he said. "You're trespassing. Go, before I call the cops."

She knew the voice—Bryan Topham. What on earth was he doing here?

"What's your name?" Symanski asked him. "Do you live here?"

"That's none of your business. You need to move away from the door and stand on the sidewalk."

Jones tapped the kitchen window, shouting, "Sally, people have a right to know if the Poster Killer is active again."

Sally couldn't bear it—she had to get out of there.

There was a screech of brakes, and the sound of car doors opening and closing. Through the glass panels of the front door, Sally glimpsed another TV channel van with a satellite dish on the roof.

"Leave her alone," Topham shouted. "She doesn't want to talk to you."

A new team left the van and ran up the path.

Symanski complained, "Wait your turn! I was here first!"

Sally's cell rang. She didn't recognize the number so she let it go to voicemail. The message was from the crime reporter at the *Franklin Times*. Sally felt trapped. She started to panic, her breath shallow and fast.

Sally made a snap decision. She found her purse, took out Bryan Topham's business card, and dialed his number. He answered. Sensibly, he didn't say her name.

"Hi?" Topham said.

"I need your help to get me through the reporters and into my car. It's the Honda Civic, but I guess you already know that. In return, I'll meet you. In a public place. Somewhere we can talk."

"Agreed. When?" Topham said.

"Give me five minutes to grab some things. I'll text you when we're ready. Can you hang around that long?"

"Sure."

The call over, Sally caught Paul frowning.

"You're kidding? You're asking psycho man for help?"

"He just has to get us to our car. Please, go pack a bag."

Paul didn't move. "You don't need him. I can push them out of the way. I play football, remember?"

Shoving a TV reporter wasn't a good idea. She saw the news headline in her mind's eye. *Son of Poster Killer's next victim attacks reporter*. "My love, don't engage with them. Please do as I say. We must hurry."

Sally walked past him and took the stairs two at a time. Paul followed.

"Laptop, music, clothes for a week," Sally called over her shoulder. "Five minutes."

"I only have my sports bag."

"That'll do."

Sally dragged her rolling carry-on luggage from the closet,

threw her toiletries into a small bag, then grabbed some clothes and her running shoes. She pulled on a jacket. Then she dragged the box containing her notebooks from under the bed and carefully placed the books in the bag, cushioned between her jeans and a running top.

"Ready?" she called out.

"I don't know what to bring," he whined.

She zipped up her bag and ducked into Paul's room. In his sports bag was his football clothes, laptop, headphones, his games console, and PJs. She'd forgotten hers but she was more concerned about Paul having a change of clothes with him. She was banking on Margie letting them stay for a while and she was sure to lend Sally some PJs.

"I'll get your stuff from the bathroom. You pack underwear, tees, jeans, fleece, shoes."

In the bathroom she grabbed his toothbrush, shampoo, and electric shaver.

She found him rummaging in a pile of dirty clothes he'd dumped in the corner. "Where are my sweatpants, Mom?"

"I'll buy you new sweatpants, honey. We have to go."

Paul followed her to the living room. "You're taking me to football training later, right?"

Maybe that wasn't such a good idea now. "Can I think about that later?"

Sally texted Topham. *Coming out now. Ready?*

Topham replied: *Ready.*

Sally opened the front door. Symanski immediately shoved a microphone in her face, and Sally flinched. Paul pushed the mic out of the way.

"Hey!" complained the reporter.

Topham and Paul stood either side of Sally as she wheeled her bag onto the street, her head down.

"She's leaving—get back to the van," Symanski yelled to her cameraman.

The Channel 10 cameraman who'd been in her backyard must have heard the commotion because he ran round the corner. Sally opened her car door, and Topham acted as a buffer between her and Paul, and the crowd of reporters.

Breathless and shaken, as soon as she was in her car, she started the engine. She couldn't believe it when Jones stepped into the road, blocking her way, his TV camera pointed straight at her.

"Sally! Why is the Poster Killer targeting you?" he asked.

Sally honked the horn. "Get out of the way!"

"Is it because of your support role for the victims' families?"

"Out of the way! I'm calling the police!" shouted Topham from the sidewalk.

Sally edged the car forward until the front bumper was only a few inches from the man's knees. The cameraman hesitated, then stepped aside and ran toward a van, clearly intent on following her.

Sally gave Topham a thankful smile then drove off. As she'd feared, all the other reporters dived for their vehicles too. She sped up and barely slowed at a junction, narrowly missing a taxi. She hadn't driven this fast since she was a cop.

TWENTY-EIGHT

Margie's house was a 1950s single family residence with a basement granny flat. She greeted Sally and Paul at the top of the porch steps then beckoned them inside. Sally paused at the doorstep to look up and down the street. As far as she knew, she'd lost the reporters tailing her.

For the first time since Sally had resigned from Franklin PD, her advanced driver training had come in useful. She'd managed to lose all but one of the news crews when she'd sped through a yellow light, then she'd dodged the last van when she'd turned into a small side street and pulled up behind some dumpsters. She had deliberately led the media out of Pioneer Heights. Then, when she'd been sure she'd lost her tail, she'd double-backed to Margie's house.

Margie gave Sally and then Paul a hug. "I'm so glad you called. You know you can stay here as long as you want."

"Are you sure you're okay with this?" Sally asked. "I don't want to put you in any danger."

Margie swatted the air. "Don't be silly—that's what friends are for. To be there when you need them. Besides, I have a very loud house alarm."

"I guess there's no football training tonight, huh?" Paul said, dropping his sports bag dejectedly on the polished wooden floor.

"I guess not. There's bound to be reporters there. I'll call the coach. He'll understand."

"That's just great," Paul moaned.

"I'll show you your rooms so you can freshen up if you want. Sally, you're upstairs. Paul, I thought you might like the basement apartment."

Paul's face lit up. "Yeah."

Margie's husband, Henry, an author, who'd passed away some years ago, had had the basement converted so he could have his own space to write. After Henry's passing, Margie had added a small bathroom and started renting it out to a college student.

"It's not occupied?" Sally asked.

"I had to ask her to leave. Long story. Anyway, it means Paul has his own space. It's self-contained."

Paul knew where to go. The basement had two entrances: via a set of internal stairs and also via an exterior door which led to the backyard.

"Hey, don't open the back door, okay?" Margie called out. "It's alarmed."

The house was colorful, with polished timber floors and sixties-style furniture. Sally's bedroom overlooked the backyard and had doors opening onto a small balcony.

She went to the bathroom, splashed water over her face, and dried her skin with a soft towel. Then she set up her cell phone to charge and joined Margie in the kitchen.

Sally burst out laughing at the sight of Margie chopping onions—in swimming goggles.

"Yeah, I know, looks ridiculous, right?" Margie said. "But they stop my eyes running." She nodded toward a bottle of red wine on the counter. An empty glass sat next to it; Margie had already filled one for herself. "Yours, my friend. I expect you need it."

"I sure do." Sally sat at the kitchen counter on a tall stool and poured a large glass of Shiraz.

"How are you really doing?" Margie scraped the onions off the chopping board and into a wok on the gas stove. "Paul can't hear us. Henry had the basement soundproofed. He found any sound distracting when he wrote."

"Surviving, I guess. It's all such a shock. And I'm scared something bad will happen to Paul." Her voice cracked.

"We won't allow that to happen, okay? *You* won't allow that to happen. You're tougher than you think. Now tell me what's going on." Margie began chopping carrots into matchstick-sized pieces.

Sally told Margie about her conversations with Tiffany Blake and Lou Thompson. "And Paul questioned Bart Hower, the manager of the YMCA, who wouldn't hurt a fly. Paul wants to get involved with solving the case, and he's pissed with me because I don't want him to."

Margie stopped chopping and took a sip of wine. "Let me get this straight. You want to find the Poster Killer?"

"Yes."

"Honey, I always knew you had the talent to be a detective, but this guy is real scary. Are you certain you want to poke around? He won't like it."

"I can't rely on Detective Clarke. It's my face on the poster, even if they say it's a copycat. It doesn't matter either way. Someone killed Durrant to stop him identifying the killer. And then there's my stalker."

"Stalker!"

Sally filled her in on Bryan Topham. "...And then, just as I was beginning to believe he might actually be the Poster Killer, he arrives like a knight in shining armor and helps us escape from the hordes of reporters at my house. I promised to meet with him. He's been pestering me for days. Maybe I can find out why he's so obsessed by this particular case."

"I'd think very carefully about that, Sally. I know you've lost faith in the detectives, but maybe you should fill them in on this guy."

"I'll think about it. I'm going to see Chase tomorrow, Tiffany's husband."

"Isn't he a Hell's Angel?"

"No, he just looks like one."

"Want me to come with you?"

"It's okay. His workshop will be busy with mechanics and customers. I'll be just fine."

Margie left the knife on the chopping board and took the stool opposite her. "You said Durrant told you that you know the killers."

"That's right. It creeps me out just thinking about it."

Margie took a big gulp of wine. "There's something I need to tell you." She paused. She sounded nervous, which was totally unlike Margie.

"Margie, you can tell me anything."

"Here goes." Margie put down the glass. "Okay. It's about Scott."

"Scott?"

"He set about isolating you from your parents and your friends. You know that. He did his best to turn you against us, and I know it upset you. It only made me more determined to stick around. What you don't know is that he threatened me."

Sally gasped. "Why didn't you tell me?"

"Because you were already under enough stress. It was 2010, and the poster killer had taken two girls. Scott started with little asides that only I would hear. You know, like, *Drive carefully. You don't want to have an accident.* I know he told you I said cruel things about you to my friends. That was a lie, but it was all part of his plan to separate us. You remember the night you invited me to dinner, thinking Scott was on duty so it would be just us and the kids?"

"He came home early and asked you to leave."

"He asked me to leave *his* house. That's what he said. Not *our* house. He blamed me for making you depressed. I refused to leave, and he demanded you choose between us."

"I couldn't do it," Sally said, remembering how helpless she'd felt.

Scott had undermined her self-belief so badly that she'd been unable to stand up to him.

"So I left the house, but I told him I would never stop being your friend and that he was a manipulative narcissist and he was making you miserable."

"Yes, I remember. Zelda was crying, and I begged you both to stop shouting."

"What you don't know is what he said when he followed me to my car. He told me he would ruin my life if I came near you again. He said he would plant false evidence that would ensure a criminal record and time in jail."

"I had no idea. I... I'm so sorry."

"No, Sally, you didn't put me through it. *He* did. There's more."

Sally wasn't sure if she could bear to hear it.

Margie continued, "When that threat didn't work, he came to my office one day. Told me that if I didn't walk away from you, he'd frame Henry for the Poster Killer abductions. He'd plant evidence. Our basement would be dug up. We'd lose our jobs and our friends."

Margie waited for Sally to respond but she couldn't speak. *He seriously did that?* Even now Sally was discovering new horrors about her ex-husband. When she didn't speak, Margie continued, "Then Henry passed away. It was just me then, and

I told Scott to do his worst. He never followed through with the threat. But you see where I'm heading with this?"

"You think Scott put up the poster with my face on it to torment me? But he's in Chicago."

"Is he?"

TWENTY-NINE
SEPTEMBER 5, 2010

It seemed the glorious summer would never end. Sally and Zelda walked the trail to their favorite picnic spot at the lake's edge. It was a Sunday and the lake's water was just warm enough for kids to swim and play in. A large family who'd had the same idea as Sally sat on a picnic blanket, their food spread out in Tupperware containers, so Sally and Zelda headed for their special, quiet spot, which was further to walk but, as Sally had hoped, there was nobody around.

They skirted one edge of the lake and carried on up the mountain. The lake was in a dell, the steeper end of which had a tree-lined bank which only the adventurous would take to reach the lake's shore. Some years back, a big conifer had collapsed in a storm and its horizontal trunk was the perfect place for them to sit. In the distance, kids' laughter drifted across the water. Overhead, an eagle cried out, and Sally looked up to see the magnificent bird riding the rising air currents in search of prey.

"Look," Sally said, pointing into the sky.

For a while, mother and daughter watched the eagle circling. Sally took the opportunity to glance at her daughter's side profile. Zelda had grown tall and willowy, just as Sally had been at her age. But Zelda's cheeks were gaunter, and her waist and thighs were too thin.

For weeks now, Zelda had been avoiding her mom and dad, and when she was home, she stayed in her room as much as she could. After the debacle at the child psychiatrist, Zelda had stopped caring about herself, school, family. The only time she seemed to be happy was with Stacy and Nikki.

Nikki's mom, Bettina, had expressed concern about Zelda, hinting that she might be suffering from anorexia. But while it was true that Zelda had become furtive, she hadn't shown any signs she was stressed about her weight or her looks, as many girls her age were.

The eagle dived into the tree cover and disappeared from view.

Sally took a swig of water then offered the bottle to Zelda. Zelda brushed it away without taking her eyes off a pair of male and female wood ducks on the lake, not far from a low branch that overhung the water.

"Isn't he beautiful?" Sally said.

The male wood duck had iridescent plumage, a neat pattern of terracotta, white, black, teal, emerald, and mustard colors.

"Yes," Zelda said, her eyes fixed on the ducks.

Zelda rarely looked her mom in the eye these days, as if fearful Sally might see something in her eyes that Zelda didn't want her to see.

"I've made pita pockets with roast chicken, avocado, and feta. And there's bananas and apples." Sally pulled the food from her rucksack and laid it on the stretch of trunk between them, as if it were a table. "And chocolate-chip cookies, baked this morning."

"I'm not hungry." Zelda looked at Sally and gave her a half-smile. "Thanks for doing this."

Her voice was flat, her eyes so sad.

Sally took her hand. "I've made another appointment with Dr. Collins." The child psychiatrist.

"Dad won't let me go."

"He's on a training course that day. He can't stop us."

Sally was pathetic. She knew that, sneaking around behind Scott's back. But he wouldn't listen to her. He'd sabotaged Zelda's previous appointment and Sally had failed to persuade him to allow Zelda to see the shrink since. He was having none of it. Caroline Blake, the cause of Zelda's depression, had been abducted three months ago, but if anything, Zelda was deteriorating. She certainly wasn't recovering from the trauma as Scott claimed.

"There's no point," Zelda said, drawing her hand away.

"Of course there is! She's a lovely person, and she can help you."

A fly landed on the Saran-Wrapped pita sandwich. Sally swatted it away with the back of her hand.

Zelda got up and walked toward the water; Sally followed, a few steps behind.

"Please talk to me, Zelda. You can confide in me. Whatever's making you unhappy, I will do everything in my power to fix it."

Zelda shook her head. "You can't fix it."

At the lake's edge they stopped, and Sally saw a tear roll down her daughter's cheek. She felt crushed by the weight of her child's misery. "Is someone else bullying you? Please tell me."

Zelda stared ahead and smirked. "You could say that."

It was a glimpse of the truth, and Sally took it as a gift.

Zelda's walking boots almost touched the gently lapping water. Sally stepped into the water so that she could face Zelda. Her running shoes were quickly soaked but she didn't care.

"Who?" Sally asked. "Just tell me who."

"Oh, Mommy."

"A name—please."

"Nobody will believe me."

"I will." Sally grasped Zelda's hands. "Trust me."

Zelda looked down at her mom's boots. "Your feet will get wet."

"I don't care. I just want you to be happy. And I know you're unhappy. Would you like to switch schools? Do you want to move to a new town? Anything. Just tell me what you want?"

"I just want to be left alone."

Zelda walked away, following the shoreline, but looked behind her briefly. "I won't see the shrink." Then she kept walking.

THIRTY

On Saturday morning, Sally was up early. She and Margie went for a run, avoiding their normal route just in case a reporter had worked it out. After a hot shower and coffee, Sally dithered about calling Scott to confront him about the poster. Margie's revelation last night about Scott's threats had her worried, but talking to her ex-husband could set her back significantly. Her psychiatrist had advised against it. She hadn't spoken to Scott since he'd walked out. The divorce had been managed through a lawyer—she and Scott had no direct contact.

She stared at his contact details in her iPhone. Everything about him was so abhorrent and yet she hadn't been able to delete him from her cell. Every time she tried, she just couldn't do it.

Even if Scott was back in Franklin, he wouldn't tell her the truth—and he'd get a kick out of the fear in her voice. Perhaps he was exacting revenge on Sally, but she had no proof, and Clarke had said that the fingerprints on the poster weren't in the police database. As a cop, Scott's fingerprints would be in there, so if she told Clarke her theory, he would dismiss it as ludicrous. Everyone at Franklin PD thought Scott a fine cop and a good family man. They had no idea that beneath the charm he was a cruel narcissist.

Margie left to do grocery shopping. Paul helped himself to breakfast and then went back to bed. Thankfully, he was enjoying the basement apartment so much, he didn't ask her about her plans today. Sally intended to see Chase Feinstein—his workshop was open Saturday mornings.

Sally informed Paul that she was going out and asked him not to leave the house. He was watching a movie in bed and eating waffles and could hardly bring himself to acknowledge he'd heard her.

"Margie will be back soon. Please don't open the door to anyone."

Chase Feinstein owned an auto-repair workshop that occupied a space under the brick arch of a railway bridge in the semi-industrial neighborhood of Lincoln. All the way there, Sally vacillated about the wisdom of what she was about to do. The industrial estate was on the edge of town and it felt isolated. What if Chase turned nasty? As a safeguard, Sally called Margie and reminded her where she was going.

"Are you sure about this?" Margie said. "That offer to come along is still open. I can be there in fifteen minutes."

"You know where I am. If I don't ring you in an hour, call Detective Clarke."

The first business on the estate was an importer of Persian carpets; the second was a cell-phone recycling business, which had a dumpster outside the premises full of old phones. The third was Chase's Auto Repairs. She took a parking spot opposite his workshop. A train sped over the bridge with a deafening rattle. She got out and was immediately buffeted by a cold wind that whipped her jacket around her.

The workshop's roller door was raised, and the sound of

music blared out of the workshop. An electric impact torque wrench screeched, and a car engine reverberated in the confined space. Two vehicles were raised up high by hydraulic hoists. There were three men and a woman working there, all in short-sleeved overalls.

Sally approached the woman, who was working under the hood of a gold 1970 Ford Mustang Boss.

"Beautiful car," Sally said.

"Boss's car. She's a beauty," replied the female mechanic.

"I'm looking for Chase."

She pointed in the direction of a black Chevrolet Express cargo van that was raised up high. Beneath it was a lean, muscular man with tattoos the length of both arms. His hair was shaved so short Sally could see the scars on his skull. He was pointing a flashlight under the chassis.

"Chase?"

He turned his head. Chase had a protruding brow and was rumored to have used it to headbutt people he picked fights with. "Hey, Sally, long time no see."

"Can we talk? I need your help."

Chase grabbed a cloth and wiped his oily hands on a patch that was relatively clean. "Come to my office."

He escorted her up some metal steps to an office raised above the workshop on steel girders. It was no more than a box with smeary windows and a door, and it stank of axle grease. He lit a cigarette and inhaled. He didn't ask her if she minded. An ashtray on his desk was piled high with cigarette butts.

"This about the new poster?" he asked. "I hear he's looking for you." There was an amused glint in his eyes.

She fidgeted in her seat. "That's why I'm here."

He took a deep drag on the cigarette. "I don't know the guy."

"I saw Tiffany yesterday."

Chase sat up. Now she had his attention. "How is she?"

"Not good. She's being sexually abused."

He frowned, and his eyes receded behind his sharp brow. "You sure?"

"She told me she was, and I believe her."

"Tiffany imagines things, right? But this? I don't know, it could be real. Can't the prison shrink do something?" he asked.

Not the kind of reaction she'd have expected from a devoted husband. Then again, he wasn't a devoted husband.

"Tiffany won't report it,' Sally said. "She says they'll kill her if she does."

"Look, there's something you should know." He rested his muscular forearms on the desk, which was covered with paper invoices. "Tiffany and me, we're over. Have been for a long time. I know she's got mental problems, but she killed my kid. I'll never forgive her for that." He shook his head. "Never."

"Do you visit her?" Sally asked.

"Nah. Can't bear to look at her. You understand, right? My little Madison. She was so perfect. And Tiffany took her from me."

Chase ground the barely smoked cigarette into the ashtray as if he were grinding her memory into the dirt. He stared at the ashtray, and it wasn't until he looked up that Sally realized his eyes were watery.

"Do you see much of Tiffany's family. Her sisters?" Sally didn't want to come out with what Sophie had implied. She wanted to hear Chase's version of events.

"They moved to Idaho, except Sophie of course. She's at college here."

He picked up a biro and tapped it on the desk. "I guess I should be straight with you." The pen tapping stopped. "We're living together, me and Sophie. I've asked Tiffany for a divorce, but she won't give me one. She's got this mad idea that when she gets out, everything's going back to the way it was."

"Does Tiffany know about you and Sophie?" Sally asked.

"Look, it started a while back. Tiffany found out. Went totally crazy. Smashed up the place. Threatened Sophie. Sophie and me, we stopped seeing each other for a while. But after Madison's death, we got back together. There was no point telling Tiffany then. I just told her that I wanted a divorce."

"When did your affair with Sophie start?"

He looked down at the pen and tapped it on the desk again. "That's not important." He looked up and gave her a warning glare. "You were good to Sophie's family and me when it all happened. So tell me what you need. I don't have all day."

"Is it possible Tiffany killed Caroline?"

"Killed her baby sister?" He shook his head. "Tiffany admired Caroline for the way she got exactly what she wanted from people." He paused. "You know Caroline got into trouble for bullying?"

"Yes."

"Did you know your husband threatened to kill Caroline if she didn't stop?"

"Kill her? He wouldn't do that."

He wagged a finger at Sally. "Your ex is a piece of shit. It was maybe a week before Caroline got taken. Scott picked Caroline up in his cop car after school and took her for a ride, said he knew how to commit the perfect crime and if she didn't stop bullying Zelda, he'd make her disappear."

"How do you know this if you weren't there?"

"I don't know for sure, but Caroline came to our house, bawling her eyes out. She told me and Tiffany what happened. I do know for sure that Scott took her for a ride because I saw him. I drove past the school that day and saw her get into the patrol car. His friend, the black cop, was with him."

Walt Jackson was there? Why hadn't Walt ever told her this?

"What else did Caroline say?"

"She confessed she'd bullied Stacy and Anna, but not Zelda."

There it was again. Both Sophie and Chase had now claimed that Caroline hadn't bullied her daughter. This contradicted everything Sally thought she knew.

"Did anyone else see Scott and Walt take Caroline for a ride?" she asked.

"Nikki Jackson. She said hi to her dad, but she didn't get in the car. I guess she'll deny it. She won't want to land her dad in the shit."

Sally suddenly felt lightheaded. She put out a hand and held on to the edge of Chase's desk.

"Are you all right?" Chase asked.

"I... I have to go."

Sally took the metal steps carefully, fearing she might fall, then dived into her car and burst into tears. If Zelda wasn't being bullied, then why had she killed herself?

THIRTY-ONE
OCTOBER 27, 2010

It was a little after 7 a.m., and Sally was in the kitchen making breakfast. It was fifty degrees Fahrenheit outside, and her ears, nose, and hands were cold from her run. She enjoyed the warmth rising from the hot pan as she stirred the scrambled egg, making sure it didn't stick to the bottom. Scott was already at work, which meant it was up to Sally to coerce Paul and Zelda out of bed and get them to school on time, before she drove on to the DA's office. She had a tough day ahead. Lindsey Green, the mother of the third Poster Killer victim, was making a formal statement to Detective Clarke and it was Sally's job to support her through the ordeal. She had already prepared the kids' lunch boxes and the scrambled eggs and toast were now done.

"Breakfast is ready!" she called up the stairs.

Sally had already knocked on both their bedroom doors earlier. Neither kid had responded.

Exasperated, she climbed the stairs again, hoping the eggs wouldn't turn rubbery. If Scott had been home, Zelda and Paul would be downstairs by now, because neither of them dared to disobey their father. Sally, they knew, was the soft touch.

First, she knocked on Paul's door and yelled for him to get up. She heard him groan, so she went in and threw his drapes open. The room had a musty, wet-sports-shoe smell. And there were clothes all over the floor. She resisted the urge to pick them up and dragged the duvet away from his head.

"Up you get!" She stood there until he sat up. "Breakfast is getting cold."

Sally then knocked on Zelda's door.

No response.

Sally knocked again.

Not a sound. Did Zelda have her earbuds in?

"Zelda, I've made breakfast. Please try to eat something," Sally called out.

Zelda had turned painfully thin. And she no longer made any effort to do as she was asked. It was like she was a different girl.

Sally knocked again—louder this time.

"Zelda? Honey? I'm coming in."

She opened the door and immediately noticed a strange smell. Zelda's room usually smelled of sweet fruit like strawberries, but this morning it smelled musty—no, sour. The room was in darkness, the blackout drapes drawn. She could just see Zelda's outline on the bed.

"Zelda, honey, your scrambled eggs are getting cold," Sally said. She patted the wall for the light switch. When her fingers found it, she flicked it on.

Zelda was curled up in her bed, her long fair hair fanning out over the pillow behind her. She was facing away from Sally. Resting near her head was her left hand, and her beaded bracelet caught the light.

"Zelda?"

The bedhead was cream-painted wrought iron in a semi-circular shape. Zelda had intertwined some fairy lights through the bars which she liked to have on at night when she was reading in bed. On the nightstand was a pile of novels, her cell phone, and a pink nail file. There was also an empty glass plus some white tablets scattered across the surface. They were the wrong shape and color for the antidepressants their GP had prescribed. Had she taken painkillers last night?

Sally tripped over one of Zelda's shoes as she walked to the other side of the bed. Then she gently pulled back the duvet to reveal the upper half of Zelda's nightie: it was her favorite one— pink-and-white striped with two cute pugs on it.

"Honey, wake up."

Sally reached over to brush away a lock of hair that had fallen across Zelda's cheek and discovered her skin felt tight and cool. Her parted lips had something white crusted on them, and there were dried bubbles of white foam at the corner of her mouth that had spilled onto the pink pillowcase.

She gave her daughter a little shake, but Zelda's eyes stayed closed. Not even a flutter of her eyelashes.

"Zelda!" she shouted. "Please! You're scaring me!"

Dread chilled her to her core.

She leaned over her daughter's mouth, desperate to feel her warm breath on her cheek, then reeled back because there was none.

Sally stumbled backward and trod on something small and hard. It cracked underfoot. Dazed, she stooped to pick it up. It was a plastic pill bottle. Sally knew the shape. Saw the label with her name on it. Temazepam. The bottle was empty.

"No, no, no, no!"

Sally took Zelda by her shoulders and shook her. "Zelda! It's Mommy!"

Bile surged up Sally's throat. She swallowed. *Phone? In the kitchen.*

"Paul! Get my phone!" Her scream shattered the quiet of the house.

Sally knew CPR. She had to get Zelda onto her back, then

place the heel of one hand in the center of Zelda's chest, with her other hand on top, and push down one hundred times per minute.

Edging her hands under Zelda's hips and shoulder, she tried to roll her onto her back, but Zelda's limbs stayed in the fetal position, her muscles locked in place. Sally's breath caught in her throat. Her head told her that she was too late, but her heart told her to keep trying. Sally stooped, trying to shift Zelda, and held her tight.

"I love you, I love you."

"Why are you shouting?" Paul mumbled from the doorway, bleary-eyed.

THIRTY-TWO

MAY 9, 2015

Sally didn't drive far. She pulled over where a forest trail began and wiped her tear-stained cheeks with a tissue, then blew her nose. The memories of Zelda's suicide flooded back along with the terrible sense of helplessness that had followed. She couldn't save her child. The paramedics couldn't either. When Scott had arrived with Walt and found Sally clinging to Paul, both of them sobbing at Zelda's bedside, he'd had to drag them from the room and persuade them to go to the living room.

"You don't want to see this," Scott had said.

"I want to be with her," Sally had protested, as he led her downstairs.

"Stay with Paul. He needs you."

The paramedics had come and gone. Paul broke free from her embrace and ran to his room. She would never forget his loud sobbing. She wasn't sure how much later Scott had run down the stairs, his face puce with fury.

"That little bitch killed her!" he'd cried, holding up a transparent evidence bag.

Inside the bag had been Zelda's suicide note.

A note that had broken Sally's heart.

And now Paul, Sophie, and Chase had put doubts in her mind about its authenticity.

Emotionally wrung out, Sally left her car and walked for a while. The birdsong and the chittering squirrels scampering from tree to tree helped her to regain some composure.

Back in her car, she drank from her water bottle. She was torn between her deep need to know why her daughter had died by suicide and her more urgent mission to identify the Poster Killer before anything more sinister happened.

I'll find a way to do both, she thought. *Detectives juggle multiple cases. So I can too.*

Her phone rang. It was Bryan Topham, surely calling to arrange their meeting. She wished she hadn't agreed to it. She let the call go to voicemail because she didn't want to think about it just now. She sent him a brief text message.

Thank you for your help getting us away from the reporters. I need time out today. It's been very stressful. Can I call you tomorrow?

She leaned back against the headrest and turned her attention to the Poster Killer—or killers. What did she know?

Theo Durrant could have used his criminal network to organize Sally's missing-person poster, but, having met him, she didn't think he was the actual killer. There were two killers, not one, he'd said, and she knew them.

Topham texted a reply.

I'm glad I could assist. I understand your trepidation about me. I'm no threat. Google me. I'm the founder of Blazer and Topham, the advertising agency. I retired last year. They'll vouch for me. I'd like to meet you as soon as possible. Tomorrow morning would be perfect, Bryan.

Bryan Topham was on her suspect list. She googled Blazer and Topham and found he was telling the truth about founding the advertising agency. He'd worked with an impressive list of clients. But that didn't rule him out as a serial killer. She didn't understand why he so urgently wanted to talk to her and why he'd been tailing her.

Next, Sally considered Tiffany Blake and Chase Feinstein. They could only have worked as a team up until Tiffany's arrest. Chase could then have continued killing girls, either operating alone or with a new accomplice. Could Sophie Blake be that accomplice?

Sally shook her head. She just couldn't believe that Sophie, who'd turned sixteen in 2010, was a serial killer.

Chase was certainly a suspect though. He clearly liked young women, and it was possible his relationship with Sophie had begun when she was underage. As a mechanic he could also easily have used a different vehicle each time he'd picked up his victims. There would always be a car or two that had to stay overnight in his workshop.

Lou Thompson was an unpleasant man, but he'd been thoroughly investigated at the time. The victims had all bought snacks from his corner store, but so had hundreds of other kids.

Paul had mentioned Bart Hower, the YMCA manager. Sally hadn't been back there since 2011—after Scott left, she hadn't been able to face running the evening teens club on her own. She'd always found Bart went out of his way to be helpful, and he was passionate about his job. The police had contacted all the club members and no new suspects had surfaced.

Sally closed her eyes. Solving crime sure was difficult. Was she making progress? Feeling a little disheartened, she phoned Paul.

"Hi, just checking you're okay?"

"I'm good. Reilly rang. Can I invite him over?"

"It's best if nobody except Margie knows where we are. You didn't tell him, did you?"

"No, Mom." Paul sighed loudly.

"Maybe we can drop by Reilly's house later. I'll talk to his mom and see what we can do." He was a teenage boy—she understood how frustrating this must be for him. "I'll be back in an hour, I promise."

"Why do you get to do what you want, and I have to stay here?" he moaned.

"That's a fair point. I'll call Reilly's mom now."

Sally did as she'd promised and discovered Reilly's mom was very happy for them to drop by this afternoon. Sally asked if they'd been contacted by the media; she replied that they'd had a couple of phone calls to which they'd said no comment, and that was it.

Their planned visit put time pressure on Sally. There were two people she wanted to talk to: Nikki Jackson, Zelda's best friend, and retired detective Richard Foster. Nikki might hold the key to why Zelda had died by suicide. Foster might offer guidance as to which of her suspects were worth looking into further and which were a waste of time. It would take her twenty minutes to reach the Jacksons' house, whereas Foster was much closer.

She dialed Foster; he picked up.

"Sally, I've been expecting your call. What took you so long?"

"Been kinda busy, Richard, avoiding rabid reporters and trying to work out why the hell I'm on a Poster Killer poster."

"I've been wondering that myself."

As always Foster sounded cheerful. British born, he'd been a Metropolitan Police officer for seven years before he'd gone on an exchange program with Franklin PD. Foster had liked it in Franklin so much, he'd never left, and worked his way up to the lead detective in Homicide until Clarke had taken over the role.

"I need someone to brainstorm with. That's why I'm calling. Can I pop in?"

"I'm not sure I'll be of much help but always happy to see you. When were you thinking?"

"How does ten minutes sound?" Sally said.

"Sounds good to me."

THIRTY-THREE

It took her only eight minutes to reach Richard Foster's 1960s house on a half-acre block at Pine Crest. Sally recalled when she and Scott had been invited to a celebration at the house when Foster had been promoted to detective. The house hadn't changed much: it had been built to accommodate the existing pine trees, which camouflaged it from the road. It was painted a grayish-brown that matched the tree trunks and the exposed rock of the front yard. It was as if the trees and the house were one. She remembered the dense forest and the creek—remembered thinking it was a lovely place for the Fosters' son Aiden to grow up.

Foster must have heard her approach because he was waiting on the front deck and waved at her, a black Labrador at his side. He stooped like an old man, although he'd only just turned sixty. Heart problems had forced him to retire.

Sally left her car in the gravel driveway and climbed the paved steps up to the porch, which was a simple wooden deck. "Hello, Richard!"

Up close, his skin had a yellow tinge, but he sounded robust. "Good to see you. Come on in."

The interior was a myriad of corridors and stairs on three levels that followed the slope of the hill. If the decorations and furniture had been updated since she'd last been there twelve years ago, she didn't notice. Each room had a pine wall, all the built-ins were pine, and so were the decks and the floors. In the kitchen was a diner-style booth with Formica table, shaped like a kidney bean. The red leather semi-circular seating was long enough to seat six people easily.

"Coffee?"

"Please. No sugar. Cream."

"How's retirement?" he asked, pouring coffee from a percolator.

"Not what I'd expected," Sally replied. "And you?"

He handed her a mug of coffee and a small jug of cream. "Hate it. What am I supposed to do? I walk the dog, read the paper, then what?"

He led her into the lounge, which had an unlit log fire surrounded by a rough-hewn stone mantelpiece and cream leather sofas and chairs. She took the L-shaped sofa, he took one of the chairs, and the dog settled at his feet.

"Does Aiden still live with you, or has he flown the nest?" Sally asked.

"He has the lower level to himself. Own entrance, like it's his own house. One day he'll move out, when he meets a nice girl and marries. Billy will stay with me, won't you, boy?" he said, scratching the top of the dog's head.

Billy wagged his tail, thumping the pine floorboards.

"Is he home?"

"No, working."

"So, the poster..." Sally said.

Foster nodded. He had a square face, a flat-top haircut, and a thick horizontal mustache. Even his shoulders were wide and level. She had forgotten how angular he appeared.

"It doesn't make any sense," he said. "The killer went to

ground in 2011. Why would he return, after all this time, and then target you? It's bullshit. The Poster Killer is dead—anyone can see that."

"So you still think Theo Durrant was the Poster Killer?"

"Oh yes, he's the one. I've no doubt about it. The killings stopped when he went to jail."

"Clarke seems to agree with you, although he's reopened the case."

"He doesn't have much choice now the new poster is all over the news, but this was all part of Durrant's plan. He used you to create doubt that he's the killer. The poster scared you into meeting with him, right?"

"Right." She paused. Foster seemed well informed about the latest developments, but she guessed Aiden kept him in the loop. "How much do you know about my meeting with him?"

"Let's say I'm kept informed."

"So you know Durrant told me two things?"

"There are two killers and you know them." Foster laughed. "What a load of crap! There is *no* evidence there were two killers. Again, he's deflecting attention away from himself. He knew there was a hit out on him. He knew he was as good as dead. He wanted his legacy to be the cartel his son would take over. The sick bastard was proud of what he'd achieved."

"Any idea why he was murdered?"

"It wouldn't surprise me if Christos, his son, was behind it. He wanted to run the business and wasn't going to wait until papa died of natural causes."

Sally sipped her coffee. Foster seemed so certain, but she had more questions.

"Can I throw a theory at you?"

"Sure."

Foster patted the cushion next to him and the dog jumped up. He lay partly across Foster's lap; Foster stroked the dog's head.

"Durrant used the term 'he or she' when talking about the Poster Killer. This got me thinking about male and female child abductors like Ian Brady and Myra Hindley. A young girl is more likely to trust a woman and to get in the car with a woman. What if Chase Feinstein is the rapist and killer, and Tiffany was his accomplice?"

"Tiffany was serving time by the end of 2010 so that rules her out."

"What if another woman filled her shoes?" Sally asked.

"Who?"

"Sophie Blake. Are you aware that she and Chase are in a relationship? And I'm not certain but it might have started up when she was underage which suggests he likes his sexual partners young."

"Where's your evidence?" Foster asked.

Sally looked down. "I don't have any. Yet."

Foster shook his head. "Chase had a nutty wife who killed their child. If he was going to kill anyone, I'd have thought it would be Tiffany. I'm sorry, Sally, I just don't see him as a serial killer."

Sally's confidence in her own suspect list melted away. All she had were theories. There was, however, one more question she wanted to ask him. She would never dare ask a serving police officer this, but Foster was retired.

"I've recently learned that someone I know, who was a cop at the time, threatened to frame someone for the Poster Killer abductions." Sally tapped the handle of the mug. Was she about to sound like a bitter ex-wife?

"Did that cop follow through with his threat?" Foster asked.

"No."

"Are you going to give me a name?"

Sally shook her head. "It doesn't matter. It's a stupid idea. Forget about it." She changed the subject. "Am I safe now Durrant is dead?"

"It's always good to be careful, Sally. There will always be a question mark over Durrant in the file, but I think you should stop worrying. My biggest regret was not finding the missing girls' bodies. I wanted to bring closure to their grieving families. They need a body to bury, a gravestone to cry at. Only one of the families was able to hold a funeral—the others live in hope they'll see their child again. Sometimes hope is too painful to live with."

"Do you think the bodies will ever be found?"

"Not now Durrant is dead. You know, I went to see him several times after I retired. I asked him where the bodies were. He claimed he didn't know. May he rot in hell."

Sally felt lighter; the tension in her neck unwound a little. If Foster was correct, with Durrant dead, she and Paul had nothing to fear. But there was more at stake than their safety. What if the girls were still alive? Or at least some of them? Even if they were now dead, at least she could help their families to discover the truth. It was something positive she could do—free them from the hell of never knowing what happened.

"What can I do to help find the girls' bodies?"

"Oh, Sally, leave well enough alone. Durrant may be the only one who knew where he buried them. If he dumped them at sea, like Francesca Molinari, they're unlikely to be found."

Sally tapped her fingernail on the tabletop. "Can I ask you something that has nothing to do with the case? It's more of a personal matter."

"Sure."

"I need you to promise you won't breathe a word of it to anyone, not even Aiden."

"This must be serious. You have my word."

"How much do you know about the girls Caroline Blake bullied?"

"All the girls she allegedly bullied were questioned at the time she was taken, and that included Zelda, as you know."

"How did you know who Caroline bullied? She always denied doing it."

"They told us she bullied them. Anna Moorehouse, Stacy Green, and Zelda. There were a couple of others, but their names escape me."

"What if I was to tell you that I have new information that suggests Zelda wasn't bullied?"

"Then why would she say that she was?"

"Good question, and I don't know the answer."

"Your husband was convinced. In his statement, he said Caroline confessed to bullying Zelda."

"Maybe Scott got it wrong. He was wrong about a lot of things."

"There was a suicide note, wasn't there?"

"Yes, and now I'm beginning to doubt it's genuine."

"Oh, Sally, don't do this. People tend to tell the truth when they're about to leave this world. Accept it as genuine and move on."

"I can't. What if there was another reason? Something I totally missed."

"Sally, Sally. Sometimes it's best not to know."

It was easy for him to say, but Foster had never lost a child. Sally had to learn the truth.

THIRTY-FOUR

NOVEMBER 9, 2010

The gathering after Zelda's funeral was held at the Fairburns' house. Sally insisted on preparing the food because if she was busy, she could briefly escape her desolation. This was the only part of the funeral that Scott had allowed her to manage—everything else, from the invite list to the choice of coffin and the words engraved on the headstone had been his decision.

"It's too much for you to think about, darling," he'd said. "Leave it to me."

Sally hadn't wanted to be excluded from the arrangements, but she'd had no energy for a fight. She was an empty woman, like a dead, hollow tree. Her roots were barely holding her upright.

Paul, nine, followed Sally around like a lost puppy. He kept asking when Zelda was coming home, refusing to accept that she wasn't. The night before the funeral he'd flown into a rage and would have trashed his room if Scott hadn't stopped him.

Scott did his best to ignore Sally, neither accepting nor giving her love. He'd taken on the role as the public face of the family's grief with a vigor that Sally found disgusting, positively basking in the attention. With friends, family, and work colleagues, he blamed the bullies for Zelda's depression. At home, he blamed Sally for Zelda's suicide, flinging insults like *useless mother* and *selfish. Why didn't you see it coming?* he'd demanded. *You're supposed to protect victims, so where were you when our daughter needed you?* He never took any responsibility for what had happened.

The day before the funeral, Sally had struggled with even the simplest of tasks, such as pushing a trolley at the grocery store or acknowledging the kind people who came up to offer their condolences. With every kind word, she crumpled into tears. At the funeral, she'd cried quietly into a tissue and tried to take Scott's hand, but he pulled it away. The gathering afterward was excruciating. Sally wanted everyone to leave so she could grieve in peace. But people needed feeding, and so Sally carried trays of sandwiches to their guests in a dream state, inwardly screaming.

"Have you seen Paul?" she asked Scott, who was drinking a beer with Walt.

"No, he's around somewhere."

Sally guessed where he would be. She climbed the stairs and knocked on Paul's door.

"Go away!" he said.

She went in. He lay on his bed, clasping a scruffy blue teddy bear to his chest. Sally closed the door on the voices downstairs and lay on the bed next to him; Paul rolled into her, and she held him tight as they both cried.

Paul's weeping eventually stopped and he fell asleep, but Sally stayed holding him. Gradually the voices downstairs diminished.

Bettina knocked and poked her head into the room.

"The guests have gone," she whispered so as not to wake Paul. "Kitchen's cleaned and sandwiches are Saran-Wrapped."

"Thank you," Sally whispered.

"We're going now. If you need anything, just call."

The stairs creaked, and from the thump of the shoes, Sally knew it was Scott. He peered over Bettina's shoulder.

"Is Paul okay?" he asked too loudly.

Their son woke, blinked, and when he realized he had an audience, he rolled away from Sally so his back was to Bettina and Scott.

"Go away!" Paul said.

Sally sat up. "Let's give him some space."

A wave of dizziness hit her as she lowered her feet to the carpet. She ushered Bettina and Scott away from the doorway and closed Paul's bedroom door behind her. "He needs rest," she said.

"Honey, have you thanked Bettina?" Scott said.

She hated it when he talked to her like she was a child.

"Yes, darling, I have."

"Oh, it was nothing," Bettina said. "Scott's been amazing. A tower of strength in these terrible times. You're so lucky."

Lucky?

Sally would have yelled into Bettina's face if she hadn't bitten down on her lip.

Lucky my daughter killed herself? Lucky my husband treats me like a disease he keeps at arm's length? Lucky my son is traumatized? Lucky how?

Scott went with Bettina downstairs and waved her, Walt, and Nikki off. Sally waited for him at the top of the stairs, clinging to the banister for support. But he went into his study. Was he going to shut himself away?

"Scott?"

He didn't answer. He appeared with his laptop in hand and climbed the stairs. They faced each other on the landing.

"Scott, please. I'd love a hug."

"You! It's always about you! Why do you have to be so needy?"

He strode past her and into their bedroom then slammed the door.

Needy? Was she needy? Right now, yes, she needed him. She'd always put Scott and the kids first. People at work described her as selfless; her friends saw her as a dedicated mom and wife. Only once had she put her needs above Scott's: when she'd taken the job of victim advocate. Scott had wanted to start a family as soon as they were married and Sally had been happy with that, but she'd also wanted a career. Scott had done all he could to dissuade her, and when Zelda was born, he'd ramped up the pressure for her to become a stay-at-home mom.

Sally had almost caved to Scott's will in the ensuing months, then her boss had rung and asked when she was returning to work. There was a daycare center in the building adjacent to the DA's office, and Sally's parents had offered to contribute to the cost of childcare so that Sally could return to the job that she loved and be close to her kid, which she'd gratefully accepted.

The relationship between Scott and her parents had already been strained, but defying him made Scott furious. He kept finding reasons not to invite Ellen and George to family events. And then he banned them from attending Zelda's funeral.

Sally had wanted more than anything for her parents to be with her at such a terrible time and had begged Scott to mend bridges with them, for Paul's sake as well as hers. But Scott wouldn't relent.

Mend bridges...

Sally stared at the door that had been slammed in her face. She had to be the one to mend bridges because Scott wouldn't do it. She would apologize for being needy. And bear his fury for "causing" Zelda's suicide.

It took a moment to build up the courage but finally, she knocked, walked in, ready to pacify Scott. She stopped dead.

On their bed was a suitcase. It was the large one they used for long vacations. The case had Scott's shoes, shirts, jumpers, socks, and underwear in it.

"What are you doing?" she asked.

He paid no attention to her, folding his smart jacket and putting it in the suitcase, then pushed past her and went to the en-suite bathroom, where he took his black toiletries bag from the cupboard under the basin and filled it with his shampoo, deodorant, hair gel, hair clippers, cologne, toothbrush. He took the toothpaste they shared.

"Scott? Are you going away?" Her voice quivered.

Just when she'd thought her life couldn't get worse, it did.

In stony silence, he brushed past her and returned to the bedroom. His jaw was clenched tightly. The toiletries bag went into the suitcase.

Sally followed him around the bed so she might force him to look at her.

"If you need some space, I understand. But we have to work through this as a family."

He glared at her and stabbed a finger into the side of her skull. "Get this into your stupid head. I don't want you or this family. I'm done."

"What?"

Stupefied, she watched him fold his shirts and put them in the suitcase. Then his pants. He didn't touch his three sets of Franklin PD uniforms.

"You don't mean that. You're grieving. It's okay to be angry —" Sally began.

"Don't give me that psych shit. I've had enough. Have you any idea how much I hated being married to you! I deserve a fucking medal."

Scott could be cruel, but this was beyond anything he'd said before.

Scott zipped up the suitcase and clutched the handle.

Sally was reeling. "I love you! I thought you loved me?"

Suddenly, he was right in her face, jaw jutted forward, his eyes dark, angry slits. "You make me miserable. You bore me. I'm leaving you."

Scott strode from the room.

Paul opened his bedroom door and peered out. "Mom? Dad?"

Scott didn't even look at his son. He didn't hug him or say goodbye. He just jogged down the stairs, grabbed his coat from the peg on the wall, popped his baseball cap on his head, and picked up his car keys and sunglasses. He closed the house door behind him and drove away without a backward glance.

THIRTY-FIVE

MAY 9, 2015

Paul was enjoying showing off *"his* apartment" to his buddy Reilly, which he did through video on WhatsApp.

"It's all mine," Paul said.

He moved his phone's camera slowly around the space so that Reilly could take it all in. "Big bed." The bed was a rumpled mess, but Reilly wouldn't care. "Own TV with every channel."

"Getting seriously jealous," Reilly said, his image a small rectangle on the bottom left of Paul's phone.

Paul pointed the camera at the bathroom. "My own bathroom." He kept turning. "Refrigerator, but I can take what I like from the fridge upstairs." He moved on. "Huge backyard, and you'll never guess what else..."

Paul walked through the exterior door, across the stone patio, and into the warm sunshine. He pointed the video camera at the outdoor swimming pool, the blue water sparkling.

"Oh man! Why can't I come to your place?" moaned Reilly, who then moved his phone so that Paul saw a close-up of his friend's nostril. As usual, Reilly was messing around.

"Ew! Stop doing that. Hey, how was football practice?"

"Okay, until John shoved his stinking ass into my face during the team huddle. Hate that guy."

Paul laughed. "He's got it in for you."

Paul heard the crunch of gravel underfoot. It was coming from the driveway. "Hey, Mom's home. Gotta go. See you later."

He knew he wasn't supposed to have shown Reilly his location, but it had just been the interior with a bit of the backyard too. Either way, he didn't want his mom getting pissed at him.

Paul was dressed in a T-shirt, jeans, and sneakers, ready to go see his buddy as soon as Sally came home. He ran up the internal steps which led to the hall.

"Mom? You home?"

The house was quiet. Just the tick of the funky atomic age wall clock in the hall. Margie hadn't set the burglar alarm—he could tell because the box on the wall had a light that blinked when it was active.

He ducked into the living room and looked out of the window. The only car in the drive was Margie's and she'd gone to help a neighbor after returning with the groceries. He couldn't remember why the neighbor wanted help, but it occurred to him that maybe it was Margie that he'd heard on the drive and not his mom.

"Hello?"

Irritated that everyone else was out and about except him, he helped himself to a packet of chips and a Coke and headed back down the internal stairs to the basement. He would play a video game until his mom came back.

Sitting with his feet on the coffee table, he opened the Coke and drank, then pulled open the packet of chips and pushed a handful into his mouth. He selected *Star Wars: Battlefront*, not bothering to channel the sound through his headphones— instead, he turned the TV volume up high and let the sound fill the room.

A shaft of sunlight through the open door behind him made

it difficult to see the right-hand side of the TV. He was about to get up and close the door when the sunbeam disappeared. Maybe the sun had gone behind a cloud? But it would come out again. He got up.

A man in a black ski mask stood in the exterior doorway, blocking the sun.

His heartbeat surged. Ski mask? This had to be bad. His whole body tensed.

"Who are you?" Paul asked.

Then he spotted the knife in the man's left hand. *Holy shit!*

The intruder headed straight for him, pulling back his knife-holding hand, ready to stab Paul.

Paul instinctively dived to his left, just as the knife swiped through what would have been his chest, then stumbled, very nearly losing his balance. Between him and his attacker was nothing but a coffee table.

Paul desperately looked around for a weapon, anything he could hit the guy with. A small red fire extinguisher was mounted to the kitchen wall. He edged toward it. The intruder stepped in his path.

Sweat trickled down his temple. "Take anything," Paul said. "Just leave me alone."

The man said nothing. He just edged closer. The weapon had a black handle and a long blade and looked like a kitchen knife.

Paul backed away. "Help!" he shouted.

His butt hit a chair that screeched as it scraped the floor. Paul picked up the chair and held it high, ready to hit the knife-wielder.

"Stay away!"

But the intruder kept coming.

Paul was a strong guy—if he could swing the chair hard enough, he might knock the knife from the attacker's hand.

Then man crept closer, and Paul swung the chair, aiming at his middle, but his opponent had fast reflexes and jumped aside, then jabbed the knife at Paul's stomach.

THIRTY-SIX

The last person Sally expected to hear from on a Saturday was Dr. Buss, and to her relief he had some good news—Tiffany was being moved to the secure wing of a psychiatric hospital the next day.

"She's asked if you'll come and see her. Are you able to visit today?" Buss asked.

Sally had only just left Foster's house and she was on her way to Margie's place to pick up Paul. "Can it wait until tomorrow?"

"Tiffany won't be able to have visitors on day one. She'll need to settle into her new environment."

"I really can't do it today." She needed to get back to her son. "Can I speak to her by phone?"

"Yes, although she tends to be more confused when she's on the phone. Never mind. If you can hang on, I'll pass the phone to her. She's in the prison hospital."

"Wait up. Why's she in the hospital?"

"Black eye and broken rib."

Sally was exasperated. "Who did it?"

"She won't say."

Sally could overhear Dr. Buss explaining to Tiffany that Sally was on the line.

"Sally?"

"Hey, Tiffany!"

"Did you hear the news? I'm leaving tomorrow. Chase is coming to get me."

"You're going to a much nicer place, Tiffany. People won't beat you there. It's a special hospital, with pretty gardens."

"What are you talking about? Chase is taking me home. We're going to make babies. Everything is going to be great."

"It's good to hear you so happy," Sally said. "Dr. Buss told me that you wanted to speak to me."

"Have you read *To Kill a Mockingbird*?"

"Um, yes, at school."

"Me too," Tiffany said. "Didn't like it much back then. But I love it now. If I'd had an attorney as good as Atticus, I wouldn't have ended up in jail. He'd have saved me, I'm sure of it."

For a while Sally and Tiffany talked about the story and characters of *To Kill a Mockingbird*, and Tiffany was lucid and knowledgeable—a good sign.

"Tiffany, do you have something you want to tell me?" Sally asked.

"This is a secret, okay?" Tiffany whispered. "If they find out I told you, they'll kill me."

The setup of the prison hospital was four beds in a ward. Who else might overhear what Tiffany said? "Are you alone?"

"No, Jane's here but she's asleep."

"Okay, can you speak quietly?"

Tiffany whispered. "I saw him. He got out of his car and talked to Caroline. I don't know what he said, but I saw him."

It took a few seconds for Sally to comprehend what Tiffany was saying.

"You saw the man who abducted your sister?" Sally said.

"Yes. I didn't tell anyone. I didn't want him to take me too."

Had Tiffany's lucidity gone? Was she now delusional? Or was this Tiffany's secret? Sally had to know.

"Who was he?"

"It was twilight. Not sure."

"Did you see his face?"

"A little. The hat hid most of it."

"What about his face?" Sally asked again. "Can you describe it?"

"It was a nice face."

"Why was it a nice face?"

"I saw his smile."

"What happened?"

"Caroline got in his car and he drove away."

Sally's heart thumped hard and loud. "What did the car look like?"

"Just a car. Maybe black. Don't tell anybody. He'll find me if you do."

"How will he find you? Did he see you?"

"I don't know. Stop asking more questions. You're confusing me."

"I won't ask any more. Thank you for telling me this."

"It's our secret, right?"

"This is important information, Tiffany. I'm not sure if I can keep it a secret but I can keep you, as the source, anonymous."

"You promise?" Tiffany said.

"I promise."

Sally noticed a call coming in from Detective Clarke. She really wanted to speak to him so she said goodbye to Tiffany and then took Clarke's call.

"Sally, Paul is missing," he said.

"Missing? No, he's at Margie's place." She rattled off the address.

"Are you sitting down?"

"I'm driving."

"Then pull over." His voice was different—a forced calmness.

"No, tell me now!"

"Margie Clay dialed 911. Said she saw a man in a balaclava enter her backyard. She was next door at the time. Said he had a knife."

"Where's my son?"

"We don't know. We're searching for him."

Sally slammed her foot down on the accelerator.

THIRTY-SEVEN

Sally threw the car door open and ran straight for the uniformed officer who was busy keeping people away from Margie's house. Dread twisted in her stomach when she saw the yellow crime-scene tape strung across each end of the street.

All the way there she'd hoped Margie had made a mistake. But the tape told her loud and clear that a serious crime had been committed. Two squad cars and Clarke's unmarked suburban were parked outside Margie's home. Neighbors stood on porches or in their front yards watching the commotion, and a small crowd had gathered in the street.

"Let me through!" she yelled, but her voice was drowned out by an approaching police car's siren.

Sally shoved her way through the onlookers. A man was haranguing a young cop patrolling the tape.

"I live here, for Christ's sake!" the man complained. "That's my house!"

Sally's legs felt like jelly but, regardless, she squeezed past the moaning man and called out.

"I'm Mrs. Fairburn, Paul's mom. Clarke told me to come here!"

He lifted the tape and pointed to where Clarke was talking to Lin. She ducked under the tape and sprinted across the street. Lin saw her first. Then Clarke turned.

"Have you found my son?" The words burst from her lips.

All around them was a whirl of cops.

"We're searching now," Clarke said. "We're doing everything we can."

Did he have any idea how it felt to fear your child might be dead?

Lin said, "We'll find him." She gave Sally a sympathetic look then walked over to a couple of cops and briefed them.

"It's been over thirty minutes," she shrieked. Driving there, she'd counted off the minutes and broken every speed limit. "Why haven't you found him?" She didn't care that she sounded panicked.

"I need you to calm down and tell me what you know of his movements this morning."

"I wasn't with him. He was here. In the basement." She looked around, frantic. "I thought Margie was home. You've spoken to her?"

"Yes. Lin is interviewing her."

She followed his line of sight. Margie sat on the next-door neighbor's steps, her arms wrapped around her knees, a blanket over her shoulders. She had that wide-eyed, dazed looked of somebody in shock. Detective Lin was talking to her, a notebook in her hand.

"Who attacked him?"

"We don't know yet. Although we know the assailant was masked. And we found this."

Clarke held out his phone so she could see the screen. When she saw the photo, it was like she'd been plunged into freezing water. Her heart almost stopped.

"No, no, no, not my boy!" she breathed. The photo was of a missing-person poster, and Paul was on it. "He's got Paul!" She looked at Clarke pleadingly. "He'll kill him, just like the others!"

"Sally, look at me." He pocketed his phone and stepped closer. "We'll find him, okay? But you have to stay calm and leave us to do our jobs."

She was only half-listening. It was the Poster Killer. It had to be. But why Paul? He'd never targeted boys before. It was because of her. It had to be. She'd poked her nose where he—or they—didn't want her to and he'd taken her son to punish her.

"The poster. Where was it found?" Her voice was brittle.

"On the bus stop at the end of this street. Sally, can you tell me when this photo was taken?" He raised his phone again and held it at her eye level.

She stared at the image on the tiny screen, but her brain just couldn't take it all in. *Concentrate! Help them find him!* "He wore that sweatshirt yesterday."

"Okay," Clarke said, "tell me about Paul's movements yesterday."

"Um, I kept him at home. I went out in the morning. He went to the YMCA. He had this idea that someone there could be the killer. I didn't know he was going to do that. I told him to stay home. Oh my God! Is that why he was attacked?" Sally was finding it difficult to breathe.

"Who did he speak to there?"

"He mentioned Bart Hower."

"Okay, anything else I should know about? Anyone suspicious hanging around?"

"An old guy called Bryan Topham has been stalking me. Claims he's writing a book about the Poster Killer. He came to my house. He followed me to the jail when I saw Durrant. I know he's spoken to Lou Thompson."

"Who? Slow down, Sally. Describe Bryan Topham."

"Looks about seventy. White hair and goatee. Well spoken. About my height."

"I doubt that's the man who pursued Paul. Margie Clay described him as athletic and tall. He sprinted after Paul with no difficulty."

Sweat stung her hairline and the back of her neck. "Sprinted? Where?"

"Thataway." Clarke waved his hand down the street. "Any idea where he might go?"

Again her brain moved painfully slowly.

Sally looked around. Large houses on big blocks. In a valley. Forest all around. "I don't know," she said despairingly. "Ask Margie."

He'll be okay. He's strong and fast.

Detective Lin jogged over. Her chiseled face was a picture of grim determination. "Sir, Margie says she thought they headed into the woods. There's a trail that starts a little way down this street." She pointed in the direction.

"Show me," said Clarke. "Lin, I want every cop with us except Santiago and Singh. They keep the crowds away." To Sally he said, "Stay here."

"No, I'm coming with you. I can help."

"As you wish, but don't get in our way."

Sally, Clarke, and Lin walked down the center of the street, followed by two plainclothes detectives and four uniformed cops. Why hadn't Paul run into the neighbor's house? Why keep going down the street?

It took them five minutes to locate the start of the trail, but it felt like hours to Sally. The forest was mainly Oregon ash. Further up the hill, the cover became mostly paper birch and lodgepole pine. The forest stretched for miles. Sally almost despaired. It would take days to search the area properly. By then her son could be dead.

"Gather around, people."

Clarke dictated how he wanted the search done. Sally's pumps were totally wrong for straying off the paths into the forest proper. No matter. She would walk barefoot if she had to. She had already lost a daughter—she wasn't about to lose her son too.

We will find him, she told herself.

The search began. They spread out in a line and stayed in that line as they walked forward. Sally picked up a stick to poke at bushes and potential hiding places. The ground cover in some areas was thick with ferns and brambles, which made progress slow. The bramble thorns ripped at her ankles. It was a warm day, but under the thick tree canopy it felt much cooler.

Sally tripped over a root, and Lin, who was next to her in the line, asked if she was okay. Sally was grateful for the detective's concern, but wild horses wouldn't drag her out of the forest until Paul had been found.

As the minutes ticked by, Sally fought back negative thoughts. *He's a strong boy and a fighter—he'll be okay. We just have to find him.*

"Sir! Fresh footprints," a cop shouted. He was at the far end of the line where the pines left their needles on the forest floor. It was muddy there.

Sally's heart almost burst from her chest. She broke the line and jumped fern branches to reach where the cop stood. Clarke got there first.

"Two different sizes of shoe. Look here." Clarke pointed. "They overlap."

"What does that mean?" she asked, frantic.

"Means we're on the right track," Clarke replied. "It may mean he has Paul. Are you sure you want to continue?" he asked her.

"Certain."

Clarke made a phone call requesting two dog handlers, but they were an hour away. Clarke set off again but much slower this time, following the muddy footprints through the dense forest. Sally tried to keep her breathing regular to fuel her body.

She inhaled the rich pine-sap smell and powered onward. The gradient grew steeper and rockier. Sally stumbled and cut her hand on a sharp stone, but it wasn't deep. If only she was wearing her running shoes. The question she kept asking herself was who had known their location? Had Paul told one of his buddies? Reilly Doyle came to mind.

"Clarke," Sally said. "Only me, Paul, and Margie should have known our location. Either Topham followed me to Margie's house, or Paul told a friend where he was staying. Reilly Doyle would be a good bet. Perhaps he innocently told someone he shouldn't have?"

"Thanks, Sally."

Over the phone, Clarke sent a cop to interview Reilly.

When he was done, she said, "I have something to tell you."

Clarke glanced at her.

"Chase Feinstein. I don't have proof, but I think he might have started a sexual relationship with Sophie Blake when she was underage."

He frowned deeply. "Why do you say that?"

"Sophie and Chase were together before Tiffany went to jail. Sophie turned sixteen on May 1, 2010, but it might have begun before that. Either way, it means Chase likes young girls."

Clarke flicked a sideways glance at her and smiled. "You know, you should never have left Franklin PD. You might have made detective."

"Scott had the potential to be a detective. Not me. But thank you for the compliment."

"Scott? No offense, Sally, but Scott was only good at rounding up violent criminals. He didn't have the brains to be a detective."

Before Sally could react, Lin shouted, "Over here!"

Sally looked in her direction. Lin was kneeling next to some large ferns.

"Blood!" Lin said.

Clarke put out an arm just as Sally darted forward. "Stay here. I don't want the evidence contaminated."

He then jogged over to where Lin was crouched. Sally ignored his order—she had to see for herself.

Something wet and bright caught her eye on a fern leaf. The drops of blood looked more brown than red on the green foliage.

"He's hurt," Sally whispered.

She yelled his name. All she could think of was that her son was bleeding. How badly was he wounded? She turned in a circle, but she could only see never-ending trees.

"It's Mom! Paul, where are you?" she cried. "Paul!"

Then she heard a scratching noise.

"Quiet!" Clarke ordered.

Nobody moved.

"Paul? Is that you?" Sally shouted at the top of her lungs.

It sounded distant, but he was calling out, "Help!"

Heads swiveled. Where was the voice coming from?

"This is Detective Clarke. Keep talking, Paul!" he shouted.

"Over here! In the hide."

Sally spun around, searching for a hide, but it had been well camouflaged.

Paul kept calling out. They followed his voice to the left of the trail where the muffled sounds grew stronger.

"There!" a cop said, pointing.

It was a five-feet-high-by-six-feet-long hut with a narrow rectangular opening at eye level through which hunters and birdwatchers could see the forest. Sally ran. She lost a pump. She kept running. Clarke caught up with her and pulled her away from the hide's entrance.

"Paul, is anyone with you?" Clarke said.

"No."

Sally tried to open the hide's door, but the cop pulled her back. "It could be a trap."

When the hide was surrounded, a cop kicked in the door and went in. "Clear!"

"Paul Fairburn?" Sally heard the cop ask.

"Yes," Paul said.

Sally barged into the hide, squeezing past Clarke and the other cop, who was kneeling next to Paul. It was dark and musty. In its close confines, all she could smell was his sweat and the damp earth.

Paul lay curled up on his side.

Sally took his hand. "Paul, are you hurt?"

"Twisted my ankle. Maybe broke it. He cut my arm."

"Son, there's blood near the trail," Clarke said.

"I jumped him, smacked him on the back of the head with a rock. Then ran. Stumbled over a tree root. Hurt my ankle, but he'd lost me by then. I crawled in here."

"Where is he now?"

"Gone."

THIRTY-EIGHT

Sally stared at the cream linoleum on the hospital corridor floor. She was seated on a chair outside pale blue double doors waiting for the X-ray of Paul's ankle to finish. In her hand was an empty bottle of sparkling water she'd bought from the vending machine and drank thirstily. She must look a mess. Her hands and feet were grimy with mud. A nurse had taken pity on her and given her blue booties that were usually used to protect the shoes she didn't have anymore. She wasn't sure when she'd lost the second shoe.

She was still reeling from the attempt on her son's life. On top of the injured ankle, the knife wound on Paul's arm had needed stitches, and his ribs were bruised, but otherwise he seemed to be unhurt. If he hadn't been resourceful and a fast runner, he might be dead. The knife-wielding intruder had lunged at Paul's stomach, but Paul had turned to run, the blade slicing his arm instead.

Sally straightened her back and peered down the corridor to where a nurse was helping an elderly patient walk to a vacant chair. She then opened her wallet and pulled out a passport-sized photo of Paul, taken after a victorious football match. He looked so proud and happy. It was hard to comprehend that she had almost lost her darling boy today. The assailant had to be stopped. Clarke said she could have made detective if she'd stayed with Franklin PD. Well, she was damn well going to be a detective and hunt down the man who'd attacked her son, and she was pretty certain that person was also the Poster Killer—or one of them at least.

"Nobody hurts my child," she said to herself, her voice steely.

Sally was done with living in the shadows. She was done with people telling her what she could and couldn't do. She was a mother, and every mother had the right to defend their child.

The question she grappled with was how best to do that.

One of the people she'd come into contact with recently either was the serial killer or was an accomplice—and she wouldn't rest until they were behind bars.

The familiar bullish figure of Clarke barreled down the corridor and sat heavily on the seat next to her.

"How is he?" Clarke asked.

"They're X-raying him now. Otherwise, a few bruises, stitches in his arm. Any news?"

"Forensics are all over the crime scene. We have to hope the assailant left some DNA."

"It's the Poster Killer. One of them anyway," Sally said. "He thinks I know who he is."

"Do you?"

"Not yet." She tapped her temple. "Somewhere in here is the answer."

"Sally, the best thing you can do is leave town. The attempt on your son's life failed this time. They may try again. They may come for you. You can't stay at Margie's house. It's a crime scene. I can find you a safe house. Some place you and Paul can hide out until the perp is arrested."

"I don't want to hide. I want to help you find him."

"Let me finish. I'll assign officers to be with you twenty-four-seven. You and Paul mustn't use your phone, the internet, social media, email. Basically, anything the killer can use to locate you."

"You're effectively cutting me out of the investigation."

Clarke threw his hands in the air. "I'm trying to keep you alive. Here's what's going to happen. You and Paul are coming down to the station to make statements. In the meantime, we'll allocate a safe house to you. I can't force you to go there, but at least talk through the idea with Paul."

The door to the X-ray room opened and Paul, in a wheelchair, was rolled out by the radiologist.

"There are no fractures," the radiologist said. "But the ankle's severely strained. It needs to stay raised for a few days. And you should pack ice around it to ease the swelling."

Clarke stood. "We have ice at the station. Paul, how do you feel about making a statement while it's fresh in your head." He took hold of the wheelchair's handles.

"I'm beat," Paul said. "Can we do it another time?"

"Now's the best time, Paul. And, Sally, I want you to tell us everything you know, every person you've spoken to about this case. And I mean everyone."

Two hours later, the detectives took pity on Paul and Sally and brought in some takeout food and soft drinks while Clarke and Lin took a break. When the detectives returned to the interview room, Lin had a document and a pen in her right hand.

"We've found a suitable safe house, an hour's drive from here," Clarke said. "I want to be very clear. Your lives are at risk, and you should take the offer. You are within your rights to refuse, and if that's what you want, then you sign this piece of paper and you can leave."

Detective Lin placed the document and a pen on the table.

Clarke said, "I'm going to give you time with your son to talk it over."

They left them alone.

"Can I go to Reilly's house? Pleeeeease. You can come too," Paul said.

"I wish it were that simple. But everyone knows you and Reilly are buddies. I hate to say it, I think we have to go to the safe house."

Paul complained but by the time Lin returned to the room, Sally and Paul had reached an agreement.

"What have you decided?" Lin asked.

"We'll go with you to the safe house, but I'll drive my car. Paul and I will get burner phones, and we don't need cops babysitting us." Sally wanted the freedom to search for the man who attacked her son and with police watching them all the time, she wouldn't be able to. "Besides, don't you need every police officer you have to find the killer?"

"It's for your protection."

"The safe house is enough. No babysitters."

Lin sighed. "Okay, I'll send someone to your place to pack your clothes."

"I'd like to let Margie know what's happening."

"We'll contact her for you. From now on, it's best you don't communicate with anyone other than me or Clarke."

THIRTY-NINE

Detective Lin took the freeway out of Franklin. Sally tailed the unmarked Chevrolet Suburban in her Honda Civic. Paul was dozing in the back with his foot up on the seat. On the seat next to Sally were two new burner phones, which had already been activated and programmed with any numbers they might need.

"Where are you taking us?" Sally mumbled to herself. She had been instructed to stay on Lin's tail. Any time it looked as if Lin was about to lose them, the detective slowed down, allowing Sally time to catch up.

This stretch of freeway was raised above the surrounding suburban and industrial sprawl of Lincoln, and the next turn-off was the one she'd taken to reach Chase's auto-repair workshop.

She glanced to her right. A train line ran parallel to the freeway and across a bridge. There had once been a river beneath the bridge, until it had been diverted. Now it was a light industrial zone.

The strobing lights of a police car grabbed her attention. It was parked outside Chase's workshop. Sally took her foot off the accelerator so she could see better what was going on. Had they gone there to arrest Chase? She now wondered if she'd done the right thing telling Clarke about him and Sophie.

Then a thought entered her head that caused her to shudder. Had Chase become the killer's next victim?

Sally made a split-second decision—she grabbed the burner and called Lin.

"What's going on at Chase's Auto Repairs?" she asked.

"We're handling it. Keep following me."

"I have to know. Is he all right?"

Her raised voice woke Paul in the back. "What's up?" he asked, yawning.

Lin replied to her question. "Chase isn't hurt."

In Sally's rear-view mirror, a similar Suburban to the one Lin was driving zipped past them with sirens blaring. It took the turn-off to the industrial estate.

"I'm taking a look," Sally said, taking the turn-off at the last minute.

Lin had already driven past the exit. "Sally! No!"

"Sorry, Esme, I have to know what's going on."

"Jesus, Sally! Clarke will be livid." She sighed. "I'll take the next turn-off. Don't you dare leave there, you hear me?"

Paul leaned forward. "Are we there?"

"I'm making a quick stop on the way."

At the end of the ramp, she took a right. Paul could now see the police cars in the industrial park.

"You're investigating, right?"

"That's right."

Paul grinned at her in the rear-view mirror. "You go, Mom!"

When Sally came to a stop outside the auto-repair workshop, Clarke was in conversation with Chase. They were gathered close to his workshop doors. A uniformed officer was unrolling crime-scene tape.

"I won't be long," Sally said as she got out.

Paul lowered the window. "What am I supposed to do?"

"I'll be quick. Promise."

A uniformed cop saw her heading straight for Chase and stepped in her path. "This is a crime scene. Can you step back please?"

"I want to speak to Detective Clarke."

The female cop raised an eyebrow when she mentioned the detective's name.

Clarke had spotted Sally and came straight up to her. "Sally, what the hell are you doing? Where is Lin?"

"She's turning around. Is Chase okay?"

He took her arm and pulled her aside, then hissed in her ear, "You shouldn't be here. As soon as Lin arrives, you leave with her, you got it?"

"Just tell me what's going on."

Clarke ran a hand through his hair. "There's another poster."

Sally suddenly felt lightheaded. "With Chase on it?"

"Nope. Tiffany."

"Tiffany? Is she next?" Sally's mind was racing. Someone had managed to kill Durrant in jail. Was the same fate awaiting Tiffany? Or was she already dead? "Where is she? Is she at the psychiatric hospital?"

Clarke's phone rang. He told Sally to hang on and walked away from her.

The call was brief. The color drained from his face as he listened. "Don't touch anything, you hear me? I'm on my way."

Clarke made another call, then he faced Sally. "Tiffany is dead."

Sally groaned. "How?" was all she could manage.

"Not sure. By the time she arrived at the hospital, she was complaining of abdominal pain. She collapsed and died."

"Had she been punched in the stomach?"

"The doctor suspects poison."

Sally stared at Clarke. Had someone administered poison to her meal before she'd left the correctional facility? How could that happen? Had someone overheard Tiffany telling Sally what she'd seen the night Anna had been taken?

"Detective, Tiffany confided in me that she witnessed Caroline's abduction." Her voice was reedy with shock. "I wish I'd told you before."

"Jesus Christ! Tell me now."

Sally explained how Tiffany had described the man and the vehicle.

"Get out of here, Sally." She wasn't surprised he was angry. "I now have to break the news to Chase and to Tiffany's parents." He hesitated, as if he were psyching himself up for the grim task, then headed back over toward Chase.

Back in her car, Sally was shaking. "I made a mistake."

"Mom?" Paul leaned through the gap between the two front seats.

Sally told him what had happened.

"Maybe we should head on over to the safe house?" Paul said. He suddenly looked like a scared little boy.

"We will. We have to wait for Esme to get here," Sally said, trying to sound calm. "I think Tiffany's dead because she saw the killer abduct her sister."

She frowned, mulling it all over. "Something's wrong. So far there have been three posters: me, you, and Tiffany. And two people have been killed: Durrant and Tiffany. And there was the attempt on your life. It doesn't make any sense. I'm the common denominator and yet, so far, knock on wood, there's been no attempt on my life." She swiveled in her seat so she could regard her son. "Is this my fault?"

"Mom! Don't say that," Paul said with fear in his eyes.

"I promise I'll keep you safe."

"What if the psycho comes after you? What are you going to do?"

Sally cupped her son's cheek. "I won't let him take me. And I won't let him take you. You hear me?"

FORTY

Detective Lin's Suburban turned off the freeway and followed a winding country lane, then took a left up a sloping drive lined with fir trees. The nearest house was a quarter of a mile back the way they had come.

Sally inhaled the scent of fir needles and damp leaves through the open window. It was late afternoon, and little sun penetrated the forest surrounding the property.

When the drive came to an end, she had a first glimpse of the uncared-for house and the overgrown front yard. Her heart sank. It looked dilapidated. The concrete drive was so cracked that tall grass had grown through the gaps. The A-frame roof was green with moss, the gutters piled high with twigs and leaves. Behind the house was a steep hill, thick with grand firs and Sitka spruces. The area was known as Grand Ridge.

"What a shithole!" Paul said from the back.

Sally followed Lin's car until she pulled over to one side of a garage that had also seen better days. The roller door was raised, and the interior was full of dead leaves, storage boxes and junk.

Sally let the engine idle as the detective left her vehicle and came over. The entrance to the house was up some steps to a wide porch that ran the length of the front wall. Every surface was gray with dirt.

"Park in the garage and close the door," Lin said. "You should always do that, in case Paul's assailant knows your car."

It took Paul a while to maneuver his painful ankle out of the car. The hospital had given him crutches.

"Are you serious?" Paul said to Lin. "*This* is the safe house?"

"Wait until we get inside."

He leaned on the crutches and hopped toward the steps, a look of deep concentration on his face.

The garage was built to house two cars, but with the junk piled up on each side, it was barely wide enough for Sally's Civic. Paul was on the porch by the time she and Lin had carried the suitcase and other bags up the wooden steps, which creaked as if they were about to snap under their weight.

Sally took a breath and looked around. Next to a pillar was a dusty walking frame, while a pair of rubber gardening shoes sat next to the house door. There was a table, covered with a cheap plastic tablecloth, with four plastic chairs around it—the kind you'd buy from a discount store—and a sofa with faded cushions faced the view beyond the wooden railings, although said view was little more than miles and miles of trees topped with a cloudy sky. There were four plant boxes that were overgrown with weeds. A rusted gardening trowel stuck out of the soil of one box.

"Did an elderly person live here?' Sally asked.

"Yes. When she died, Franklin PD bought it."

"Is the house full of her stuff?" It felt like they were invading someone else's life.

"Mom, can we go to a motel. This place sucks," Paul said, balancing on his one good leg.

"Take a look inside before you decide," Lin said.

She pulled back the screen door, which looked to be a

recent addition, then unlocked the front door and walked in. They followed.

Inside, things were very different. The floors were polished to a shine, and the paintwork was new. The ceiling was white with wooden beams in black that formed squares—a dated look that reflected the age of the house. The kitchen had cheap but functioning pine cupboards, and the stove looked new, as did the large refrigerator.

"We keep it looking trashy on the outside so nobody will bother you. We want it to stay looking like an old lady's house."

Lin left the suitcase in the kitchen, then showed them around. The four bedrooms had double beds made up with clean and warm bedding.

"Beds are new, so's the bedding," she said.

The furniture in the living room was basic but clean, and there was a large TV. The bathroom was dated, but there was a separate shower cubicle, and everything was sparkling clean.

"You have gas heating. I have some food in the car. It'll keep you going for a few days. If you need more, head for the grocery store in Preston, two miles north. Use cash, and don't talk to anyone in the store." Lin paused. "You have cash?"

"Yes."

Lin continued, "Don't give anyone your name. If somebody comes here, you dial 911 and then get in the panic room. Remember to dial 911 first, because once you're in the panic room, there's no phone signal and no internet. Got that?"

"There's a panic room?" Paul asked. He sounded excited for the first time since they'd arrived.

"This way."

In the middle of the house was a study with a tiled floor. No window, just ceiling lighting. A desk took up most of one wall. There was no chair, but on top of the desk were dusty boxes. Inside them were printed photos, old letters curled and yellowed, mildew-covered paperbacks, and board games, the boxes discolored and aged. Lin leaned over the boxes, picked up a remote control, then pressed a button—there was a click, and the desk and the wall behind it shifted, as if it were hinged at one end. It was like watching a giant door open. The desk's legs, Sally now realized, were on rollers so they slid across the tiled floor easily.

"Don't put anything in front of the desk, okay? You may have just a few seconds to get this open, and you don't want to have to shift stuff out of the way."

The door-cum-wall came to a halt. Sally could see that it was a foot thick and lined in steel, like a bank vault. The interior was about the size of the bathroom. The walls were padded with a soft material, and the floor had a spongy covering. In one corner there was a folding single bed and two folded chairs. In a crate on the floor were two dozen bottles of water. In another corner was what looked like a composting toilet with a pack of toilet paper next to it.

"Is that what I think it is?" Sally asked.

"Toilet? Yes. No flushing of course. The whole point of the panic room is that you can't be seen or heard."

Paul stepped into the space and looked around. "Cool! I've always wanted to see inside one of these."

Sally stayed back. "I suffer from claustrophobia."

"There's nothing to be afraid of. It has air-conditioning. The units that power it are hidden under the house. If there's a power outage, a backup generator kicks in. It's not meant to be used long-term. Just long enough for us to get here."

Paul looked around the panic room. "Is there a camera or something so we can see what's going on in the house?"

"See here." Lin pointed to a screen on the wall then pressed a button. "There are three cameras. All hidden. One each for the front and back of the house, and one points at the entrance to this room."

"Is there a phone line?" Paul asked.

"No. As I said, you dial 911 before you shut the door."

Sally felt hot and panicky—she needed to get some air. "I'll see you outside."

She heard Paul ask how the police could afford to install a panic room. "It must have cost a fortune."

"We didn't. Last year, there was a billionaire banker who needed witness protection before and after he testified. He was holed up here for months. He insisted a panic room was installed, at his own cost."

"So this billionaire knows it's here?" Paul asked.

"He lives on the other side of the world and has no contact with anyone in this country. He can't. If he does, the people he sent to jail will find him and kill him. I assure you this is the best place to go if you're in danger."

FORTY-ONE

After Lin drove away, the unfamiliar house descended into a quiet that Sally found unnerving. No airplanes in the sky, no passing cars, no familiar neighbors' voices. Just the creak of floorboards as she moved about the house.

Sally busied herself with getting Paul's ankle iced, then put the groceries in the fridge, and selected a bedroom overlooking the drive. As a light sleeper, if anyone were to enter the drive at night, she was bound to hear them.

Paul began playing a game on the PlayStation that he'd brought with them, and she made coffee, which she drank in the kitchen. Outside, the sky was getting darker—a storm was building.

Sally took her six color-coded notebooks out of her bag and laid them on the table, then added another. This notebook she dated *May 2015*. She proceeded to make notes on the recent murders as well as the attempted murder of her son, outlining everything she'd discovered so far in the course of her investigation, then leaned back in the pine chair and thought about what to do next.

She had three clear goals.

First, keep her son safe.

Second, discover the truth about Zelda's suicide.

Third, help the police locate and arrest the Poster Killer. His reign of terror had to end.

On one level, it was all about her children. Even though it was too late to save Zelda, she would do all she could to stop anyone hurting her son again. But it was way more than that. Sally was so involved in the case that she almost felt as if the six missing girls were her kids. The Poster Killer was murdering anyone who he, or they, believed could identify them. Durrant said that Sally knew the killers. Therefore, she was in the best position to solve the mystery. She owed it to the missing girls to work it out.

In the living room, Paul made a whooping sound. "Gotcha!" he shouted.

His video game must be going well.

Sally thought back to the day before when she and Paul had argued. He'd blamed her for not doing more to prevent Zelda's suicide. He'd also questioned the validity of the note she'd left behind. Paul had a point—why hadn't Zelda handwritten the suicide note? Why didn't she name Caroline Blake as the bully? And now she thought about it, when Sally had cleared out Zelda's belongings, her current diary wasn't there. She'd found the other diaries hidden in a shoebox. Had Zelda destroyed it before she'd taken her own life? Sally had never asked Paul about the missing diary. Might he know why it was gone?

Her cheeks flushed red with shame. Did Paul know more than he'd told her?

Sally left the kitchen and stood before her son, blocking his view of the TV screen.

"Paul!" she said. "Please switch that off. I have to ask you something."

He didn't protest as he would usually—he took one look at

Sally's face and paused the game, then put the controller down "What's up?"

Sally sat next to him. "I want to talk about Zelda."

"O-kay." He folded his arms defensively.

Sally cleared her throat, unsure how to continue. "I know you've been through a lot. I thought I'd lost you today. I love you —I want you to know that."

"Love you too." He frowned. "If you want to ask me something, ask!"

This was the conversation they had to have. But it was like she was entering a minefield.

Paul saved her from chickening out. "Is it about the suicide note?"

"Yes. You asked me if I thought it was weird that the note was typed. I hadn't thought about it that way. But now I can't stop thinking about it. What do you think it means?"

"You're not going to like it, Mom."

"Tell me anyway."

"I don't think it's her note."

"Whose note is it?" Sally asked.

"I don't know. I guess there are only four people who could have used her laptop and printer after she passed. You, me, Dad, and maybe Walt."

"I didn't write it and I can't imagine the paramedics did either."

"And I didn't," Paul said. "I guess that leaves Dad and Walt."

Sally and Paul stared at each other. It was windy outside, and it blew in under the front door, making a whistling noise.

Sally spoke first. "Why would they create a fake note? Maybe Scott did it to be kind and Walt went along with it?"

"Kind? When was Dad ever kind?" Paul's nostrils flared with anger. "The only time he was nice to us was when there were people around and he pretended to be nice. Mom, seriously? Dad was a total shit."

When Paul was born, Sally had been so sleep-deprived she'd believed anything Scott had told her. At first, Scott had adored Paul, but Paul's constant crying had got on his nerves, so he'd begun avoiding his baby boy. Only when they'd had visitors had Scott held Paul in his arms.

"You're right," Sally said. Why did she still make excuses for Scott? She thought she had gotten past doing that. "He only ever cared about himself." She paused, deep in thought. "Do you remember when an anonymous letter was sent to the middle-school principal? The one about Caroline and the list of girls she bullied?" Sally asked Paul.

"Not really. I was nine."

"Chase and Sophie are adamant that Caroline left Zelda alone. They said she was a bully, but not to Zelda." She shook her head. "I'd love to know who sent that accusatory letter."

Paul had a faraway look. "I once saw Caroline push Stacy around. And she stole Anna's lunches. But whenever I saw her with Zelda, they just seemed to chat."

"I wish you'd told me."

"So you could bite my head off? No way."

Sally rubbed her tired eyes. "Any idea what happened to Zelda's diary? The one from 2010?"

Paul shrugged. "Ask Dad? He and Walt were in her room for a while after the paramedics left. You were downstairs with a neighbor, and I had my room door open. When he noticed me watching, he shut Zelda's door. It was ages before he came out with the suicide note."

"No point asking him. He won't tell me the truth."

"I think Dad faked the suicide note, Mom. He was always hiding something."

FORTY-TWO

MAY 10, 2015

It was a rainy Sunday morning as Sally drove into the neat, tree-lined street where the Jacksons lived. Already she was regret-ting leaving Paul alone in the house, but she'd lain awake all night, desperate to know why Scott or Walt would create a fake suicide note. Walt was still loyal to Scott, and she doubted he would tell her the truth. But Nikki on the other hand had loved Zelda, and Sally hoped to convince the girl to tell her what she knew.

The houses were small but neatly presented. Bettina's Beetle was parked in the drive of a red house with a porch with white pillars. Sally parked out of sight of the house and dialed Franklin PD on her burner phone and asked to speak to Walter Jackson. She was told that he wasn't on duty today, which meant that he might be at home, which wasn't what she'd hoped for. The last time she had seen the whole family together was at Zelda's funeral, and a lot had happened since then.

Sally procrastinated for a while.

Just do it! You have to know the truth.

Their doorbell had a loud chime. Sally fiddled with a coat

button as she waited. Violin music, soft and sweet, drifted from the house, and it lifted Sally's spirits.

Bettina opened the door and stared at Sally, lips parted in shock. Then she recovered herself.

"Sally! What a lovely surprise!"

But she didn't step aside to let Sally in.

"Bettina, hi. I hope you don't mind me dropping by. There's something I wanted to ask you. May I come in?"

Bettina looked down the hall as if searching for an excuse to say no. "Um..." She turned her head back to look at Sally. "We heard about Paul. How frightening."

Anger sped through Sally's veins—Bettina hadn't picked up the phone to find out how her son was. "He's shaken, and I'm terrified. We don't know why we're being targeted."

"I don't see how we can help."

"That's not why I'm here. I need to talk to you and Nikki. Is that her playing the violin?"

"Yes, um, we're about to go out."

Sally wasn't the kind of person to rake over the past, but now was the time to build bridges. She had never understood why Walt and Bettina had dropped their friendship straight after the funeral.

"Whatever I did to upset you and your family, I'm truly sorry. Can we start again? We used to be such good friends."

"We were," Bettina said. "Can we make it quick?" She stepped aside and invited Sally in.

The house was pristine, the furniture ultra-modern, the paintings on the walls bright and abstract. Bettina led her to the open-plan kitchen-cum-living room where Nikki was practicing the violin, a sheet of music on a metal stand. Nikki's hair had been straightened, and she had a bobby pin holding her shoulder-length tresses from her face. The girl had inherited her mother's good looks. She stopped playing as soon as Sally walked in.

"That was one of Bach's violin concertos?" Sally asked.

"Yes. You know it?" Nikki said.

"I love classical music. And jazz and blues. You play beautifully."

"Thank you, Mrs. Fairburn." Nikki paused.

"Call me Sally, as you used to do. I hear you're a star at school. Are you planning on going to college?"

"She certainly is," Bettina interrupted. "Can I offer you coffee or homemade lemonade?"

Sally took the lemonade.

"Take a seat. Nikki, go and get changed. We're going out shortly."

Sally sat on a brown leather corner sofa and noticed Nikki giving her mother a questioning look. Sally suspected Bettina had fabricated the appointment as an excuse to get rid of her as soon as possible. She felt her chest and neck flush red with embarrassment.

"Nikki, please stay. I need your help with something." Sally patted the sofa cushion. "It'll take five minutes."

Nikki glanced at her mother, who nodded, then the girl perched on the edge of the sofa opposite Sally, looking like a bird ready to fly away. Bettina sat next to her daughter.

"No Walt?" Sally asked.

"He's walking the dog. He'll be back any minute. You had something to ask us?" Bettina said, crossing her long legs.

Sally took a sip of lemonade to wet her dry mouth. "I've already lost my daughter. The incident with Paul... almost losing him to a killer, it got me thinking." Sally felt as if she were wading through syrup. "Nikki, can I ask you a question about Zelda?"

Nikki blanched. "Zelda!"

"Yes. Can you think back to when you were thirteen and friends with Zelda and Stacy. Before Caroline was taken by the Poster Killer."

Nikki glanced at her mom, her eyes pleading.

Bettina said, "Do you really need to bring this up? Nikki suffered survivor's guilt and has only recently got past it. I really don't see the point in going over this."

"Please, Bettina. It's... important. There were allegations made that Caroline was bullying Zelda, Stacy Green, and Anna Moorehouse. Information has now come to light that puts doubt on this. I need to know what really happened, Nikki. Did Caroline bully my daughter?"

Again Nikki glanced at her mom, but this time Bettina responded with a nod.

"Yes," Nikki said.

"Did Zelda tell you this or did you witness it?"

"I... I can't remember." Her eyes wandered to the bookshelf behind the sofa.

She does remember, Sally thought.

"When did Caroline start bullying Zelda?"

"I, um, don't remember."

"Did Caroline bully you?"

Nikki looked straight at Sally. "No."

"Why not?"

"Excuse me?" said Nikki.

"You were a close-knit group. You, Zelda, and Stacy. Why did Caroline bully them and not you?"

Nikki shrugged. "I... I don't know. Stacy was timid, I guess."

"How did Caroline bully my daughter?"

Bettina spoke. "You know how, Sally—she took Zelda's lunch money. She pushed her in the school corridor. She called her a weirdo."

"Yes, that's what I was told." *By Scott, most of all,* Sally thought. Was it Scott who sent the anonymous letter to the school, accusing Caroline of bullying girls, including Zelda? "Nikki, tell me what you actually saw Caroline do to my daughter."

"I... I can't."

Bettina piped up again. "Sally, we were all devastated about Zelda, but there's no point going over it all again. And Nikki has choir practice."

Sally ignored the comment. "Nikki, did you actually witness Caroline bullying Zelda?"

"I don't know—it's too long ago."

It was an evasive answer.

"Nikki, did you see Scott regularly pick up Zelda after school?"

"Yes, so what?"

"Was Zelda excited about being picked up by her dad?"

"Not really. I think she was kinda embarrassed. He'd sometimes turn up in a cop car. That was so not cool. Zelda started leaving school early to avoid him."

"Was your dad with Scott?"

"Sometimes, why?"

Sally leaned forward to try and close the distance between her and the girl she desperately needed the truth from. "Did Zelda tell you why she was depressed?"

Nikki wrung her hands. "Not really."

"But you have an idea why, don't you? Please, Nikki, I have to know."

"I don't think I should."

Bettina stood. "She's told you all she knows, Sally, and we have to get moving."

"One more question. Nikki, did you see Scott pick up Caroline from school a few weeks before Zelda took her own life?"

"Oh yes. He was angry. I've never seen Caroline so scared. He was yelling at her that if she didn't stop, he'd—"

"That's enough," Bettina said, cutting Nikki off.

"Please let her finish," Sally said.

"We really have to get moving. I'll show you out."

Bettina ushered Sally down the hall and opened the front

door. Bettina and Nikki were hiding the truth, but Sally knew she wasn't going to get anything more out of them today.

Still, she paused, just inside the house door.

"Why did you end our friendship after Zelda's funeral?" Sally asked.

Bettina flinched—Sally had never been this direct before. "I didn't end it. I guess we just drifted apart, you know, once Scott went to Chicago."

The old, malleable Sally would have politely accepted the excuse; the new, stronger Sally wasn't going to.

"You were a good friend. One of my best friends. My daughter had just died and my husband had left me. I needed you, Bettina. Where were you?"

"Don't you dare blame me! You want to know the truth? I couldn't stand to be with you! You know why? Because when Zelda needed your help, you didn't give it. Scott told us all about it. How you refused to acknowledge that she was deeply troubled. How he wanted Zelda to see a psychiatrist and you told him they would do no good. We know that you locked her in her room and didn't feed her because she skipped school. How could you be so cruel? Scott had to take her meals when you were asleep. What kind of mother were you?"

Sally had to lean against a wall to stop her legs from buckling. Clearly, walking out on his wife and son wasn't enough. Scott also spread vindictive lies. Did his cruelty know no bounds?

"None of that is true. I swear. Every time I raised Zelda's changed behavior, her lethargy, her depression, Scott dismissed it. He called her a moody, spoiled princess. I tried arguing with him, but he wouldn't listen. I never locked her in her room. Not once. I was the one who carried her meals upstairs when she refused to come to the table. I begged Scott to let me take Zelda to a psychiatrist. He kept saying no. In the end, I took her to see one without telling him. You can have Dr. Collins' number if you don't believe me. Scott somehow found out and put a stop to it. Every move I made to help Zelda, he thwarted. I'm beginning to think that he was the cause of her despair, not Caroline. Two people have told me categorically that Caroline liked Zelda and didn't bully her. I think Nikki knows what really happened." Sally looked at Nikki. "I have to know."

"I don't know anything," Nikki said weakly.

"You're lying."

"How dare you!" Bettina, said. "Get out of my house!"

As Sally stepped over the threshold, still reeling from Bettina's appalling accusations, Nikki's voice echoed down the hallway. "Scott said that if we didn't say Caroline was bullying Zelda, he'd tell everyone I was gay."

"Shut up!" Bettina snapped.

"Bettina? You knew?" Sally asked, all the color draining from her face. Scott had lied. And her friend hadn't told her.

Bettina scrunched her eyes tightly shut and turned away. "I was protecting Nikki."

"Protecting her from what?" Sally said. "Why does it matter if Nikki's gay? We're not living in the dark ages. Why aren't you proud of her for being true to herself?"

Bettina snapped her head up and glared. "You have the impudence to criticize me? Our church doesn't agree with same-sex relationships. And they've agreed to sponsor Nikki to go to music college. They're paying for her tuition."

Sally stared, utterly astounded, then rubbed her brow, trying to take it all in. "Nikki, are you saying Zelda wasn't bullied, not by Caroline or anyone else?"

"That's right. Zelda knew I was gay—so did Stacy. I don't know how Scott found out. Zelda kept a diary. I guess he could have read it."

"Thank you for your honesty."

Sally turned her back on them and walked down the drive. The street, the sky, her whole world had just been drained of its color and vibrancy. Now it was sepia, poisoned with lies and deceit. There was a bitter taste in her mouth like rust, which nothing other than the truth could remove.

There was no doubt in her mind anymore that the suicide note was a fake, and there were only two people who could have typed it and placed it in Zelda's bedroom: Scott and Walt Jackson. Paul was nine at the time and he simply wasn't capable of fabricating such an authentic-seeming suicide note. Scott, as she was discovering more and more, was capable of all sorts of diabolical lies. Did Walt help him do it? Sally knew that Scott wouldn't take her calls. Her best bet was Walt Jackson.

FORTY-THREE

As Sally drove away, she spotted Bettina peeking through the blinds, no doubt checking that Sally hadn't hung around. She was probably already on the phone to Walt. Sally didn't care. She was going to find Walt and hear his side of the story, and she had a good idea where he'd be walking their German Shepherd, Prince. There was a two-mile, circular forest trail that—at least when she'd known him—had been Walt's favorite walk. When Prince was young, Walt would walk the one mile from his house to the start of the trail, but now Prince was a senior dog, Walt tended to drive to the parking lot.

The muddy lot was easy to find, and near the trail's entrance was Walt's silver Honda CR-V. Sally parked far enough away so as to be inconspicuous, then left her vehicle and took a quick look through the CR-V's windows. The trunk didn't have a shelf, so she was able to see muddy dog towels and a harness. Stuffed between the two front seats was Walt's old baseball cap, sporting the emblem of his team, the Franklin Falcons. She headed back to her car to wait—the spot she'd picked would let her see him as soon as he approached his vehicle.

She didn't have to wait long.

Walt wore a rain jacket and rubber boots that were splashed with mud. Prince was on the leash, moving more languidly than Sally recalled. His muzzle had turned white near the nose.

Walt opened the trunk, and the dog jumped in. Sally startled him when she called his name. He turned fast to discover her standing just five feet away. He didn't show surprise: he'd always been the kind of guy who stayed cool in a crisis.

"Sally! I didn't know you walked this trail." He shut the trunk. The dog squished its nose against the rear window and looked out at them. Dog breath fogged the glass.

Sally moved closer. "I don't normally. I've just come from your house. But I guess Bettina already told you that."

"She did. You've upset her."

That was when Sally lost it. "*I've* upset her? Are you serious? If anyone deserves to be upset, it's me. You've all lied to me. Zelda wasn't bullied, and you and Scott fabricated the suicide note."

"I don't have anything to say."

"Well, at least your daughter was truthful! I already know you were with Scott when he took Caroline for a ride. He wasn't threatening her because she bullied Zelda. He told her that she was going to be blamed for Zelda's bullying and she had to suck it up. Am I right?"

Walt walked to the driver's door. "I can't remember."

Sally gripped his arm and spun him around. "How dare you treat me like an idiot! Caroline never bullied Zelda, right?"

Walt looked away, then finally made eye contact. "I can't betray a friend. We worked together longer than I can remember. He had my back, and I had his. There's nothing I can say that will bring back your daughter, and I won't land Scott in trouble."

"How would you feel if Nikki took her life and the whole

story about why she killed herself was a pack of lies, designed to ensure that your wife would never know the truth?"

Walt dragged a boot across some small stones in a puddle. The unsurfaced lot was full of puddles.

"I thought he must have had a good reason for what he did. When a buddy asks for a favor, you do it."

"And Zelda? Did you even stop to think about her? Or the hell you put me through?"

"You should ask Scott, not me."

Sally stepped so close that her chin was a mere couple of centimeters from him. "You expect me to get a straight answer from Scott? The man who lied to me. The man who was prepared to lie about his daughter. The man who told you that I was an abysmal mother. Told you lies about me, when all the time he was blocking all my efforts to help Zelda."

"Bettina told me about that. Look, we didn't know, okay?"

"You and me, we've been manipulated by Scott. This is your chance to put things right. Please!"

Walt looked up at the cloud-filled sky.

"Jesus!" He was quiet for a while, his eyes following the clouds. When he finally gave her his attention again, Sally had ripped a fingernail with her teeth and the skin beneath it was bleeding. She held a tissue over the wound.

"Scott blackmailed us, okay? On my salary, it'll be tough to cover Nikki's tuition fees. Our church offered to pay. She sings like an angel, and she plays the violin like a professional. The church has connections, orchestras she can work for. But if they ever found out Nikki is gay, there would be no college fund. He was going to tell the pastor. I couldn't let that happen."

"Why did Scott lie about Caroline and Zelda?"

"So you wouldn't know the real reason." Walt shook his head. "I can't tell you. He'll destroy Nikki's life."

"Who wrote the suicide note?"

Walt turned away.

"Answer me!"

He didn't speak.

"I believe you're a good man, Walt. Help me. Who wrote the suicide note?"

He spoke with his back to her. "It was Scott. He made me stay outside her room so I could stop anyone who tried to get in there, until he'd typed and printed it."

There—at last. The truth.

"What was the real reason for Zelda's depression?"

He shook his head. "That's all I've got to say."

The dog in the car barked and paced in the small space. Walt got in his car and switched on the engine, then reversed out of the parking spot and wound down the window.

"You tell anyone about this, I'll deny it. It's your word against a cop's. Who do you think they'll believe?"

FORTY-FOUR

By the time Sally reached the safe house, it was raining heavily, the tree-lined driveway full of deep puddles, and she had the windshield wipers on the fastest speed.

She drove around the side of the house to the parking garage, and her breath caught in her throat. She slammed on the brakes, startled by what she saw. The car engine stalled and everything went quiet, except for the *tick-tick-tick* as the engine cooled and the faint sound of the TV coming from the house. Ahead, was a parked car she didn't recognize. They weren't supposed to have any visitors. So who did the car belong to?

"Oh my God!" Sally couldn't release the steering wheel.

If it belonged to a plainclothes detective, why hadn't Lin told her? Or had Paul asked a friend round? No, he wouldn't do that, not after his near-death experience. This didn't feel right, and her injured son was in the house, helpless. Instinctively, Sally centrally locked her doors then phoned Paul.

Before he said a word, she spoke.

"Paul, whose car is outside? Are you okay?"

"Yeah, Mom, it's cool. Aiden's here. We've playing *The Witcher 3: Wild Hunt*. He's kicking my ass."

Sally studied the car ahead of her. It was a Hyundai Veloster Turbo, the kind of vehicle a young man would drive.

"How did he find us?"

"He's a cop, Mom. How do you think? And it's not like he's a stranger. Will you come in and stop embarrassing me?"

"Okay."

But Sally didn't go in. Her belief in the integrity of cops had been shattered that very morning—if Scott and Walt were prepared to lie, then so might Aiden.

She dialed Detective Lin, who answered immediately. "You okay?"

In the background, a man was talking. It sounded like a briefing. It was a Sunday and yet they were hard at work.

"Aiden Foster is here. Did you give him our address?"

"No. Only four people know where you are—me, Clarke, Rodriguez, and Florakis." All detectives on the homicide team. "Have you told anyone where you're staying?"

"No, and Aiden is in the house. What should I do?"

"He's a cop, right? So no need to panic. Hang on while I find out." Lin put her on mute.

Sally had known Aiden for a long time, and his father, Richard, was a good man. She was probably jumping at shadows.

Lin came back on the line. "Florakis told Aiden. He shouldn't have done. He assures me he hasn't told anyone else. It won't happen again."

"I know you're doing your best, but this makes me nervous."

"I understand. The boss is livid. If we think your location has been compromised, we'll move you someplace else. Give us some time to discuss it."

Sally hung up, took a big breath, and left her car, then entered the safe house to find Aiden and Paul glued to the TV, yelping with delight as they battled the monsters in the video game.

"Hi, guys!" Sally said, trying to sound calm. She locked the door behind her.

Aiden stopped playing and looked at Sally.

"Hey, don't stop!" Paul complained.

Aiden put down the PlayStation controller and stood. "Sally, I hope I didn't freak you out. Dad would have come if he could, but he's not feeling too good. I said I'd come over in his place. I hope that's okay?"

"It's always good to see you, but you shouldn't be here. How did you find us?" Sally wanted to be sure that nobody else knew.

"Conrad told me." Florakis's first name. "My bad. I pressured him into it. Dad wanted to get hold of you. He's got some leads. Clarke wasn't interested so Dad wanted you to have them. I left a voicemail."

Sally had her personal cell phone off, as instructed. She'd been using the burner phone instead, and Aiden wouldn't know that number.

"I appreciate Richard's help. But if it's that easy to find out where we are, this safe-house setup isn't working."

"I swear, I haven't told anybody. I'm sorry, Sally, I feel bad. Dad tried calling you, but you didn't call back, and he doesn't trust email or Messenger or anything online."

Aiden looked mortified. Sally felt sorry for him and asked if he'd like some lunch. Aiden declined.

"Dad wanted you to have this." He handed her two printed images. Poor quality but clear enough.

"Hey, I want to see them," Paul called from the sofa.

Aiden and Sally sat close to Paul.

The first page was the printout of a photo of a middle-aged man with a big, tattooed guy in an alley. They were both smoking.

"Lou Thompson and Chase Feinstein," Sally said. Paul and

Aiden whipped their heads round to stare at her. "Why does Richard think this is important?"

"There's a theory that the Poster Killer is two people," Aiden said. "Maybe Lou and Chase worked together."

"Did Richard take this?"

"Yes."

"When?"

"Yesterday."

"I still don't see why this is incriminating. They're having a smoke. It's the alley behind the corner store. So what? Richard told me he was certain it was just one person—that there was no evidence of it being two people. Has he changed his mind?"

Aiden shrugged. "I'm just the messenger boy."

Sally stared at the second printout—it was a close-up of Zelda, Stacy, and Nikki, taken in a McDonald's. Sally recognized the floral dress Zelda was wearing and smiled. There was a man with them, in the background—gray hair, clean-shaven, big smile and perfect teeth, maybe in his sixties.

"Who's the guy?" Sally asked.

"That's Stacy Green's granddad, celebrating Stacy's birthday."

"Ah yes. He was supposed to collect Stacy from school the day she was taken," Sally said. "But he was late, and she took the bus."

"That's right. You really know your stuff, Sally."

"Thanks, Aiden."

Sally drew the image closer and studied the face. Stacy's granddad had refused any help through the victim support program so Sally hadn't met him. The man's features suddenly clicked into place.

"That's Bryan Topham!" She looked up. "Bryan is Stacy's grandfather?"

All this time he'd been pestering her about a book he was allegedly writing. Not once had he mentioned that he was a close relative of one of the missing girls. Why keep that fact to himself?

"Yeah, Bryan pestered Dad about a book he said he was writing. In the end, Dad felt sorry for him and they met up. I gotta tell you, he asked some weird questions. Dad wants you to be careful if he comes near you."

Paul leaned forward to look closer at the image. "That's the creepy guy who came to our house."

"It is," Sally said.

Aiden said, "You should know that Bryan kept asking my dad about you."

"Me, why?" Sally said.

"He wanted to know where you were when the girls disappeared."

"Me?"

"Yes, you."

FORTY-FIVE

Redmond was a neighborhood for the wealthy, and Bryan Topham's house didn't disappoint—four parking garages, manicured box hedges, at least six bedrooms upstairs, and a backyard big enough for a gymkhana. Why would a retired, single man live alone in such a big house?

Sally stopped her car diagonally across the street. His Audi wasn't in the sweeping driveway, but that didn't mean he wasn't home.

Now that Sally had arrived, she wondered if she was out of her mind for coming here alone. Initially, she'd taken Topham for a well-meaning man obsessed by a hobby—writing his book. Now she knew he was the grandfather of one of the Poster Killer's victims, she had to be very careful. This might be about revenge. Equally, Topham could be the killer.

She'd left Paul with Aiden playing video games—it was good for him to have some new company.

Sally locked her car and crossed the street. There was no movement behind Topham's windows, and all was quiet. The house next door had the windows open, and laughter danced on the breeze.

His narrow porch was shaped like a sentry box with a steep A-shaped roof. She found the front door slightly ajar. Did that mean Topham was home and expecting someone? Or could he have forgotten to close it?

"Hello! Bryan!" Sally shouted.

She listened. No voices—no sound at all.

"Bryan! It's Sally Fairburn!"

High up on the porch wall was an alarm system. Why go to the expense of an intruder alarm and then leave your front door open?

To the left of the door was a bell. She pressed it. The chime was startlingly loud.

She waited. No one called out. No footsteps.

A deep sense of unease crept over her. Should she call the police? They wouldn't thank her if it turned out Topham was safe and well and simply hadn't shut his front door properly. Perhaps he was in the backyard and hadn't heard the doorbell or her shouts?

She headed round to investigate. The earlier rain had made the grass wet underfoot, and there was no footpath to the side gate and fence separating the front and back yards. Sally wore sturdy walking shoes so the sodden grass didn't bother her, but the locked side gate was a problem.

Returning to the porch, she pulled her burner phone from her jacket pocket and dialed Topham's number—she'd moved her contacts list from her personal phone to the burner last night.

A sharp trill came from inside the house. When she ended the call, the trilling stopped. Should she close the front door and drive away? What if Topham was hurt—had an accident and couldn't reach his phone?

Just inside the hallway was an umbrella stand. Amongst the umbrellas was a walking cane with a beautifully carved handle shaped like a swallow on the end of a branch. Sally guessed it was solid ash.

Removing her muddy shoes and leaving them on the porch, she pushed the front door open enough to squeeze through the gap. Then she picked up the walking cane and held it over her shoulder, ready to strike anyone who might attack her.

Her heart thumped so loudly she could hear it. "Bryan? It's Sally. Your door was open."

On a hall stand of polished walnut was Topham's cell. She recognized the case: it was a dark burgundy. He had some unopened mail. The hall runner was Persian, with swirling patterns of blues and black and cream. The walls had framed photos of awards for his advertising campaigns, and photos of him with Stacy and Stacy's mother, Lindsey, perfectly styled and no doubt professionally shot.

Each room she went through was neat and tidy, almost like a show home, but there was no sign of Topham.

Through the dining-room windows she saw a tennis court, and beyond that, fir trees.

She paused at the bottom of the stairs. Should she go upstairs? She felt like an intruder. What would he say if he arrived home to find her there?

The banisters were polished wood that swirled like a snail shell at the bottom and top. She gingerly walked upstairs then poked her head into each room.

"Bryan? Hello? It's Sally. Are you okay?"

No sign of him.

There was a set of stairs leading to an attic room. It was the only room she hadn't searched. She hesitated, then told herself to stop being a baby and take a quick look.

After knocking on the door and receiving no answer, she tried the handle and the door opened.

The first item she saw was a desk under a skylight. In stark contrast to the rest of the furnishings, the desk and everything in the room looked as if it had been bought from IKEA. There was a large computer screen and a tablet set up with an additional keyboard. Perhaps the tablet's small keyboard was tricky to use now that Topham was elderly?

Sally pushed the door wide open and gasped at the row of posters stuck to the wall: all six of the 2010–11 Poster Killer's posters. Beneath them were three more posters, and to her horror, hers was the first in the second row, followed by one of Paul and then Tiffany.

Cold dread filled her, like ice in her veins, and she shivered. Was Bryan Topham the freak Paul thought he was, or worse? How could he have replicated them so perfectly, unless…?

Sally looked behind her, suddenly terrified that Topham might be in the house and hiding from her. A voice in her head urged her to run and call Clarke, but the box files stacked on a bookshelf drew her deeper into the room. Each file was labelled with a name.

Her heart spasmed when she saw a file named PAUL FAIR-BURN. She stretched out a hand, then pulled it back. Did she want to know?

Another look behind her, then she laid the box file on the desk and opened it.

At the top of a pile of loose documents was a printed photo of cops at Margie's house after Paul had been attacked but before he'd been found. She vividly remembered seeing the same scene when she'd arrived. How had Topham gotten there so fast? And how had he known about the attack at that point? It wasn't public then.

Beneath it was a photo of her with Clarke and Lin. There were printouts from online news sites about the attempt on Paul's life and also images of the hide in the forest. Topham must have gone back much later and crossed the crime-scene tape to get them. Was this the work of an overzealous author or a killer gloating about the havoc he'd caused?

"Bryan's too old," she said aloud. Paul's assailant was tall and fit. Topham was neither and too old to keep pace with Paul. "It can't be him."

Sally put the box back on the shelf and then took out the one titled STACY GREEN. There were printed photos of the bus stop where the poster had been found and of cops searching the area. Topham's notes described how he'd retraced her movements on the afternoon she'd been abducted. He blamed himself for not collecting Stacy. He blamed the police for failing to locate her. He even had a copy of his own statement to the police. How on earth had he gotten hold of that?

She scanned it fast. Held back in a client meeting, he'd tried to contact the school secretary and then Lindsey, but neither had answered his call. When he'd reached the school, he'd been told that Stacy had taken the school bus home. But when he'd arrived at Lindsey's apartment, Stacy wasn't home, and their neighbor hadn't seen her since that morning. He'd then walked from the apartment block to the bus stop: no Stacy. Then he'd found the missing-person poster stuck to the side of the bus stop.

"You poor man," Sally murmured. She could only imagine the horror of finding that and realizing that his grandchild had been taken by whoever had taken Anna and Caroline.

At the bottom of the box file was a diary decorated in pink and pale blue flowers with an illustration of a girl holding a pen and a notebook. She opened the cover. Stacy had written her name and age in it. A pink ribbon marked the page she'd been up to: it was the day before she'd been abducted.

A selfish thought filled Sally's head: Could Stacy's diary explain what had driven Zelda to suicide? Perhaps Zelda had confided in her? And could it help Sally understand why Topham was so keen to talk to her?

Sally laid the diary on the desk and turned the first page. On January 1, Stacy had made some New Year's resolutions. As Sally read them, she felt an overwhelming sadness.

In 2010 I will:
    Be brave
    Tell Caroline I won't do her homework anymore
    Do my chores
    Tell mom I love her every day

It was a lovely list and Sally's eyes welled up.

A floorboard creaked behind her. Then pain exploded in her head and everything went black.

FORTY-SIX

Paul was worried about his mom. Aiden had gone home ages ago and she hadn't called like she'd promised. He dialed her burner phone, but it went to voicemail.

"Mom? You didn't call." He paused, hoping she might pick up, then ended his message.

Paul slapped his palm onto the sofa cushion. That Bryan Topham guy was a real weirdo, stalking Sally the way he had been. And this big old house was cold and spooky—not that he'd ever tell his mom he was scared. He stared around the gloomy room then at the TV screen, where he'd paused a movie partway through. What if Topham had captured his mom? Or was he being a baby, panicking like this?

He moved his leg off the sofa and tried putting downward pressure on his sprained ankle. A shooting pain raced up his leg, and he winced. Okay, so his ankle was no good.

Swallowing two more painkillers, he tried to think what to do about Sally. He was in the middle of nowhere. If they'd been at home, he could have caught a bus to that creep's house. Then Paul realized that he didn't even have Topham's address.

He left Sally another message: "Mom, I'm getting kinda freaked out. Maybe I should call a detective?"

Paul stared at his ankle, still swollen, with major black-and-green bruising. It was kind of impressive. But he couldn't just sit there and do nothing.

He dropped his phone into the pocket of his sweatpants and used his crutches to help him stand.

His first attempt failed. The sofa was too low, and the coffee table was in the way.

He pushed the table aside and tried again, and this time he was successful. Then Paul hopped to the front window, which looked out over the porch that stretched the width of the house and down the driveway. It revealed nothing that he didn't already know. Sally wasn't there, and Paul had no way of reaching her. He felt useless.

He tried sending a text message. No response. He stared out the window at the never-ending trees and sky.

"Fuck it!"

He called Detective Lin, the nicer of the two cops. She'd put her cell number in his burner phone as a precaution.

"Hey, Paul! What's up?" Lin said.

People were talking in the background.

"It's Mom. It could be nothing, but she's not answering my calls and she promised to phone me, and she hasn't."

"Guys, keep it down, will you?" Lin yelled out to the people making the noise. Then to Paul she said, "Where did Sally go?"

"She just found out that Bryan Topham is Stacy Green's granddad. Did you know that?"

"Yes, so what?"

"You know he's been harassing Mom about the case."

In the background, a man shouted an order. It sounded like that dipshit Clarke.

"Hold on a minute." Lin put Paul on mute.

Paul yelled at his phone, "Don't do that!" But Lin didn't hear.

When she took him off silent, she asked, "Is she at Topham's house?" There was tension in her voice.

"That's what I'm trying to tell you. Yes. She wanted to know why he's been asking where she was when the girls were abducted. Look, I'm stuck here. Can you go to his house? Mom promised to call in an hour and it's been two now."

Lin called out to the people with her. "She's at Topham's place." Then she turned her attention back to Paul, "Don't leave the safe house. Lock all the doors. Cars are on their way to Topham's house."

"What's going on?"

"There's another missing-person poster. And this one is of Bryan Topham."

FORTY-SEVEN

Zelda was running away from Sally through a pine forest. The light was fading, and a dense fog was creeping closer. Sally screamed at Zelda to stop, but every time she did, a shot of pain filled her head, causing Sally to stumble.

Sally was fit—she ran most days. But her legs wouldn't move fast enough. She tried to speed up, but Zelda kept getting further and further away.

Suddenly, Sally's arm was caught in a snare, the kind made of wire with a loop that snapped tighter and tighter the more she struggled. Zelda kept running and the dark fog engulfed her.

"Stop! Zelda! Please!"

Somebody grabbed Sally's wrist. Frozen with fear, she watched a knife slice open her artery and the blood begin to spurt.

Sally woke from her nightmare, panting with fright. She was in darkness and totally disoriented. Was the forest real or a nightmare? Groggy and confused, she couldn't understand how it had become night so fast.

Behind her eyeballs, pain pulsed. When she turned her head to search for clues as to where she was, what felt like an electric shock zinged down her neck and spine. She froze in agony and focused on breathing deeply to dissipate the pain. It subsided a little, enough for her to think clearer.

There was a damp, moldy smell, but it wasn't the natural earthy smell of a forest. It was of damp rooms. There was another smell too—she recognized it from her time volunteering at the YMCA youth center, when she'd caught three boys at the back of the building inhaling pot through a bong. It was the stench of filthy bong water she could smell.

Sally tried to remember where she'd been before she'd fallen asleep and drew a blank.

Nearby, water dripped on a hard surface as if from a leaking gutter. There was the distant rumble of cars moving, but they sounded far away. Why was she sitting in the dark on a floor that felt cold and gritty to the touch? Although, only one of her hands was on the ground—her right shoulder ached, and she couldn't feel her right hand. She couldn't wiggle her fingers.

Alarm turned to panic. Sally attempted to bend her elbow and met resistance. Why was her arm raised above her head, and why couldn't she lower it?

Sally tried again, and when her arm didn't budge, she slowly raised her left hand and extended it toward her right. When she felt the cool, hard surface of the metal cuff around her wrist, fear shot through her veins like fire.

Who had done this?

The answer that came to her made her gag. Was it the Poster Killer? Was the silent promise of the missing-person poster coming true?

A flash of memory exploded inside her brain, and she saw the pages of a handwritten diary. The writing was childlike, larger than an adult's would usually be.

That was it! Stacy's diary. Sally had been flicking through it, searching for references to Zelda. But where?

Sally recalled an attic room, a big skylight in the slanted ceiling. It had been daylight: there had been sun streaming in. Beneath it, a desk. Posters on the wall—the Poster Killer's victims and targets lined up in neat rows. Bryan Topham's house. There had been a sharp pain in her head, and then she'd blacked out. She must have been hit from behind.

Was Topham her jailer? Was he the serial killer? Or had there been another person in the house all along?

Sally clawed at the handcuff that held her right wrist to what must be security bars. It clanked against metal.

She tried to pull her hand through the narrow gap around her wrist, but the cuff was too tight.

A powdery substance fell on her arm—it smelled like rust.

Desperate to find some defining features in the room, she peered into the darkness, her eyes now having had time to adjust.

There were two sources of subdued light. Behind her, a narrow slit helped define a small section of the room. Perhaps it was a window that was partially covered? Ahead, was a door with a glass panel, and through that panel, some muted light entered the room. Near the door was a pile of junk on the floor, all angular edges. Further along were what might be the outline of stacked chairs.

Using her unfettered hand, Sally searched the floor for a tool to help her escape. She touched what felt like laminated card and brought it close to her eyes. There was an illustration of a woman on it. Holding what? A pen? Some chalk? Was it a blackboard behind her? A teacher perhaps.

She held the laminated card up higher so that the chink of light behind her would hit the shiny surface. The lettering was big and it said *Step 2: name on the board.*

Was Sally in a school? If so, why did it smell damp, and why was the floor covered in dirt?

She dropped the laminated sign into her lap and felt further across the gritty floor. She found something like a small wooden brick and held it up. She couldn't make out the color, but it reminded Sally of a toddler's building block. Perhaps it was an abandoned school or a daycare?

Her scalp prickled. She was handcuffed inside a derelict building, far away from anyone who might help her. Would screaming do any good?

Just then, Sally remembered her phone. She dropped the wooden toy brick then used her free hand to feel her pockets. She couldn't remember where she'd put it so she tried her jacket pockets then, finding nothing but a tissue, patted all the pockets of her jeans. No phone.

Her fear grew.

She stretched out her arm as far as the handcuff would allow to feel the floor for her purse. It was a vain hope.

All she found was more kids' building blocks and some scrolls of paper.

Only Paul knew where she was. He would notice that she hadn't called him, wouldn't he? He'd call the cops, right? And if they turned up at Topham's place, what would they find? Had anything of hers been left behind? Would her car still be there?

Panic surged and her breathing quickened. What if she was trapped here and nobody found her?

A scream rose up her throat, but it burst from her mouth as a husky exhale, barely loud enough for her to hear, let alone any possible passerby.

She forced herself to turn her head, to ignore the pulsing pain behind her eyes, and look as far over her shoulder as possible. The handcuffs were locked to a rusting metal grille that covered an entire window. And behind the grille, the window was covered in weatherboard. It was poorly fitted, hence the sliver of daylight.

Sally screamed, loud and shrill. "Help! Somebody, help!"

She paused, listening.

"Hello, Sally."

Sally's body jolted. He was there with her. He had been the whole time.

FORTY-EIGHT

A voice in the darkness.

As a child, Sally had been afraid of the dark. When it was nighttime and her mom switched off the bedroom light, leaving her alone, little Sally would cower under her blankets. If moonlight caused leafy shadows to move across her wall, she would scream. Her dad told her to stop being silly; her mom came up with a practical solution: she draped muslin over the lampshade, leaving the bedside lamp on at night to allay Sally's fears. Even so, Sally always checked her closet and under the bed before she went to sleep.

All her childhood fears of terrifying monsters lurking in the dark were with Sally now but multiplied a hundredfold. The voice just a few feet from her, in an enclosed room, was that of a serial killer.

"Who?" Sally said in a trembling voice. She wanted to say *who are you?* but the last two words evaporated on her tongue.

"You're better looking in real life than in the photo."

Her flesh crawled, and she instinctively backed as far up against the wall as she could, tucking her legs close.

What photo did he mean? The one on the missing-person poster?

She clawed at the floor, trying to find something to defend herself with. Kids' building blocks. No good. A textbook. Scrolls of paper. A pencil. Could she stab him with it?

A sudden point of light blinded her. It was aimed at her eyes, and it felt as if it had seared a path through her brain. She yelped and turned her head away.

"What are you looking for, Sally?" His voice was muffled, as if he were talking through a scarf or mask.

"You're hurting my eyes!"

The flashlight was lowered. "Drop the pencil."

She hesitated then did as he said. She looked askance at the man, hoping to avoid the searing light. But all she could see was a black smudge in the shape of a man.

The flashlight did more than illuminate her—it cast a dull light across the room. On the walls were colorful kids' paintings. She looked to her right and saw wire mesh in large rectangles screwed to window frames. It had to be a derelict school.

With a dreadful sinking feeling, Sally knew where she was. Four of the six abducted girls had gone to the same school as Zelda—Ronald Reagan Middle School. The remaining two victims, Francesca Molinari and Tazeen Ibrahim, who'd been eleven at the time, had attended Pioneer Elementary School. The latter had been shut down in 2012, the pupils transferred to another state-run elementary school that had recently been expanded with new classrooms and gym. Pioneer Elementary had remained vacant since then; nobody would buy the land because of its association with the missing girls.

"Why am I here?" Sally asked.

"Here?" He was toying with her.

"This is Pioneer Elementary, right? Please tell me what you want?" Her voice cracked with terror.

Her captor had to be the Poster Killer. He'd been circling

her for a while, killing those who posed a threat, and now he held her captive. She was alive, but for how long?

"I want the truth," he said.

Was this a game?

"Okay."

"Tell me why you lied for Scott?"

"What do you mean?"

Why was he interested in Scott? For one muddled moment she thought he was referring to Zelda's suicide note and Scott's campaign to frame Caroline as the bully who drove Zelda to it.

"You gave him a fake alibi the afternoon Stacy Green was taken. You lied about the time he got home."

She remembered that day. It was October 25, 2010, and she was off sick from work with influenza. Scott, who was off duty, had gone to the pharmacy to buy cough medicine and nasal decongestant for her. Because he had been seen driving past the bus stop where Stacy was abducted, he had to make a police statement, which Sally had confirmed.

"I didn't lie."

There was an ear-splitting *wham!* A metal pipe hitting the wire-mesh frame. Sally cringed.

"You did!" he yelled. "You claimed he got home at 4:30 p.m. when in fact it was an hour later. Plenty of time to abduct and kill Stacy."

"You can't think..." Did her captor seriously believe that Scott was the Poster Killer? "My ex-husband was many things, but a killer? No way."

Wham! Again, he slammed the metal pipe into the wire window grille. "You knew and you lied for him. And you're still lying."

He was getting angrier and the angrier he grew, the more likely he was to hurt her.

"I'm... I'm sorry. You're frightening me—I can't think."

"You still can't see it, can you? How he manipulated you,

lied to you, and you believed it. You think you've gotten past it."
He was yelling. "But you can't see him for the monster he is."

How did her captor know so much about her? "I... I'm
making progress."

"Is that what your shrink told you?" The man in the darkness snorted contemptuously. "Did Scott tell you that you
remembered things wrongly?"

Why was he humiliating her? She wasn't the only person to
have fallen for Scott's version of reality. Friends, neighbors,
colleagues had all fallen for his lies. However, it was true that
she had doubted her memory and come to rely on his version of
events.

"I... don't want to talk about Scott."

"I do!" he yelled. "Scott knew *all six* girls. They all went to
the YMCA. They all trusted him. If he asked them to get in his
car, they would. He brainwashed those poor girls, just like he
brainwashed you."

Her mind was in turmoil. If her captor truly believed that
Scott *was* the Poster Killer, then who had brought her to the
derelict school?

"How can you be so sure that Scott came home later than
he said in his statement?"

"I saw him."

Sally shuddered. "How?"

"It doesn't matter how. I saw him at 5:31 p.m. driving along
Fifth."

Who was this psychopath who had been monitoring her
ex's movements? Sally shut her eyes. The flashlight was blinding, and his voice was terrifying. Why had Sally been so sure
that Scott came home at 4:30 p.m. on the day Stacy Green
disappeared? Sally had been feverish. Had she been mistaken
about the time? Then she remembered Scott sitting on the bed,
handing her the cough medicine and the nasal decongestant.
He'd told her that he'd had an easy drive to the pharmacy. He'd

made a point of telling her it was 4:30 p.m. And she had simply accepted it as the truth.

"So what if I was wrong about the time? That doesn't prove anything. Scott was cruel and manipulative, but he'd never kill a child."

Her abductor laughed. "The YMCA was his hunting ground and you stood by and let him do it."

Sally's head pounded. She couldn't think straight. Had she ever seen Scott behave inappropriately towards Stacy?

She thought back to the teens club that she and Scott had managed. The outings they'd done with the kids. She thought about Anna Moorehouse, Caroline Blake, Stacy Green, Tazeen Ibrahim, Vinesh Kapoor, and Francesca Molinari. Zelda had known all of them. They'd either been in the teens club with her or the tweens club with Paul, and occasionally Sally had driven one or more of the girls home. Scott had done the same. Safety was key, and they'd always liked to be sure the girls had reached home safely.

"Sometimes Scott drove the girls home, and so did I. Is that what you mean?"

"Did it ever occur to you that Scott was doing more than driving them home?"

Her stomach churned. "No!"

"He liked young girls, Sally. You knew and you turned a blind eye."

"No!"

Sally yanked so hard at her handcuffs that a trickle of hot sticky blood ran down her inner arm. The wire grille gave a little. Perhaps the screws would come loose from the wooden frame if she kept tugging?

"Stop that!" he shouted.

"Why are you making these terrible accusations? You have no evidence!"

"Oh, but I do."

FORTY-NINE

Doubt gnawed at Sally. Had she been blind to Scott's depravity?

On the night of Stacy's abduction, Sally hadn't paid much attention to the time. Why should she? She'd been sick in bed with influenza. She had gone along with Scott's version of events, never once doubting him. Now she recognized how her mistake in trusting Scott's word had ruled him out of the investigation into Stacy Green's disappearance.

As she cowered in the darkness, Sally's captor claimed he had evidence that Scott was the Poster Killer. She prayed it wasn't true. The thought that she might have been married to a serial killer and not known it, made her feel faint. Her vision momentarily blurred.

There was a snap underfoot as the shadowy figure shifted position. He kept the flashlight pointing at her, but as he drew closer she was better able to see through the white halo of light to the man behind it. He was dressed in black and wore a black balaclava. Her heart almost burst out of her ribcage. He must be the knife-wielding man who'd attacked Paul.

An adrenaline rush fueled an instinctive urge to flee, and she struggled to stand. Was this it? Was he going to stab her?

Sally's legs felt shaky as she slid her back up the steel grille. She managed to get upright, leaning into the grille for support. She had one free arm and two legs she could kick with. If only she could find a way to free herself from the handcuffs.

"You attacked my son!" she said. "You won't get away with it. Or what you're doing now."

He stood less than a foot away. His eyes were somehow familiar. There were deep age lines at their outer edges.

"You're going to write a statement," he said, and held out a lined notepad and a pen. She noticed that the pen was an unusual chunky shape, which made it impossible to stab him with it. "You'll say how Scott lied about the time he reached home on the day Stacy was abducted. You'll say it was after 5:30 p.m. and you'll say that Scott was overly familiar with the girls in the teens club."

Right now, Sally would sign anything, if it meant she would be freed.

"If I do that, will you let me go?"

"Maybe." He shoved the notepad and pen at her, and she took it. "If you don't, I will leave you here. Nobody will find you, and there's no point screaming. You'll die here."

A mewling sound slipped from her lips—she didn't want to die alone in the dark. She had to stay strong. "I can't see."

"You can see." He directed the flashlight onto the notepad.

Sally hesitated. "For pity's sake, promise me you won't kill me when I've done it?"

"I won't kill you, Sally. I want more from you."

Fear gripped her throat. *Keep him talking. Just keep him distracted.* Sally had always been good at connecting with people. Could she create a rapport with her captor?

"I didn't notice the time Scott came home. I promise," she pleaded. "I didn't intentionally lie."

"Just write."

Now that her handcuffed arm could hang at waist level, feeling was returning to it—pins and needles stung as the blood started to flow back.

"I can't do this unless you undo the handcuff."

"You're a bright woman. You'll find a way."

Disappointed her ruse hadn't worked, she suggested that he hold the notepad. He agreed. This meant she was uncomfortably close to her captor.

In one hand, he balanced the notepad. In the other, he held a flashlight so that it pointed at the paper. She started to write. Amongst the stench of the decaying building, he smelled clean. Was he wearing aftershave?

"This doesn't prove that Scott is the Poster Killer," she said as she wrote.

"I think you know more than you realize. We're going to keep talking until you help me prove his guilt." His eyes narrowed. "He's pure evil."

Sally looked into his eyes. They were familiar. Through the mouth slit in the balaclava, she saw the tip of a white beard, with hints of copper.

She must have frowned because he asked, "What are you staring at?"

She knew a man who had a well-groomed white beard and mustache with a hint of copper through it. That man was Bryan Topham.

He must have been hiding in his house the whole time she'd been snooping around and then knocked her out when she'd found Stacy's diary. There was one thing she was certain of—if she could get out of the handcuffs, she stood a good chance of running away fast enough that he couldn't catch her.

She continued to write, all the time considering if she should confront the man with his name. Did this knowledge give her power or was Topham crazed enough to kill her so she wouldn't be able to identify him?

"If you truly want to find the killer, I'll help you," Sally said. "Free me and I won't tell anyone about this. Helping people is what I do. I'm good at it."

"I tried that."

Sally was certain she was talking to Topham. "I was too afraid to talk to you. I'd become a target, my son was almost murdered, and I thought you were the Poster Killer. I'm sorry, Bryan."

He took a step back. His flashlight dangled low in his hand.

Sally kept going. "Bryan, you're a good man. I'm so very sorry for your loss. But kidnapping me won't help."

"You don't understand. I have to have justice for Stacy. My beautiful grandchild. At least I can do that for her."

"I *do* understand. I blame myself for Zelda's suicide. I carry that guilt with me everywhere, every day. But kidnapping me isn't going to bring Stacy back. Please, Bryan, undo the handcuffs and we can solve this together."

Topham said nothing. He was little more than a dark outline again. All Sally could see were his shoes because the flashlight was pointed downward.

"There's nothing to solve. It's all in Stacy's diary. And together with your revised statement, that no-good detective will have to take Scott in for questioning," Topham said.

Sally had started to read that diary just before Topham had thumped her on the back of the head. At the time, she'd had no idea that the diary might contain evidence that Scott was a killer.

"I want to know what's in her diary,' Sally said.

Topham disappeared into the blackness at the far end of the room then reappeared holding up a small book.

Topham turned the diary's pages, then began to read. His

voice resonated through the derelict room. *"February 1, 2010.
Teens club night. The group split in two. Some of us went with
Scott to shoot hoops. I went with Anna even though I'm no good
at sport because Anna asked me to. Zelda stayed in her mom's
group. They were going to chill and listen to music.*

*"Scott was weird tonight. It's like he's flirting with me. It's
real creepy. I told Anna and she laughed. Said I was being
stupid. When I missed the shot, he came up behind me and
helped me make the shot. Then he whispered in my ear. I
couldn't believe it. He said I was beautiful.*

"How can I be beautiful with my ugly freckles?

*"He drove me and Anna home. When Anna was gone, he
touched my thigh. It could have been a mistake, but it felt wrong.
He's old enough to be my dad. Eww!"*

Topham looked up. "See what I mean. She was thirteen
years old!"

Sally felt as if the floor beneath her feet had cracked wide
open and she was falling down, down, down into a chasm. Scott
had flirted with Stacy? She tried to remember if she'd ever
noticed Scott doing it. But she couldn't trust her memories. It
was true that teenage girls often fantasized about older men or
women they found attractive. But the extract from Stacy's diary
sounded heartfelt.

"I... I don't know what to say. I didn't know about this. If I
had, I would have done something, said something. There's a
possibility that Stacy may have been fantasizing about Scott,
especially as she had no father figure in her life."

"Stacy was an innocent. She was thirteen but she thought
more like an eleven-year-old. If Stacy said Scott was flirting, he
was flirting," Topham said. "Listen to this."

Topham turned the pages and, using the flashlight, he
selected the bit he wanted to read out loud. *"June 4, 2010.
OMG! Caroline and Scott had the biggest fight. It was after
school. Caroline followed me down the road, then she shoved*

me against the fence and told me to write her essay for her, and I said yes, because I was scared. Then Scott turns up in his police car with Nikki's dad and Scott tells Caroline to get in the back of the car. I don't like Caroline. I was secretly glad she looked frightened. Now she knows what it's like to be bullied. Ha-ha!

"*Anyway, Caroline said she wouldn't get in the car and if he made her do it, she would tell her dad that he was a pervert and he'd f**ked me! Me!!!! I would never do that. NEVER EVER! He's flirted a bit, that's all.*

"*Scott shouted, told me to go, and I ran. I'm so confused. I have to tell Zelda.*"

Topham stayed silent for a moment. "Do you believe me now?"

Caroline again. At the center of everything. This time she was accusing Scott of rape. Stacy denied it. Where were these diary entries heading?

"Did he?" Sally began, then tried again. "Does she say he sexually assaulted her?"

Topham turned the page.

"*June 5, 2010: I told Zelda he touched me in a way I don't like and she cried. I told her I was scared. I told her I wasn't going to the YMCA anymore. I think I broke her heart.*

"*June 7, 2010: I'm so afraid. Caroline has gone missing.*

"*July 2, 2010: OMG! Zelda told her dad she knew he wanted to have sex with me. She said that he killed Caroline. OMG!!!!!!!!! She told me that he threatened to KILL HER if she ever talked like that again. She was shaking all over. She said he would do it too.*

"*I feel bad. This is all my fault. Scott will know that I told Zelda. I'm scared too.*

"*August 29, 2010: He came to our apartment. He was in his cop's uniform. He told me he had to interview me about Caroline. I didn't want to let him in and I wanted Mom to be with me but Mom was at work. He told me it was okay for us to talk without Mom.*

"It was my fault, he said. I'd flirted with him, he said. He told me he liked me because I was quiet and so very pretty. He made me do things I didn't like.

"I hate myself."

Topham snapped the diary shut.

"See what a monster he is!" he shouted. "He's a filthy pedophile!"

Sally wanted to cover her ears, but the handcuffs didn't let her. Her stomach was writhing like a snake. Hot, acidic bile and the remnants of her breakfast shot out of her mouth and onto the floor. Her eyes stung and all she could smell was the foul odor of her vomit. A voice in her head told her that Stacy was imagining things—that none of what she was hearing proved anything.

It was Scott's voice. She consciously shut it out and searched her heart. The diary entries were true. Every word.

"You're right. He's a monster," Sally said.

Topham raised the diary so he could see the pages better. "This is Stacy's last entry, the day before he abducted her. *October 24, 2010. Zelda told me to tell Granddad. He would know what to do. Granddad is picking me up from school tomorrow. I'll tell him then. He's rich and powerful and the cops will have to believe him..."*

Topham's voice faded to a sob.

Silent tears dripped down Sally's face. She felt broken. Ashamed. "You must give Stacy's diary to Detective Clarke."

"It's a boys' club. Cops protect cops. If I hand in her diary, it'll mysteriously get lost."

"Okay, make copies and hand in the copy." She paused. "Ah, I see. The diary itself might not be enough to motivate Clarke to investigate Scott but if I withdraw my statement about the time Scott arrived home, he has to investigate. Am I right?"

"Yes. You'll write the statement?"

"Yes," Sally said.

She had enough self-control to sound composed, but her skin burned with fury and shame. She wanted to tear Scott limb from limb.

FIFTY

Sally had never felt hatred before. Anger—yes. Resentment—
yes. But not hatred. She'd believed it to be a destructive emotion
that would corrode contentment and a person's ability to love
and forgive. Sally had always given people the benefit of the
doubt and striven to be understanding. How wrong she had
been about Scott.

Her hatred for Scott burned through her, destroying every
ounce of forgiveness. Now she was convinced that Scott had
driven Zelda to take her own life. How could a thirteen-year-
old cope with knowing her father was sexually assaulting her
friend and yet she was powerless to stop it? He had threatened to kill his own daughter if she reported him. No wonder
Zelda had suffered from depression in the months before
she'd died. To carry the burden of such a terrible secret. To
have to face a father every day who she must have despised.
And feared. And then when Stacy was taken by the Poster
Killer, it must have been more than she could cope with. Did
Zelda blame herself for not speaking up about Scott? Did she
believe that her father was the Poster Killer? Dear God! And
how stupid she must have thought Sally to be. If only Sally

had been stronger, would Zelda have shared her terrible secret?

"Take off the handcuffs, Bryan." Her voice was chilling, even to her own ears.

His shoes crunched over grit. He dodged her vomit and took a set of small keys from his black pants.

"I was wrong about you. I had no idea how much he had you in his thrall. I'm so sorry I did this to you."

"I'm not. You've opened my eyes."

"Please forgive me. I was out of my mind with grief."

"There's nothing to forgive."

Topham leaned across her and fiddled with the tiny key. The sharp metal ring holding her wrist sprang open, and Sally pulled her bruised and bloody wrist free.

"I wouldn't blame you if you ran away, but I'd appreciate your company to see the detective."

Sally had already planned what she would do once she was free of the handcuffs. She wished Topham well with his case, but she didn't dare risk staying with him.

She ran.

She jumped over the pile of vomit and sent kids' blocks flying. She dragged the door open with such force it slammed into the wall, then she sprinted down the dimly lit corridor, hands out ahead of her to stop her slamming into any large objects. Beneath her feet, glass crunched—the glass from a smashed door panel. She passed a classroom in which the floor was littered with schoolbooks. On her left, yellow storage areas for the kids' coats and bags lay empty, but their name labels remained in bold letters. Ahead was a classroom full of old, shattered computers.

She turned a corner. More light crept in where a board was missing from a window. She ran past a stained mattress on the floor and a pile of stinking clothes. Someone had made this derelict school their home. Up ahead she could make out the exit sign. Beneath it was a door. A broken chain dangled from it. The door was ajar.

Sally leaped through the opening and collided with metal railings. Winded, she squinted into the bright daylight. A concrete ramp led down to the school basketball court. The hoops were still there, but there was no net. The wall to her left was covered in colorful graffiti. She heard an airplane fly overhead and birds sing. The air was clean. No mildew and rot, or filthy clothes, or the stench of bongs.

She ran down the ramp and across the schoolyard. An old stroller sat abandoned in the middle of a basketball court. Beyond the fencing was a street. She would flag down a car —any car.

She heard Topham shout her name, but she didn't look back. She sprinted down the ramp, her side hurting, her leg muscles aching.

A grocery store truck drove down the street, followed by a family car. She shouted for help—they didn't seem to hear her. The side of the street was lined with parked vehicles.

The school's chain link fence was hip height. She climbed over it then staggered into the road, waving her arms in the air.

"Help!" she shouted.

A car horn sounded to her left. A black four-door sedan. A man got out—solid build, flat-top haircut.

"Sally! Over here!"

"Richard! Thank God!"

Sally ran to him, pulled the Nissan Sentra's passenger door open and dived into the leather seat almost before Richard Foster could get back into his vehicle. He slammed his door shut and centrally locked the doors.

"I've been looking for you everywhere. Paul called Aiden. He was so worried about you. We've been driving around searching everywhere."

Sally's hair was plastered to her scalp and sweaty neck. "Get me out of here!"

"What happened?"

Sally turned her head to see Bryan Topham standing stock-still on the basketball court, staring at her. "Just drive. I'll tell you later."

Foster's gaze focused on Topham then he turned the key and pulled out of his parking spot.

"There are cops crawling all over Topham's house," Foster said. "There's a poster with his face on it. They're assuming he's been kidnapped. But I'm guessing it's the other way around?"

"You could say that." She tried to catch her breath. "Sorry about stinking out your car." In the enclosed space, the stench of vomit on her clothing was too pungent to ignore. "I just need time to think."

Sally looked over her shoulder. Topham hadn't moved from the deserted schoolyard, his balaclava in his hand. An old man driven to do foolish things. Sally didn't want him arrested for abducting her. She wanted him to hand in Stacy's diary to Clarke.

"Can I use your phone? I have to tell Clarke about something important."

"In my jacket on the back seat. Can you reach around and get it?"

Sally twisted her upper body and stretched out a hand, but the jacket was beyond her reach.

"I'll pull over," Foster said.

He indicated and turned into a quiet residential street, then came to a stop and got out.

Sally's nerves jangled. She willed Foster to hurry. He opened the rear door and leaned into the car.

"It's in here somewhere."

Sally peered around—Foster had his hand in his coat pocket. "Got it."

He popped it in his jeans pocket and then got into the driver's seat, once again centrally locking the doors. He swiveled in his seat so he could look at her more easily. "There you go." He held out an older model Motorola Moto that looked like it was due for replacement.

Sally took it. It wouldn't unlock without a passcode. "How do I unlock—?"

A sharp sting in her neck, then something cold slipped into her veins. She sank back into the seat and fell into a deep sleep.

FIFTY-ONE

Sally and Zelda were at the movies. They were eating ice cream: Zelda had chocolate and Sally had vanilla. It was a Saturday afternoon, and they were watching the movie *Middle School*. Sally glanced at her thirteen-year-old daughter's profile —her perfect snub nose, her smile, the way her shoulders shook when she laughed.

The auditorium was packed, mostly parents with kids and some groups of girls. Sally wondered for how much longer Zelda would ask her mom to come with her to the movies. She was growing up so fast, becoming particular about the clothes she wore and so incredibly knowledgeable about books. She was reading novels way beyond her age, and she loved to discuss the stories with Sally.

Zelda turned her head and looked at her mom.

"Why are you staring?" Zelda whispered.

"Because I love you so much," Sally whispered back.

Zelda smiled and snuggled into her mother's side, as best she could, given there was a chair arm in the way. Sally tilted her head so hers rested softly on her daughter's.

"Love you too, Mom."

Sally felt a cold draft behind her and she shivered. Where was that freezing air coming from?

She turned her head. Seated behind them, a black shadow in the shape of an elongated person stretched arms like tendrils over Zelda, as if the shadow was claiming her.

Sally squeezed Zelda closer. "Don't leave me," she said.

"Shush!" said Zelda, eyes glued to the movie, oblivious to the threat behind her.

Long dark arms wrapped around Zelda's body. Sally clung to her daughter, but the strength of her opponent was too much. Zelda was lifted up and over her seat as if she were light as air.

Sally tried to scream. But she couldn't make a sound.

Zelda was dragged by the monster along the row of seats to the aisle. Not one person noticed him. Nobody objected. They kept watching the movie as if nothing unusual was happening.

Sally jumped up to give chase, but the aisle she was in was blocked: legs, bags, piles and piles of books. Where had all the books come from? Regardless, she surged forward, stumbled, and fell. When she looked up, Zelda was gone.

When Sally woke, she felt as if she'd been in a deep sleep. She had that groggy feeling in which she was only semi-conscious and could so easily fall back to sleep.

She lay on her side in a relaxed fetal position with a sheet tucked under her chin. Her muscles were so floppy she was reluctant to move her limbs. A cough tickled her throat. When she licked her lips, her mouth was so dry that her tongue stuck to their dry skin. She needed some water.

Opening her eyes was like tearing apart Velcro. Her eyeballs were gritty. Near her face was a bedside table in pine and a small lamp with a frilly shade that gave out a pinkish glow. There was a plastic beaker of water next to the lamp. She caught a glimpse of floral wallpaper and pink drapes, which were drawn across a window.

Sally struggled to sit up, her muscles weak and useless. A

wave of dizziness caused her to sway. She stayed still until the feeling subsided, then, with a final effort, managed to sit up. She reached out a hand, lifted the small beaker, and drank all the cool water within. Then she looked around the room.

She was on a classic, black-coated metal bed with rectangular bedhead that had vertical bars. A patchwork quilt lay over the sheet. In a corner was an eight-drawer dresser with a dated three-way mirror and an array of make-up, necklaces, and bangles scattered across it. A woman's scarf was draped over one end of the mirror. On a cane chair was a teddy bear and a white toy dog. Whose room was this? The safe house wasn't decorated in pinks or frills.

Her whole body spasmed at the flash of memories. Bryan Topham holding her prisoner. Fleeing the derelict school building. Richard Foster. She'd been in his car. Then… then… here.

She rolled back the bedding and put her bare feet on a cold concrete floor. Her long legs were uncovered. Her nightdress was too short and too tight across the chest. She looked down at it. It was pink with little black-and-white hearts dotted all over it. On the center of her chest was a large white love heart with the word LOVE inside it. It was the kind of nightie that Zelda would have worn. Was this another crazy mixed-up dream?

How had Sally ended up here? Foster had rescued her from Topham. A respected retired detective with a son in the police force. And yet, the fine hairs on the back of her neck stood up.

Panic propelled her into action. Ignoring her lightheadedness, she shuffled across the floor and turned the round doorknob.

The solid pine door was locked.

She spun around and ran for the window, but when she threw back the drapes, her heart sank. The window was covered with security bars, and when she tried to open the casement window to call out, she found it was locked.

Sally took a step back and tried to calm her pounding heart.

Beyond the window was a rocky backyard and beyond that, pine forest. She thought she could hear the sound of running water in the distance.

A floorboard creaked above her. She looked up. The ceiling hadn't been painted like the rest of the room. It was made of pine timber, and her captor was walking around the upper level of the house.

Sally's legs almost gave way, and she staggered to the cane chair, the soft teddy bear and white dog at her back like cushions. She knew who lived in this house, but she couldn't come to terms with it.

Richard Foster, the lead detective on the Poster Killer, before Clarke had taken over, owned this house—she recognized the view of his backyard. With a crippling sense of dread, Sally realized this room was where the six missing girls had been taken—Anna, Caroline, Stacy, Tazeen, Vinesh, and Francesca. No wonder the police investigation had gone nowhere. Foster had directed it away from the real Poster Killer.

She covered her face with her hands and groaned. Scott might be guilty of raping Stacy Green, but it was Richard Foster who'd abducted the six girls.

Foster had used his Franklin PD badge for his own terrible purpose. Told them he was a police officer. Maybe he'd made up a lie, perhaps creating an emergency that meant he had to drive the girls somewhere. Then he'd driven them here, an isolated house surrounded by forest, and put them in this prison cell of a room. If they'd screamed, nobody would hear. They must have been terrified.

And now it was Sally's turn.

Only Francesca's body had been found, floating in the harbor. Where were the other bodies? Just thinking about it made Sally tremble. A pedophile was unlikely to be sexually interested in her, but that wasn't why she was here. Foster would find out what she knew and who she'd told, then kill her.

Sally thought back to the girls' faces on the missing-person posters, their lives ended to satisfy Foster's perversions. At that moment, an anomaly she'd noticed on the Francesca Molinari poster made sense. It was a spelling error which could just as easily have been a typo. The word *color* was spelled the British way, *colour*. On the other five posters, the American spelling had been used. Perhaps Foster had created Francesca's poster in a rush and failed to correct it?

Above her, floorboards creaked again. Was he waiting for her to wake from what must have been a sedative? She had to find a means of escape before he realized she was awake.

She tugged open each of the dresser's drawers in turn, searching for anything she could use. She found clothing made to fit a girl around twelve. How long had Foster kept them imprisoned as his toys?

A pair of baggy pajama bottoms with an elastic waistband might just fit. She tugged them on. She searched for shoes and found none—Foster had never intended the girls to leave this room.

The footsteps grew louder and nearer. Sally frantically searched for a weapon, her heart in her mouth with fear. She had no luck. The cane chair wouldn't do much to hurt a man like Foster.

Clomp, clomp. The sound of shoes on wooden stairs.

The footsteps stopped on the other side of the door. She heard a click as a key was turned. The door opened inward, and Richard Foster stood in the doorway pointing a FN 509 pistol at her, which she recognized from her police training.

"Don't try anything, Sally. I don't want to have to clean up the mess."

FIFTY-TWO

Paul wasn't good at waiting. But the not-knowing was driving him insane. Why wouldn't the cops tell him what was going on? What had that psycho, Topham, done to his mom?

He called Detective Lin. It went to voicemail. He dialed Clarke. No answer. He ground his teeth in frustration as he called Franklin PD's main switchboard and demanded to speak to either detective. The operator told him that she would pass on a message.

"That's not good enough!" he shouted.

The operator ended the call. Paul glared at his bruised ankle as if it were Topham himself. Here he was, stuck in a house in the middle of nowhere, unable to help his mom.

He looked around the dismal living room and saw Sally's cardigan draped on the back of a chair. He had never felt so alone. She irritated the hell out of him sometimes, but she was always there with a soothing word or a loving hug.

He gnawed a stunted fingernail. He had to do something! Maybe Reilly's mom would drive here to pick him up and then help him look for his mom?

He was about to make the call when he heard the rumble of tires on the potholed driveway—Sally, or a detective.

He rose clumsily from the sofa and hopped to the window. It was definitely a car—he could hear the engine, but the trees hid his view of the vehicle. Then a Hyundai Veloster Turbo emerged, the powerful engine growling. The car was Aiden's.

Why was he back?

Aiden left his car. He was in police uniform, his police-issue Glock 17 in his belt holster. If he was on duty, why wasn't he driving a patrol car? Had Aiden been sent to deliver bad news?

Paul hopped to the front door, unlocked it, and threw it open.

"Hey, Paul." Aiden smiled affably.

"Tell me what's going on? Is Mom okay?" Paul asked.

"Can I come in? We should talk."

That didn't sound good. Paul stepped aside then closed the door behind Aiden.

"Take a seat, Paul." Maybe it was the uniform but Aiden came across as older than his years. "Is anyone with you?"

Aiden doubled back and locked the door. "You're in danger, remember. Always lock it."

"Enough already. Is Mom okay?"

"Take a seat, Paul."

"I don't want to take a fricking seat! Just tell me!"

Aiden gestured to the sofa, his face deadpan.

"Okay, okay," Paul said, exasperated.

He moved too fast and his crutch caught on the edge of a rug. He lost his balance. Aiden caught his arm just in time.

"Steady there," Aiden said.

Paul sat clumsily on the sofa. "What's going on, Aiden?"

"Bryan Topham is holding Sally hostage."

Paul felt as if he'd been hit by a truck. Hostage?

Aiden continued, "Bryan's demanding Stacy Green's diary. He thinks Sally has it. If we give him the diary, he'll let Sally go." Aiden studied Paul's face. "This is important, Paul. Do you know where Stacy's diary is?"

"Why would Mom have it?"

"Topham thinks she does. Does she?"

"I don't know."

"Try to stay calm, Paul. You know your mom better than anyone. Where does she keep her notebooks?"

Paul ran his fingers through his uncombed hair. "She had them on the kitchen table."

"Stay here."

Aiden hurried to the kitchen and Paul lost sight of him. Seconds ticked by.

"Found them?" Paul called out.

"Yeah," Aiden called back. "Give me a mo."

Paul couldn't stay silent. "Where is he holding Mom?"

"At a disused school." Aiden appeared in the kitchen doorway. "No diary. Where does Sally sleep?"

"First room on the right."

Aiden darted down the hall and into her bedroom.

Paul hated being useless. Using his crutches, he hobbled down the hall after Aiden. When he reached the room, he found Aiden dragging her clothes out of drawers and dropping them on the carpet.

"Hey, buddy. Be careful with those."

Aiden picked up a corner of the mattress and shoved it off the bed. Then he scrutinized the wooden slats of the bed's base.

"You think your mom would go to the trouble of hiding it?" Aiden asked.

Paul didn't answer.

Aiden flipped the mattress. Not finding what he wanted, he kneeled next to her suitcase and checked the pockets.

"Why's the diary such a big deal?"

"Don't know."

"I'm coming with you," Paul said.

"No can do," Aiden replied, darting past Paul and ducking into the living room.

Paul stared in dismay at the mess Aiden had left behind. What the hell was he doing trashing the place?

Paul hobbled into the hall. He could see into the living room, where Aiden had now thrown the sofa cushions on the floor.

His phone vibrated. He realized that he had it on mute. "Stupid," he muttered, chastising himself.

It was Detective Lin. Maybe he could get some sense out of her. Paul hobbled back into Sally's bedroom.

"Paul, I have some bad news," Lin said. "Your mom is missing. Bryan Topham is dead. We're concerned for Sally's safety."

A crash came from the kitchen. It sounded as if a cutlery drawer had been emptied onto the linoleum. What the hell was going on? Aiden had said Sally was a hostage, not that she was missing. A trickle of sweat ran down the back of his neck.

Aiden slammed a cupboard door. The guy was going totally overboard with his search.

Paul closed the bedroom door.

In a hushed voice, he said, "Aiden's here. He's searching for Stacy's diary. Says he's been ordered to bring it to you guys."

"Diary?" Lin said. "No, we're not looking for a diary."

"He's trashing the place. Told me Topham was holding Mom hostage and demanding Stacy's diary."

Lin hesitated. "That's incorrect, and Aiden is not on duty."

What the hell?

"He's in uniform," Paul hissed. "I don't like this. Something doesn't feel right."

"You're right. Get into the panic room, Paul. I'll send someone over right away."

Paul didn't need to be told twice.

He opened the bedroom door as quietly as possible and limped into the study across the way. Aiden didn't see him enter it: the banging and crashing told him Aiden was still in the kitchen.

He shut the office door behind him. The remote control for the panic room was on the desk between the boxes of photos and memorabilia that the previous house owner had left behind.

In the process of picking up the remote control, one of his crutches became dislodged and fell to the floor with a thump. Paul cringed, his heart hammering in his chest. Had Aiden heard the noise?

He clicked the remote control, and the giant door to the panic room began to open.

"Paul?" Aiden shouted.

With his remaining crutch, Paul hopped as fast as he could into the padded space and clicked the remote again. The steel door began to close. Paul anxiously willed it to close quicker.

"Paul! Where are you?"

Footsteps on the hallway floorboards. The panic-room door was only half closed. Paul looked at the remote, searching for a button that would make the door close faster, but there wasn't one.

"I'm leaving now. You want to catch a ride?" Aiden said.

His heavy footsteps paused outside the study. Paul was a sitting duck. He backed as far as he could into the confined space.

A phone rang. He thought it was his. Then he heard Aiden speaking.

"Hi, Esme," Aiden said, sounding friendly.

The panic-room door only had a few inches to go before it locked shut.

"I can't come in today," Aiden said. "I'm not feeling too good."

Lin was testing Aiden. He'd just lied to a senior officer.

As the panic-room door sealed with a muffled *swoosh*, the pressure in his ears changed. Then a metal-on-metal sliding sound as the bolts set in position. Paul could hear nothing but the gentle hum of the air conditioning and his own labored breathing.

His shirt clung beneath his sweaty armpits. What had just happened? Why did Aiden want Stacy's diary so badly? Was Aiden the goddamned Poster Killer?

FIFTY-THREE

Richard Foster entered Sally's prison and locked the door behind him, then slid the key into his top-left shirt pocket. He stood with his back to the door and kept the pistol pointed at her. He knew how to use the FN 509—he'd been known at Franklin PD as a good shot. To Sally, he looked exactly like the upstanding and dedicated detective Sally had known, with a few more gray hairs. Foster had been tasked to catch the Poster Killer, and yet all the time he *was* that killer. Ingenious and sickening.

"Richard? What's this all about?"

Sally was trembling, although she tried to act in a relaxed manner, as if she hadn't realized who he really was. She and Foster had gotten on well in the past. Sally's only hope of getting out of the locked room alive was to connect with him on a personal level.

"Sit down, will you?" He lowered the pistol and tucked it into a hip holster.

She saw no point in arguing and sat on the cane chair. She inadvertently squashed the teddy bear and had to pull it out from beneath her.

"They all liked the bear," Foster said. "I haven't washed it. It still smells of them."

Sally's mouth parted in disgust, and the color drained from her face. She opened her fingers and the bear fell to the floor. His tone had been so casual, so unapologetic. She was sick in the stomach at the thought of the six poor young girls who'd clutched the bear for comfort.

He registered her dismay and smiled wryly.

"Sally, Sally, you were way too sensitive to be a cop and, to be honest, I could never fathom how you coped with working in victim advocacy."

He pulled from his jeans' back pocket a small bottle of water, which he chucked at her. Her response was too slow and it landed at her feet. "Drink. You'll feel better."

She unscrewed the lid and hesitated. "Is it drugged?"

He smiled again. "No."

She was very dehydrated. Her mouth and skin felt bone dry, and she couldn't think straight. She peered at the bottle, then took a sip. The cool water helped to remove the sour taste in her mouth. She screwed the cap back on.

"Why?" she said.

"Why do you think? It's what I like."

"You raped and killed them?"

"It wasn't rape. They liked it."

The cold water in Sally's stomach heaved. How could he even think that? The revulsion must have been evident on her face because his expression hardened.

"Don't you dare judge me."

She relaxed her features. If she was getting out of there alive, she had to appear submissive.

"I don't do that, Richard. That's never been me. You know that, right?" Foster's steely glare softened. "Are the girls here?" Sally asked, trying to maintain some levity in her tone.

"Two are. The favorites."

Sally couldn't believe it. After Francesca Molinari's body had been found, she had assumed the other girls had met a similar fate. Her shock must have been clear because Foster laughed.

"You thought they were dead. I'm not a complete monster."

Was he serious? He had just confessed to murdering four girls! Her next question formed in her throat, but she was afraid to know the answer.

"Who are the girls you kept?"

He wagged a finger at her, a crooked smile on his face, as if this was all a game. "Wouldn't you like to know!"

Sally thought of Mary Moorehouse in her damp apartment, hoping Anna would one day be found alive. She thought of Bryan Topham, so desperate to find his granddaughter's abductor that he was prepared to kidnap Sally in the mistaken belief that Scott was the killer. Of Stacy's mom, Lindsey, who was studying law at night school so she could do everything in her power to ensure evil men like Foster would go to jail for life. Of Karen and Tom Blake, who'd lost Caroline and Tiffany. Of Tazeen's family, who no longer mixed with the community, bitter and angry that they had fled Lebanon, only to have their daughter murdered in the country that was supposed to be their refuge. Of Vinesh's family, who now refused to speak about their daughter, as if she had never existed. And the Molinaris, who visited their daughter's grave every week, weeping at her graveside. Only the Molinaris had some sort of closure. Only they knew for certain that their daughter was dead.

But none of those families had justice.

"Where are the bodies, Richard? The parents deserve to know."

"No one is coming to rescue you, Sally. You know that, right? And no one will ever know where those pretty little things are buried."

She wanted to yell at him that they weren't *things*. They

were magnificent girls, full of life and hope, until he'd snuffed them out.

"How did Francesca end up in the harbor?"

"Never you mind." Foster looked away. Had Francesca managed to escape and reached the harbor where he killed her?

"Are your two favorites here?" Sally had to know. Perhaps she could save them? But first she had to save herself.

"Enough, it's time you answered my questions."

"Please, one more. Theo Durrant and Tiffany Blake. Both prisoners," Sally said. "How did you arrange their murders?"

He looked at her, a smug expression on his face. "I was a cop for thirty years, Sally. You get to know useful people. A prison guard owed me for turning a blind eye to rape allegations made against him. So he eliminated my problems. Stabbing Durrant was easy. Tiffany was harder to get at. He picked up some extra shifts in the women's jail, which he'd done before so it didn't look unusual. He poisoned her breakfast."

Sally buried her face in her hands. His lack of remorse was astounding. He was a despicable person. She wanted to scream and rail at him, but what would be the point?

Foster stepped closer and Sally looked up, scared.

He said, "I always liked you, Sally. I'm giving you a chance to get out of here. Just one. So listen to me." He paused. She nodded. He continued, "You tell me where Bryan Topham hid Stacy's diary and I will drive you far away from here and leave you there. I know you won't ever tell anyone about me, because if you do, I'll kill your son."

She whimpered, wrapping her arms around herself and rocking back and forth. She would do whatever Foster wanted to keep Paul safe. But there was a problem—she couldn't give him what he wanted. When she'd fled the school, Topham had been clutching the diary.

"Bryan has it. I can help you get hold of it."

Foster wagged a finger at her as if she were a naughty child.

"You always were a crap liar. I'll make it easy for you. Bryan is dead. The diary was not on his body. So where would he hide it?"

"Dead?" she whispered.

How had Foster eliminated Topham? Had he gone back to the derelict school after he'd injected her with a sedative? She pushed the question aside. Right now, she had to convince Foster that she could find the diary. It was her only lifeline. If she could persuade him to take her with him to find it, she had a chance of escaping.

"How do you know about Stacy's diary?" Sally asked. "Bryan kept it secret the entire time you pretended to hunt for the killer."

"The fool interviewed me for his book. His questions set off alarm bells. I asked him how he knew so much, and he said it was through Stacy's diary. Until then, I didn't know it existed." He shook his head. "I should have stayed away from that girl. I had a feeling she was trouble. You see, Stacy was not an easy kid to lure. My first attempt failed. She wouldn't get in my car even though I showed her my PD badge. I should have forgotten about her and moved on to another girl after that, but the sheer fact she'd outwitted me made her that much more enticing. I waited until she was almost home then I grabbed her."

Sally groaned. The clever girl had almost escaped Foster's clutches.

"I'm guessing Stacy wrote about you in her diary?"

"Not me specifically. She talks about *a cop* trying to get her into his car. No name. Luckily for me, Topham thought the *cop* in the diary was *your* husband, although he queried why Stacy said the man 'talked kinda funny'. Any detective worth his salt could work out it was me. After all these years, I still have a British accent. She refers to a black car with tinted windows and leather seats, and I was absent from the department when the abductions took place."

Sally thought back to the look of despair on Topham's face when Foster had driven her away from the derelict school in that very same car. Did he realize his mistake? Did he then know that Foster was the serial killer?

"So the diary is a loose end?" Sally said.

"I can't live with the risk."

Sally had one lifeline: she had to convince Foster she knew the diary's location.

"I know where he hid it. It's hard to find. I'll have to take you there."

Richard smirked. "Nice try." He took a step forward and drew his pistol. "Give me the location, Sally."

Her voice quivered. "Don't shoot. Please. It's at Lincoln Heights Cemetery. I can't describe where. I'll have to work it out when I'm there."

"Horseshit!" He pressed the barrel of the gun against her temple.

She whimpered. "I... um... he was cryptic. Said it was some-place nobody would guess and only he knew how much it meant to him."

"It's a grave. Has to be. He was married once, right? Is she buried there?"

"I don't know where she's buried. But he said it was lot four." Sally was making things up as she went along. She was so frightened she wasn't sure if she was making any sense.

"Four? You sure he said four?"

"I'm certain." She didn't dare blink in case he realized she was lying.

Richard lowered the pistol and turned his back on her. "Be a good girl while I'm gone."

Think! Give him a reason to take you with him.

"Richard, you won't find it without me. He told me some-thing else."

"Spit it out."

"No. You want the diary, then you take me with you. When we find it, you release me, like you said."

He raised the pistol again. "Don't fuck with me."

Her bones felt like they'd turned to water.

"You kill me, you'll never find it. And you should know that Bryan sent a message to Detective Clarke." Her lies were coming thick and fast, but would he believe her? "We were in the school. I saw him do it. He said he wanted to hand in Stacy's diary. If we don't find it before Clarke does, it's all over for you."

Foster swore. His face turned a deep red. He had a heart condition. If she was extremely lucky, he might have a heart attack.

"Okay. Try anything and I'll kill you *and* your son, got it?"

"Yes."

"You'll need a coat and shoes. My wife's stuff should fit you."

"You've kept her clothes all this time?" She had passed away seven years ago.

"I like the girls to dress up in them."

FIFTY-FOUR

Paul leaned back against the panic room's padded wall, dripping in sweat and out of breath. Adrenaline surged through him. His sprained ankle throbbed like hell, and there was a killer on the other side of the door: how could his day get any worse? He opened his hand and stared at the remote control sitting in his palm. Aiden couldn't get into the room, right? That was the point of panic rooms.

He can't get to me. I'm safe, he told himself. *Just wait it out.*

But for how long? It was an hour's drive from Franklin PD to the safe house. How long would Aiden hang around?

The air in the confined room smelled weird, kind of like a new car's plastic dashboard in hot sun. What did it matter as long as the air conditioning kept working? He was more worried about the psycho on the other side of the door.

Paul hopped over to where there was a keypad on the wall next to the heavy steel door. It controlled the three spy cameras fitted to the house. The first one gave him a wide-angled view of the study. He switched it on and jumped when he saw Aiden pacing the room—he was on the phone. There was no audio feed into the panic room, but from his jerky movements, Paul guessed that Aiden was really pissed. Who was he talking to?

Paul watched Aiden kick a desk drawer, then pick up the cardboard box that contained photos and chuck it into the hall. Then he jumped onto the desktop and tapped the wall.

A knot formed in Paul's gut when he saw Aiden stare fixedly at the ceiling's light fitting. Had he found the camera?

Aiden waved; Paul drew back from the video feed in shock.

"He can't see you," Paul whispered. "Stop being a loser."

Aiden continued to stare into the camera and drew his hand across his neck, as if to say he was going to cut Paul's throat.

Paul stumbled backward and fumbled for his phone. What if psycho-boy found a way in? But his cell phone had no signal at all. He was stuck there until somebody came to his rescue.

Paul opened one of the many bottles of water and drank from it to ease his dry mouth. When he'd drunk his fill and checked the camera once more, Aiden was gone. Had he left the house?

There were two other cameras—one covering the front entrance and the other the back entrance. Paul switched his view to the camera at the front. Through it he saw the length of the porch as well as the driveway immediately outside the house. Aiden's car was still there, but Aiden was nowhere to be seen.

Paul tried the back-of-house camera. He caught a brief glimpse of Aiden taking the steps down from the rear deck to the backyard. The house backed onto a steep, rocky hill. Where was Aiden going?

One minute, two, three. Aiden didn't reappear. He hadn't gone up the hill so where *had* he gone?

Abruptly, Paul was plunged into blackness.

"Fuck!"

The hiss of the air conditioning stopped too. All he could hear was his own breathing. The security-camera feed was gone, so not only was he unable to hear, or be heard, he was blind too and trapped in an airless box in the dark. This was seriously bad!

Paul hadn't cried since he was nine years old, but he felt close to crying now. He stood stock-still, hoping the power would come back on. Aiden must have switched off the electricity supply, but hadn't Lin said there was a backup generator?

There was a churning noise, and the light came on. Air hissed into the panic room, and the cameras started working again.

Paul blinked away the brightness and exhaled a huge sigh. He felt overcome with exhaustion, and the pain in his ankle was killing him. He hobbled to the fold-up bed and opened it, then lay down on it to rest his ankle. He just had to stay calm. Lin knew the situation. It was all going to be okay.

To distract himself, Paul played with the calculator on his phone, but his mind quickly returned to Aiden. When Aiden had flicked the power switch, he must have intended to starve Paul of oxygen. The psycho had tried to kill him.

The more Paul thought about it, the more he was convinced that it was Aiden who'd tried to stab him in Margie's basement, then chased him through the woods. He was tall. Fit. But why? Come to think of it, was Aiden the basketball player he had spoken to Bart Hower about two days ago? Was he the guy Paul caught flirting with girls at the YMCA, girls who were later kidnapped by the Poster Killer? Back then, Paul had been too young to remember the guy clearly. Either way, Aiden was trying to kill him, and Paul was finding it difficult not to totally freak out.

Please hurry! Paul thought, willing the cops to arrive.

His thoughts turned to his mom. It had been three hours since she was supposed to have checked in with him. Clarke and Lin knew she was missing. They would search for her. But if Bryan Topham was dead, did that mean his mom was in grave danger?

He hated himself for dissing her all the time. He was just like his dad, putting her down at every opportunity. His mom had been braver than he'd ever imagined possible, and here he was, a pathetic coward, hiding in a panic room.

The lights went out for the second time; the air conditioning stopped humming. He sat bolt upright.

He waited and waited, willing the power to return—but it didn't. His breath caught in his throat when he realized what Aiden must have done—he'd found the backup generator and deactivated it, meaning Paul would eventually run out of air. Panic swelled in him—would the police reach him before he suffocated to death?

FIFTY-FIVE

Foster drove through the eastern gates of the Lincoln Heights Cemetery and Sally directed him west. His phone rang. He answered it and kept driving. The conversation was brief, and Sally guessed he must be talking to his son who, she now realized, must have kept him up to date with Clarke's investigation.

"You certain?" he asked.

After a brief response to his question, the call ended.

"You lied. There are no cops looking for the diary." He flicked an angry look at her. "If you're messing me about, I *will* put a bullet in your head, and then I'll find Paul and do the same to him."

Sally had to keep the lies spinning. This plan was all she had.

"I saw him send the message, I swear," she pleaded. It was a lie, of course, but Sally hoped her terror would mask her deception. "Maybe there's a reason why Clarke hasn't put out an APB. Maybe he suspects there's a leak in the department?"

Foster pulled over and used his phone to call up a map of the cemetery. Sally held her breath. He would see what she'd been trying to do—she'd hoped to direct him to the center of the cemetery where the office and chapel were located, in the hope there would be people about and she could scream for help. Lot four was due south, and the map showed that clearly. She would have to come up with another plan—and fast.

"You devious bitch." Foster raised the gun and pointed it at her. "You think I'm stupid? Think again. Lot four is south."

Foster did a U-turn and headed south.

The layout of the cemetery was easy to navigate. The lots surrounding the office and chapel were given letters; on the outer parts, the lots were defined by numbers. Lot four bordered woodland, rich with oaks, maples, and elms. Within each lot, the gravestones were numbered. It would only take a few minutes to reach lot four and then what? How long would Foster believe that Stacy's diary was hidden in the cemetery? She had to get out of the car and run. Sally was fitter and healthier than Foster, and she could run faster than him. Her biggest problem was the gun.

They passed stunning tombs and statues, some dating back to 1887. A six-foot angel with wings spread was perched on top of a rectangular marble tomb. There was a sculpture that always made Sally pause when she walked through there; it was of two toddlers lying together atop a rectangular tomb as if asleep. Carved in white stone, one child was holding the other child's hand and their faces looked so peaceful. Sally liked to believe that the carvings gave their parents some solace.

Zelda was buried here, in a pretty plot beneath a mature oak. After Scott had moved to Chicago, Sally had commissioned a local sculptor to create a marble statue of a girl leaning her back against the headstone, reading a book, relaxed and happy. This was how Sally wanted to remember her.

After the burial, Sally had visited the grave every day. She'd always come alone: Paul had been too angry to accompany her. She would sit at the graveside for hours talking to Zelda. Even if it rained, Sally would come and sit on a plastic stool she'd brought with her, crouching beneath a wide umbrella. She would always tell Zelda how sorry she was for failing her.

Over time, the topic of her lonely monolog turned to more recent events: moving to a new house, her retirement, Paul's football games. If the weather permitted, Sally would then amble through the fifty acres of memorial stones, pausing every now and again to read the words on the stone or to watch the squirrels and birds in the trees. The cemetery was in fact much bigger than the fifty acres currently assigned for cremation and burial. There was another 170 acres that was currently woodland, which would one day become the resting place for Franklin's deceased.

They drove through lot three. They were almost there. Sally's heart pounded at the thought of what she had to do next. Could she dodge a bullet?

Foster smelled rank with sweat. His face was puce. His agitation was her advantage.

"This better not be a wild goose chase," he growled.

On the way there, Foster had called the cemetery office and learned that Topham's deceased wife wasn't buried there— her memorial stone was at the town's crematorium, which had briefly caused Foster to doubt Sally's word. However, Topham was an unusual surname and the office manager directed him to the Tophams' family plot in lot four. The Topham family had migrated to America in 1891 and started a mining company, which had made the family very wealthy. This information had helped convince Foster that Sally was telling the truth.

Sally's heart almost burst through her chest when she saw a hearse ahead. The coffin was being unloaded by the pallbearers, and the mourners stood by, watching silently. Foster slowed the car respectfully, clearly not wishing to draw attention to himself. This was Sally's chance. She parted her lips to scream for help—then felt a sharp pain in her thigh. Foster had shoved the gun into her flesh.

"Don't even think about it," he said.

Sally looked down. Foster's finger was on the trigger. If he fired his pistol at point-blank range, the result would be messy. The car would be spattered with her blood, and there would be witnesses. Terror gripped her—her insides turned to water, and her voice disappeared.

Their car kept going and Sally stayed silent; soon, the mourners became just an image in the side mirror.

Lot four had many large, tombed plots. Some were shaped like little houses; others had walled flowerbeds. Some contained huge headstones on which the images of the deceased were etched, some had statues, and others were rectangular stone sarcophagi.

Foster pulled over at the side of the road and switched off the ignition. He took from his pocket a barrel-shaped silencer and screwed it onto his pistol.

"When you get out, you'll take my arm and do whatever I say. Got it?"

She nodded, although she was unsure if her legs would even function. But she had to stay strong. Her life depended on it.

Foster unlocked the car doors and swiveled in his seat to get out.

Do it. You have to run.

But she was afraid of the gun.

Through the windshield, she saw another car heading toward them with a young couple inside. This was her chance.

The moment Foster pushed his door open, Sally shoved her own door wide. She jumped out and ran, her long legs pumping like pistons. She didn't run at the car—it was too easy a shot for Foster to take; instead, she headed into the graves, darted left, then right, so as not to give him an easy shot.

"Stop!" he bellowed.

The shoes Foster had given her were too small, but she ignored their tightness, sprinting between a black memorial stone and a low wall around two sarcophagi. She flicked a look behind her—Foster was chasing her, and the couple in the car had their eyes glued to the strange scene. He must've hidden his weapon inside his jacket, but she knew he would draw it as soon as the car was gone.

Sally stopped and waved her arms in the air, shouting, "Help me!"

She didn't dare hang around. Foster's lumbering gait made him slow, but he could easily kill her with one gunshot.

Sally powered on, putting as much space as possible between them.

There was a gunshot, more like a *pfut*, the silencer doing its job. She instinctively lunged behind a statue of a mother and child, then peered around it. Her throat was so dry that sucking in deep breaths made her cough. Foster heard it and jogged in her direction.

Not far from her was a huge crypt with pillars either side of double doors. To reach it, Sally would need to duck behind whatever cover she could find—a few statues, a couple of rectangular stone sarcophagi that were maybe three feet high. She set off, zigzagging between the statues and headstones.

Another shot rang out—this time it landed terrifyingly close and Sally squeaked. A puff of white dust exploded into the air as the bullet hit a gravestone.

Faster! she told herself. *Faster!*

In her haste, she tripped over an empty vase that was lying on the path. She fell on her knees and landed hard. Pain shot up her legs and spine, but she hauled herself up, and had just reached the crypt with the pillars when Foster shouted to her.

"This is pointless, Sally! I have plenty of ammo."

His voice was breathy and tired.

Sally crept around the outer walls of the crypt to the back.

Thirty or so feet away was a road and then woodland. If she could reach the trees, she would have much better cover, and she might even find some walkers and beg them for help.

Out of the corner of her eye, Sally noticed someone approaching. The sun was in her eyes, but she saw enough to know it was a man. She inhaled a big breath and set off for the stranger, ducking and diving between whatever cover she could find. A quick look behind her confirmed that Foster had also seen the mourner and was trying to cut her off.

Sally sped up. Her leg muscles ached, and her lungs burned. Squinting into the sun, it appeared as if the man had seen her because he shifted direction and headed straight for her. He wanted to help her! He started to run and dropped the bunch of flowers to the ground.

Sally's mind did a *what the...?* She was closer now; he was wearing police uniform. A sense of unease washed over her, and she slowed her pace. Sweat stung her eyes.

The cop sped up and crash-tackled her to the ground, forcing all the air from her lungs. She couldn't move or breathe.

He rolled her onto her stomach and dragged her hands behind her. She gulped in some breaths and heard the clink of handcuffs closing around her wrists.

"He has a gun," she managed to wheeze.

The cop pushed her cheek into the gravel, the sharp little stones cutting into her skin.

"I've had enough of you messing with our plans!" It was Aiden's voice. "You're a lying pain in the ass. Just like Paul. You've got no idea where the diary is, right?"

He grabbed her hair and yanked her head up. Sally squealed, and her eyes watered as Aiden dragged her up to her knees. Paul? What did Aiden mean?

"I know... where... it is," Sally gasped.

Through her tears, she saw Foster walking toward them, his

movements awkward, the front of his shirt soaked in sweat. He put out a hand against a crypt wall—he looked close to collapse.

"She's a waste of time," Aiden said. "We have to get rid of her."

"You're right, son. We do."

FIFTY-SIX

Bound and gagged in the trunk of Foster's car, Sally's claustrophobia was bringing on a panic attack. She couldn't catch enough breath and the stinking, oily rag in her mouth only made things worse.

There's plenty of oxygen, she kept telling herself. *Breathe in and out through your nose. You can do this!*

The trunk was dark, except for a red glow. Daylight penetrated the red plastic casing of the brake lights and taillights, and Sally found this weak lighting a comfort. At least she could see a little of her cramped surroundings.

Find a way out. Warn Paul.

Aiden's earlier comment about Paul was etched on Sally's mind. If Aiden was the masked man who'd attempted to murder Paul before, had he tried again? Aiden knew the safe house address—had he gone there? Had Paul made it to the panic room in time?

Sally broke out in a sweat.

Aiden, like Scott, had fooled her and so many other people.

Aiden had appeared kind. He had managed victims of crime with understanding and what she'd thought was empathy, but empathy could be faked, she knew that now. Foster must have groomed his son to be a killer. It horrified her to think of father and son stalking their victims. And what's more, they were both highly respected cops. Durrant had told her the truth. The Poster Killer was, in fact, two people and Durrant had paid a heavy price for revealing that fact to her.

Think! There has to be a way out. A way to get help.

Now that Sally had her breathing under control, she peered into the reddish darkness for anything that could aid her escape, or a way for her to attract attention from passers-by. Her biggest challenge was the handcuffs, which secured her hands behind her back.

There was a sudden jolt, then a thud. Her head, right arm, shoulder and right hip hit the trunk's hard floor and she moaned. Her bruised body ached.

The car had gone over a speed hump. Sally knew then they were still at the cemetery. Sally thought of the young couple who must have clocked Foster chasing her through the gravestones. Would they dial 911 and report the strange incident? And what good would that do? Soon Foster would exit the cemetery. She had to hope the couple had made a note of his license plate.

The car's brake light glowed; was Foster slowing down?

A plan came to her.

The trunk was large enough for Sally to turn her body so that her feet pointed at the pocket in the car's bodywork that housed the bulbs and wiring for the brake and taillights. Beyond the wiring was the red plastic covering. She pulled her legs into her chest, then she kicked at the red plastic, hoping to crack it.

Thud!

Nothing broke. She kicked again, harder and faster.

Thud, thud, thud!

Would her captors hear the noise?

There was a *crack!* A chink of daylight through the broken

covering. Sally kicked some more. Shards of plastic and the interior electrics fell outwards, hitting the road's surface. Sally then turned 180 degrees, so her face was against the hole she'd created. The fresh air coming into the trunk smelled so good. Her field of vision was narrow but she saw gravestones. There had to be somebody about.

Sally tried to call out, but the gag did its job and all she could muster was a muffled *mmmm* sound. It was useless. How could she attract attention another way? Could she leave something of hers behind so that the police would know that she'd been there?

Her wristwatch had a leather band. It was awkward to undo with her wrists handcuffed, but she managed it, then once again she shifted position so her hands touched the jagged hole.

Foster's vehicle slowed once more. Sally tried to feed her watch through the hole, but it kept snagging in the gap between the car's interior and exterior bodywork. The effort had Sally contorting her arms into an agonizing position.

With one last Herculean effort she turned her body so her foot could kick the watch out onto the road. It dropped onto the asphalt.

Was it enough of a clue? Would anyone stop to pick it up?

The car took another speed hump then came to a halt for a second or two before it sped away. They were leaving the cemetery behind them.

Exhausted, Sally lay still, inhaling through her nose, doing her best to ignore the heat inside the trunk and her aching body. She closed her eyes and tried to plan an escape once Foster opened the trunk. Her best chance was to let him help her out of the confined space and then run, but she would be severely hampered by the cuffs locking her hands behind her back.

The journey seemed to take forever, and yet she didn't want it to end because when it did, they would surely kill her. She occasionally opened her eyes to check the view through the hole. Freeway. Winding road. Trees. More trees. They were going to take her into the forest, kill her and bury her where nobody would find her body.

The car went up a steep slope, then the engine was switched off. Through the hole in the brake and taillights, she saw an asphalt driveway that she knew to be Foster's.

A car door slammed. The slap of shoes. Richard and Aiden spoke in hushed voices, too hushed for her to hear clearly.

A clunk. The trunk door sprang open, and Sally was blinded by the bright light. Her gag was untied and removed. She flexed her jaw and opened her mouth to breathe deeply the clean air, rich with pine resin.

"What did you do?" Foster demanded, leaning over her. He pointed at the brake and taillights.

Sally didn't answer, afraid he would strike her.

"It doesn't matter, Dad. We kill her, bury her, give each other an alibi." Aiden took hold of Sally's arm. "Get up!"

"My legs. I have cramps."

He dragged her up and over the lip of the trunk as if she were a sack of potatoes. He was terrifyingly strong.

Her legs buckled beneath her, and she kneeled on the asphalt. Ahead of her was Foster's house.

It was risky bringing her here. It must be because there was a place in the surrounding forest where they'd buried the bodies. Serial killers were known for their habitual behavior. Sally now believed that Francesca Molinari had escaped from Foster's basement and reached the harbor before they caught and killed her. If Francesca could escape this place, then Sally could too.

"She goes back in the room until we're ready," Foster said. "Get digging, Aiden. I'll see to her." The cold barrel of a pistol was pressed against her temple. "Walk ahead. Don't make a sound."

Sally struggled to rise, then on shaking legs she was led

around the back of the house and into the basement room where she'd been imprisoned earlier.

"Enjoy your last few moments on this earth."

Foster removed the cuffs.

"What are you going to do to me?" Sally asked, moving as far away from him as possible.

He wiped sweat from his forehead with a sleeve. "You're not my type."

Foster locked the door behind him.

As soon as he shut the door on her, Sally looked around her. Nothing had changed. Somehow, she had to get out of there.

She ran to the window, gripped the bars, and tugged.

They didn't budge. Each corner was screwed deep into the frame.

She spun around and raced to the chest of drawers. There was a make-up bag. Could she find tweezers? She tipped out everything in the make-up bag. Foundation, mascara, lipstick, eyeshadow, even sachets of hair dye. No tweezers.

Sally studied the mirror. Could she smash it without Foster hearing it shatter? Unlikely. As she stared at the mirror she saw a reflection of Aiden as he entered the backyard from the house. She turned to watch him. He had changed out of his uniform and into olive-green coveralls. He wore gardening gloves, and in his hand was a shovel. The sight of it sent her heart rate skyrocketing—Aiden was about to dig her grave. She watched him get swallowed up by the forest.

How long would it take Aiden to dig a grave? How deep would he need to go? An hour perhaps if the ground wasn't too hard?

Sally heard a scratching sound. Was it a rat? It came from behind the chest of drawers. She ignored the thought. She had bigger things to worry about.

"Hello?"

Was Sally imagining Zelda was here? Such a timid voice. *Stay focused*, Sally thought. *How do I get out of here?*

"Hello?" The same voice, young and hesitant.

Her heart leaped. Where was the voice coming from?

Sally stood and peered behind the chest of drawers. Just dust and some long hairs. And a hole in the baseboard, just big enough for someone to call through if she were in the adjoining room.

Sally pushed one end of the dresser away from the wall and then kneeled, leaning down so her mouth was close to the hole.

"Hello?" Sally said. "My name's Sally Fairburn. What's yours?"

Silence. Was Sally going mad? Had she imagined the voice? "Anna."

In shock, Sally reared up and banged the back of her head on the dresser. Was that Anna Moorehouse on the other side of the wall? Was she one of the two girls Foster had kept alive?

"Are you Anna Moorehouse?"

"Who are you? You don't sound young."

"I'm a captive. I know your mom, Mary. I see her every week. She celebrates your birthday every year. She told me you were alive. She's waiting for you." Silence.

"Is this one of his cruel games?" Anna sounded cross.

"I know Richard and Aiden abducted you and five other girls. I'm a victim support advocate. Richard has me locked in this room because I know too much. He's going to kill me. Can you help me get out of here?" Sally held her breath.

"We can't help you."

Sally had forgotten about the second girl. "Who is with you? Caroline? Stacy? Tazeen? Vinesh?" Sally said each name, hoping to entice a response from Anna.

"Tazeen's here. She won't talk to you."

Sally tried to visualize them. Anna would be seventeen, Tazeen sixteen. "Are you locked in the room?" Sally asked.

"Yes. I'm sorry, there's nothing I can do. They mustn't know we talked. They'll kill me."

"I won't say a word, I promise. Tell me how Francesca escaped?"

"I can't." A pause. "Did she make it?"

What should Sally say? If she told the truth, she would dash any hope that Anna might have of rescue. "Yes, she made it back to her family. You can too. Just tell me how Francesca got out?"

Silence. Then scuffling. Was Anna walking away?

"Anna, don't leave me. Please. Talk to me."

Sally put her ear against the hole in the wall. She heard Anna whispering.

Sally said, "If I escape, I can get help. I can free you. I know you must be frightened. Please tell me how Francesca did it?"

She turned her head so she could better hear any response. Nothing. Sally then peeked into the hole. The light coming through from the next room began to disappear as a piece of cloth was pushed into the hole. Sally wanted to scream at Anna in frustration, but that would solve nothing.

She calmed her breathing. Two girls were alive. Who would have thought? Adrenaline began to course through her body. She had to set them free. But how?

Sally pushed the dresser back in position and then picked up each necklace draped over the standing mirror and tested each chain's strength. They were cheap trinkets that snapped easily and were of no use to her.

Adrenaline surged through her body as she searched every nook of the room, every drawer, every cushion. She checked under the bed. Nothing but balls of dust and what looked like a spider hanging from the base's wooden slats. She looked closer. The spider didn't move. Curious, she lay on her back and slid right under the bed. It was a velvet pouch. She crawled out from under the bed, then sat up and untied the pouch's drawstring. Inside the pouch was a pair of glasses. The frame was metal, and the lenses were rectangular. With a heavy heart Sally recognized them as Stacy's glasses. Why had she hidden them? Sally opened one arms of the glasses and it came away in her hand. It had been broken off the frame.

Sally looked up at the bars on the window. Had Stacy tried to undo the screws with this?

Sally stood and slotted the thickest end of the metal arm into the screw's head. She thought her makeshift tool would snap, but as she kept the pressure up, the screw turned, and she was able to remove it

"Clever girl, Stacy."

One down, seven to go. No, wait. Two were already unscrewed on the top right. That meant Sally only had five screws to remove. She tried the next screw. This one didn't want to budge. Rather than snap the metal arm she was using, she moved onto the screws on the bottom left of the bars which might be easier to move. The first one undid okay but the second one was too tight, and she pushed too hard—the tool snapped.

Sally swore under her breath, dropped it, on the floor, and then broke the other arm off Stacy's glasses.

"Please don't snap."

Every few minutes, she looked out of the window to check for Aiden's return which would signal that the grave was ready, and her time was up.

Sweat trickled down her temples. She was down to the last screw. That would have to be enough. Any moment now, Aiden would drag her away into the forest. She poked her fingers through the holes in the grille and pulled with all her might. The metal frame came away, with only the bottom corner clinging to the wooden frame, held in place by the last screw.

She took up a wide stance and pulled harder, her arm and leg muscles burning. The last screw came away from the frame.

Sally staggered backward and, euphoric, she dropped the grille on the bed.

Now to open the window.

It was a sash window with a latch in the middle which held in place both the upper and lower window frames. She flicked the latch away. But the window was still locked by a bolt encased in a circular hole. Sally tried to jiggle the frame to see if the bolt might pop out. It didn't.

There was only one option left to her—smash the glass.

Foster was clearly not a fit man and Aiden was in the forest. She might have just enough time to crawl through the broken window and run. Racing to the dresser, she found two T-shirts and then tied one to each hand to protect them from glass splinters. Lifting the cane chair high, she swung it at the lower pane of glass. The smash was deafening but too much glass remained. She swung the chair again at the glass and this time she had a large enough area to crawl through.

"What the hell?" Foster bellowed from upstairs.

Sally poked one long leg through the shattered window and then her body, using her protected hands to steady herself. Then she raised her other leg and lifted it through the gap. Beneath her shoes, the glass shards crunched.

Clomping feet on internal stairs—Foster was about to unlock the door. Sally flicked a look at the forest. No Aiden.

She bolted—around the side of the house, past a rainwater tank, down some slippery rocks, and onto the driveway. From inside the house, Foster was yelling.

Two cars were parked in the drive. Might they have left the keys in the ignition?

Sally tugged at the door handle to Foster's Nissan. It was locked. She darted around to Aiden's car. Also locked. Damn!

For a second, she considered running down the road, but that would make her easy prey for her pursuers.

The house door flew open and Foster stepped onto the front porch. He raised his pistol.

Sally ran like the wind, reaching the forest as a gunshot rang out. She ducked but kept running. The density of the pine forest would be her salvation, or so she hoped, although the ground cover was thick.

Avoiding some ivy creeping over the forest floor that could easily trip her up, she jumped a fallen tree trunk and pushed on. Behind her, there were raised voices. A car engine growled into life. Just one car. Very probably Foster. It would be Aiden who would pursue her on foot.

Sally glanced behind her and saw movement. He was hard to see in his olive-green coveralls, but his black hair and pale face was momentarily caught in a shaft of sunlight penetrating the branches.

Aiden was coming for her.

FIFTY-SEVEN

Sally sprinted through the trees, leaping over ferns, dodging rocks and ivy that could all too easily snag her feet. If she fell, he would catch her. Her shoes weren't designed for running and they were at least one size too small, and her heels already had painful blisters. Her jacket buffeted behind her, the thick material threatening to make her overheat. But it was a light brown color and therefore good camouflage because the blouse Foster had given her to wear was white, and white would stand out in the forest.

Every few paces Sally changed direction, zigzagging to make it more difficult for Aiden to follow. Somewhere to her right she heard the thrum of a car engine; it had to be Foster searching for her along the winding country lane. The sun was getting low now, and the forest shadows were elongating. This helped Sally to blend in with the trees, but it also made running treacherous.

Aiden knew these woods like the back of his hand and Sally didn't. He was twenty years younger than her too. Could she outrun him? She had no memory of where the nearest house was located but it had to be further down the lane. Sally would stay in the forest but run more or less parallel to the road. Then, when she saw a house, she would head straight for it.

Behind her, a twig cracked. She peeked over her shoulder—Aiden was gaining on her.

All around her were trees, too slim and tall to offer her a hiding place. A crow flew overhead and *caaaw*ed. She heard the sound of trickling water. There was a stream nearby. Foster used to talk about it—further down the hill it grew rockier and wider, and he'd taken Aiden swimming there in summer when he was a boy.

A bullet hit a tree trunk with a *thwack*, and splinters flew into the air only a few feet from Sally's shoulder. Aiden wasn't using a silencer because nobody was likely to hear the sound, and anyway, these woods were used by hunters.

Sally's leg muscles burned, but she found a reserve of energy and sped up.

A car engine revved. Foster wasn't far away either. With Aiden behind her and Foster to her right, she realized her plan wouldn't work—Foster was patrolling the road like a guard dog and he would stop her entering any house.

Sally changed course. She had to do something unexpected. She would cross the stream and head up the slope on the other side.

The terrain began to slope downhill. Through the trees, she caught a glimpse of bright green moss and pale boulders that glinted in the last of the day's sun.

A quick look behind: no sign of Aiden. Maybe she'd lost him.

The sound of rushing water grew louder. The banks of the stream were mushy with leaves and mud, and angular rocks stuck up above the water's surface. The bank on the other side was equally steep, and beyond it, the slope rose up a hill that was part evergreen and part deciduous trees.

She stepped into the stream, and a shock of cold water

seeped into her shoes. It was a welcome relief for her hot, sore feet. But the stones were slippery—Sally fell forward, landing with a splash. Her pants and the bottom half of her coat were soaked.

Floundering for a moment, she finally managed to get up and keep walking through the stream, but her clothes were now heavy with water and they clung to her legs awkwardly. She clawed her way up the steep bank on the other side, panting and gasping.

There was a crack as twigs broke underfoot.

Sally turned fast—Aiden was charging down the hill, looking straight at her.

Fresh terror reared up within her. She ran into the trees and began to climb the hill, willing her legs to go faster.

Sweat dripped into her eyes and blurred her vision. The low sun had turned the trees into dark silhouettes. She imagined she saw a treehouse in the branches of a deciduous tree, maybe an oak. She rubbed her eyes and looked up. A rope ladder hung from the treehouse. There were walls and holes for windows—the kind of treehouse a loving father had made for his kids. If there were kids on this side of the stream, there had to be a house nearby.

Spurred on by the thought, Sally kept running for the treehouse. She had an idea that might delay Aiden and give her the extra seconds she so desperately needed to reach help.

Tearing the sodden coat from her body, Sally threw it onto the platform of the treehouse. The saturated garment would drip water through the planks—with any luck, Aiden might believe she was hiding up there and waste valuable seconds.

Sally set off again, her lungs burning with the exertion. The hill crested and then fell away downhill, and in the valley below was the most wonderful sight Sally had ever seen: a house with a swing and a greenhouse in the backyard. The interior lights were on, and there was a car parked in the side passage. She had found help. They would call the police.

She drew on the last of her remaining energy and sprinted, leaping over rocks.

A shot rang out. A magpie screeched and flew into the sky. Aiden had caught up with her again.

Sally almost flew down the slope.

The trees abruptly stopped at the house boundary, but there was no fence. The yard was grass that grew poorly because of the pine needles. She ran up a crazy paving path, past a stone birdbath and a greenhouse. The rear entrance was a set of sliding doors. Those doors were shut and wouldn't budge.

They have to be home!

In a laundry shed, a washing machine was spinning its contents.

Her mouth was so dry she could hardly muster a voice. "Help me! Somebody help me!"

A woman in her early thirties came out of the shed, a plastic laundry basket in her hands.

"Help me!" Sally shouted. "He has a gun!"

"Oh my God!" The woman dropped the laundry basket and ran like a startled rabbit through a side door and into the house.

Sally didn't wait for an invite—she followed the woman into the kitchen and slammed the door behind her. In her agitation, Sally couldn't work out how to lock it. "Help me lock the door!"

Sally swiveled to find the woman on the other side of the kitchen clutching a large kitchen knife. "Stay away!" Then she raised her voice, "John! John!"

Sally's terror was fueling the woman's fear. But time was of the essence—Aiden would be here at any moment.

"I'm Sally. What's your name?"

"Eva. Get out of my house!"

"I can't, Eva." Sally gasped for breath. "He'll kill me."

The woman screamed. "Get out of my house!"

Through the window, Sally glimpsed Aiden running down the forest slope. He would reach them in less than a minute.

A bearded man, tall and lean, wearing a checked shirt, burst into the kitchen. "Who the hell are you?"

"Please help me. I have to call the police. Look!" Sally pointed to the window. "He's the Poster Killer. He has a gun."

"What the hell are you talking about?" the man asked.

"He'll kill me. And you. Call the police! Now!" She looked at the kitchen door. "Lock the doors!"

"Eva. Dial 911."

Eva didn't move—she just continued to stare at Sally.

John continued, "And put the knife down, will you?"

Eva slapped the knife onto the countertop with a frown then picked up her cell phone. "I need the police," she said to the operator.

John went to the window and looked out. Aiden was hard to see in his olive-green coveralls, but the movement of his legs and arms must have caught John's eye because he swiveled to stare furiously at Sally. "What have you done?"

John raced to the kitchen door and flicked the deadlock in position, then he dashed out of the kitchen and into the hall, crying, "Ben, Maddie! Where are you?"

A little girl replied from upstairs, "Up here, Daddy!"

Eva was talking to the operator. "Some crazy woman's in our house. What? Address? 193 Forest Way."

"Tell them I'm Sally Fairburn. Tell them to call Detective Clarke. I'm being pursued by Aiden Foster."

"Excuse me?" Eva stared at Sally as if she was insane.

Sally had had enough. She lunged at Eva and ripped the phone from the woman's hand. Eva edged away from her and then dashed from the kitchen to join her husband.

"Hello, Operator. This is Sally Fairburn, formerly Franklin PD. Tell Detective Clarke the Poster Killer is at 193 Forest

Way. He's armed and intends to kill us. He's Aiden Foster, a cop."

"Ma'am, slow down," said the operator. "Your name is Sally Foster?"

"Yes—I mean, no. My name's Sally Fairburn. Contact Detective Fred Clarke."

Her breath caught in her throat when she saw Aiden break from the tree line and enter the backyard at full pelt. Any moment now, he would see Sally through the kitchen window and fire.

Sally bolted for the hallway, slamming the kitchen door behind her. Eva stood in front of the stairs, as if she were guarding them to protect her children from a maniac.

Panting heavily, Sally rested her back against a wall, the phone still close to her ear.

"Ma'am, are you still there?" asked the operator.

John exited a side room with a hunting rifle, which he pointed at Sally. "Give Eva the phone and stay exactly where you are," he demanded.

FIFTY-EIGHT

Sally stared down the barrel of a Browning AB3 rifle.

Throwing herself at the mercy of the young family had been a life-or-death decision, a last-ditch attempt to stay alive. However, it wasn't working out as she'd hoped. Aiden was in the backyard, armed with a police pistol—and John had his hunting rifle aimed at her. Sally thought about her disheveled, filthy state and her wild claims. Was it any surprise John doubted her? If she failed to convince John and Eva that Aiden was a serial killer, they would all die today. And it would be Sally's fault because she'd led Aiden here.

There were kids in the house. The Fosters had no qualms about murdering kids. She couldn't be responsible for their deaths. Somehow, she had to convince John and Eva to keep Aiden out of the house until the police arrived.

Sally handed the phone to Eva.

"Please hurry," Eva implored the 911 operator. "I have kids upstairs. We don't know what to do." She listened for a moment, then ended the call. "They said twenty minutes."

"Shit!" said John. "Get the Glock from the gun safe."

John kept the rifle pointed at Sally while Eva ducked into a room, returning a few seconds later with a Glock and a box of ammunition.

"I don't know if I can use it," she said.

"Please, John, Eva, you're in terrible danger," Sally pleaded. "He'll tell you he's a cop. He'll tell you to hand me over. He's a killer. He kidnapped and murdered six girls."

"Who?" John asked.

"Aiden Foster."

"You've got to be kidding!" John said. "He's a good man. We know him, and his father."

This was going to be an uphill struggle and any moment now Aiden would find a way into the house and kill them all.

"I know it sounds crazy. But Aiden and Richard abducted and murdered six girls and attempted to murder my son."

"Shut up!" John yelled.

A little boy and girl crept down the stairs. The boy was about three and the girl must have been close to seven or eight.

"Mommy?" said the girl, peeking through the banisters. "Why is Daddy cross?"

"It's okay, sweetie—Daddy isn't cross with you," Eva soothed.

"Maddie, Ben, please go upstairs with Mommy and lock yourselves in a bedroom."

Ben began to cry.

Eva put the pistol into her jeans' waistband and the box of ammunition in her pocket. "It's a game, okay? You like games. We're going to hide until the nice police come to our house."

Eva picked up her tearful son and took Maddie's hand and they climbed the stairs. A bedroom door clicked shut.

"On the floor," John ordered Sally.

Sally knew what the rifle was capable of—Scott had owned a Browning. When he'd left for Chicago, he'd taken it with him. Over such a short distance, the rifle would blow her to pieces. She sat cross-legged on the floor.

"I was a cop. I know how to use a gun. Give me a weapon."

Footsteps outside. A fist hammered the back door.

"Hello!" Aiden shouted from the backyard. "John? Eva? This is Aiden Foster. If Sally Fairburn is in there with you, send her out. She's wanted for murder."

Sally shook her head. "Don't. Just wait until the cops arrive. I'll sit right here, okay? I'm no threat."

"I say again, I'm Aiden Foster, Franklin PD. Sally Fairburn is wanted for murder. Open the door and hand her over."

John looked at Sally as if he were trying to make up his mind what to do. "He's my neighbor. I know his father. They're good people."

"I thought so too. I was wrong. They're serial killers. You must know about the six missing girls? Four are dead. Two are held captive. You have to help them."

Footsteps clomped on the crazy paving outside. Aiden was moving around the house.

"Don't let him in," Sally begged. "Please. Just wait twenty minutes. I won't move an inch."

The sliding doors rattled—Aiden was testing the lock.

John glanced behind him at the front door, then backed away from Sally, still keeping her in his sights, until he reached the door. He quickly turned the deadbolt and Sally sighed with relief—at least he was listening to her.

"I want you to call Detective Clarke. He'll vouch for me. I can give you the number," Sally said.

Both Sally and John heard the rumble of a vehicle approaching. It was moving at high speed and screeched to a halt outside. John was near the front door. He peered through the hall window.

"Richard," John said. He sounded relieved.

Fear flooded though her. "Please, I beg you, don't open the door. Richard can't be trusted. He had me imprisoned in his house. They were digging my grave. Just don't let him in!"

"John!" he called. "It's Richard Foster. Your family's in danger. I'm here to help." He sounded so earnest.

"No!" yelled Sally. "He's a liar. Just call this number." She recited Clarke's cell number. "He's the lead detective on the Poster Killer case. Do it!"

John's left hand lowered to his back jeans' pocket—Sally watched with bated breath, willing him to pull out his phone and make the call.

The stamp of boots on the porch floor caused John to stall. Foster's face appeared at the window.

"John," he said, smiling. "You know me. Let me in."

They stared at each other through the glass and Sally instinctively knew how this would go—the time for persuasion was over. Sally was a sitting duck. She scrambled to get up, just as John unlocked the dead bolt and pulled the door toward him. Foster kicked it in and the door smashed into John's face. He staggered back, clutching his bleeding nose and moaning, his rifle at his side.

Sally ran up the stairs, two steps at a time.

Boom!

Sally didn't look back. She knew that Foster had shot John and there was nothing Sally could do to help the poor man.

Boom! A second shot rang out.

On the upstairs landing, there were four doors. Two were open—the master bedroom and the little girl's bedroom. A sign on one of the door's said BEN'S ROOM. The other must be the bathroom.

Sally tried that door.

"Eva, let me in!" she whispered.

"I'll shoot!" Eva shouted.

Sally was banking on Eva being unable to use the gun. "Please, Eva, Richard killed your husband. He's coming for you. Let me in. I can protect you."

Eva was sobbing through the door. "No, no, no. You're lying."

"Sa-lly!" Foster called up the staircase. "I can hear you. Come down here and nobody else has to die."

Eva unlocked the door and peeked through the narrow gap. Sally saw the barrel of the Glock was aimed at her but Eva's hand was shaking so much it was like a nodding donkey.

Sally said, "I know what I'm doing. Let me protect you."

Eva's face was wet with tears. "You killed him!"

Behind her, both kids sat on the bathroom floor crying.

Before Sally could answer, Foster shouted up the stairs again. "Sally! You want me to send Aiden up there? You know how much he likes little girls!"

Eva's eyes were round like saucers—she had heard his taunt. She let Sally inside, then locked the bathroom door again. The lock was a sliding bolt. It wouldn't hold if Aiden gave the door a good shove with his shoulder.

"Eva, I want you and the kids to play a game. Get in the bath, all of you." Hanging from the bath faucet was a small net bag which held a variety of bath toys including a plastic yellow duck, an orange starfish and a submarine.

Eva stared at her. "Why?"

"It's the safest place," Sally urged. "Give me the Glock and the ammo."

"Last chance!" Aiden called up the stairs. He was inside the house with his father now. "Ready or not, here I come!" he taunted.

Eva handed over the gun and the bullets, then got in the bath with the kids, holding them close.

"There's no water, Mommy," said Maddie.

As Sally loaded the Glock, she said, "To win the game you have to stay quiet. No talking, okay?"

The little boy began to cry again. "I don't want to play."

"Hush," Eva whispered. "You have to be quiet, okay? Promise Mommy." She kissed her son on the head.

The little boy sniffed back a tear, then whispered "Promise."

There were murmured voices, then a creak as someone— likely Aiden—started to climb the stairs. His father would stay downstairs and keep an eye out for a patrol car.

Sally checked her wrist for the time, forgetting that she had thrown her watch onto the cemetery road. She placed her back to the solid brick bathroom wall and said to Eva, "Lie down, as low as you can go, and no talking."

Another creak—louder and closer than the last. Sally's finger rested on the trigger. Her palms were slick with sweat, and she was afraid she might fire mistakenly if her finger slipped.

There was a thud as a door slammed into a wall—the shock of it travelled through the wall to Sally's spine. Aiden must have thrown open the closed door to the boy's bedroom. It would take him only a few seconds to be sure there was nobody hiding there. He would then try the door handle to the bathroom. In Sally's three-year career as a police officer she had shot and killed just one person and it had been a long time ago. She hoped her reaction time wouldn't be too slow. Aiden was only a few months out of the academy—he would have spent hours at the shooting range.

You can do this, she thought. *You have to.*

Aiden would probably break down the door and come in, firing in rapid succession. She would have to take a kill shot before he saw Eva and the kids in the bath. The bathroom was a simple layout: a bath with a showerhead on the wall, basin, toilet, and a bathroom cabinet with a mirror on it. Sally was positioned so that when the door flew open she'd be behind it.

The round door handle turned slowly. Sally's heart was in her mouth.

The door shook a fraction: Aiden now knew it was bolted.

There was a thud and a crack as he tried to ram the door open. The wood around the bolt's screws splintered but stayed in the door.

Sally touched the trigger lightly, her arms out ahead of her. She took a deep breath and held it.

Crack! Wham! The bolt was ripped from the door.

The door swung at Sally but stopped at the doorstop on the floor. Aiden began firing.

The mirror shattered. A bullet hit the bath with a *ding*. The kids screamed. Aiden knew where they were.

Sally banked on his taking a step forward. She fired at the door, over and over. There was a cry from the other side, and Aiden collapsed forward. His head connected with the edge of the bath, then he landed hard on the bathroom floor, face down.

Sally trained the gun on Aiden. He didn't move. A pool of blood began to appear around him. Her bullets had hit their mark, and if they hadn't killed him, the bang to the head would have.

Above the sound of the kids sobbing, Sally heard police sirens wailing.

"Aiden!" Foster called. "Is it done?"

Eva stared up at Sally from the bath, tears streaming down her face. Sally signaled for her to stay quiet, then stepped over Aiden's body and crept from the bathroom. Foster was standing at the bottom of the stairs, a gun in his hand.

"Son?" he called.

Sally stood at the top of the staircase and aimed the Glock at Foster's chest. "Drop your gun and hands up!" she shouted.

His face morphed from shock to fury in a couple of seconds, then he raised his gun. "Go to hell!"

He was too slow—Sally fired twice at the center of his chest and Richard dropped like a felled tree.

FIFTY-NINE

THREE MONTHS LATER

Sally's name was called. She stood, taking care not to catch her floor-length evening dress beneath her high heels. The seven guests at her table clapped exuberantly. To her right, Paul looked at her and smiled. He looked very handsome in his dinner jacket and black bow tie, even though he had vehemently argued that he looked a total goose in it.

"Proud of you, Mom."

It was hard to believe that she'd almost lost her son forever. If it hadn't been for Detective Lin realizing the danger Paul was in, he might have suffocated to death in the airless panic room.

To Sally's left, Mary Moorehouse reached out a hand and squeezed hers. Mary's hair had been cut and styled especially for the occasion.

Next to Mary sat Anna in a simple black dress. She kept her head down and had only spoken to Sally and her mom all night. It was testimony to Anna's bravery that she was there at all. Arriving at the event with Sally and her mom, Anna had drawn just as much attention as Sally. She had clung to Mary's left arm and to Sally's right, flinching at the crowds and camera flashes. It was Margie who had asked everyone to keep a respectful distance.

"God bless you, Sally," Mary said.

Mary had come a long way since she'd received the news her daughter was alive and coming home. She had mostly overcome her agoraphobia and spent her days doing what she could to help Anna heal.

Sally's mom and dad smiled at her proudly. It was good to have them back in her life. Seated next to her dad was Sophie Blake, who clapped enthusiastically, and, completing the circle, her dear friend, Margie Clay, cheered.

Sally turned to face the stage and wove her way between the tables of guests. She stepped onto the stage, blinking into the bright lights, thankful that she was the last of the six recipients of the Mayor's Citizen Award for Valor and Service. It had given her time to calm her nerves and go over in her head the few words she wanted to say.

Mayor Xavier McAllister quieted the enthusiastic crowd. The applause died away and all Sally could hear was the clink of dessert spoons on plates and the murmurs of hushed conversations.

McAllister gestured for her to stand closer. She felt awkward in the V-neck, chiffon dress in ink blue that Margie had insisted she buy for the occasion. With sequins down the bodice and lace along the arms, it was the most flamboyant dress she'd worn since prom night. Perhaps it was a sign that she had found her true self again and her confidence was returning?

The mayor spoke into the microphone.

"Sally Fairburn, a former officer with Franklin PD and victim support advocate, survived a terrifying ordeal at the hands of the Poster Killer duo we now know to be Richard and Aiden Foster. Against all odds, she ended their reign of terror. She rescued Tazeen Ibrahim and Anna Moorehouse, and saved the lives of Eva, Maddie, and Ben Quinn."

He turned and spoke to her directly. "Sally, I am honored to award you the Citizen Award for Valor and Service."

From a leather box he took a medal that hung from a red, white, and blue ribbon. He placed it around her neck and congratulated her.

"Thank you, Sally, for your bravery."

He stepped aside so that Sally could use the microphone.

"I am deeply honored," Sally said. "Although I fear I don't deserve it. I accept this medal on behalf of John Quinn, who died defending his family. I would like to pay my respects to Bryan Topham, who died trying to track down his granddaughter's killers, and I'd like us all to remember the victims who did not survive. Can I ask for a minute's silence to remember Stacy Green, Caroline Blake, Vinesh Kapoor, and Francesca Molinari."

Sally bowed her head and the noise in the ballroom faded. She watched the seconds hand on her watch move around the watch face. When a minute had passed, she raised her head and simply said, "Thank you."

The ballroom resounded with applause. Cameras flashed as Sally paused for photos with the mayor, then she returned to her seat, relieved to be back with the people she loved.

"Can I see it?" Paul said.

She held out the gold, cross-shaped medal so that he could take a closer look.

Margie gave her a hug. "Congratulations."

A reporter asked for an interview. Sally politely declined. Guests came up to her and thanked her for ridding Franklin of two serial killers. Anna stood and gave Sally a hug.

"Thank you," Anna whispered.

By the time Sally and Paul headed for the hotel foyer to catch a cab home, it was almost 10:30 p.m. Margie had left earlier to drive Mary and Anna home. Seated on a leather sofa next to an arch-shaped foyer window was Detective Clarke, looking neat and groomed despite his long day. He rose from the sofa and strode over to her.

"Congratulations!" Clarke smiled.

He nodded at Paul who nodded back—their relationship was still a frosty one.

"Thank you," Sally said. "I'm sorry about the fallout from all this. I know you worked extremely hard on the case."

"Not your problem. Cops don't like to believe that one of their own's gone bad. Let alone two of them. They had us well and truly fooled."

Sally was acutely aware that the publicity about her solving the case had made Clarke, and the homicide team, look bad. But the Fosters had covered their tracks meticulously. The police commissioner had been forced to resign over allegations of corruption and there was a witch hunt going on for other corrupt officers. Sally hoped that the hunt would extend as far as Chicago. Was Scott the reason why Clarke was here now?

"You're working late. Is something up?" she asked.

"Can we sit?" Clarke said.

"Sure."

She and Paul followed him to the leather sofa and sat.

Clarke took the armchair opposite and clasped his hands together.

"I thought you'd like to know that we found the last body this afternoon. Vinesh Kapoor. Hers was much deeper in the woods."

"At least her parents can mourn her now. Do they know?"

"Yes, I saw them this afternoon."

"And do you know who put up the posters of me, Tiffany, Bryan, and Paul?"

"I was partly right about a copycat. The posters of you and Bryan were created by Bryan. I think the first one was to scare you into co-operating with him, and the one of himself was to distract us from your abduction. He wanted us to think he was in danger."

"So Richard put up the posters of Tiffany and Paul?"

"That's right."

"Why?"

"I guess we'll never know. Perhaps he got a thrill out of taunting us?"

He paused.

"There's something else, isn't there?" she asked.

Clarke cleared his voice. "As you know, we've been investigating your allegation that Scott Fairburn sexually assaulted Stacy Green. However, our search for the girl's diary has proved fruitless."

A sense of foreboding rippled up her spine like a cold wave. "Bryan had it with him at the derelict school. I saw it in his hand. I told you, it must be hidden at the school."

She sounded irritated and she hadn't meant to.

"We know Aiden killed him there,' Clarke said. "He was careless and left DNA behind on Bryan's body. We've searched every nook of the school. No diary."

Sally sighed. "It's being demolished next week. Can't you delay the demolition?"

"There's no point. It's not there, Sally. We've done a thorough search."

"Is this heading where I think it's heading?"

A knot had formed in her gut.

"You should be happy that Richard Foster will go to jail for the rest of his life and Aiden is dead." Knowing Aiden was a serial killer didn't make it any easier to live with the fact she had taken a life. Richard was lucky to have survived the bullet wound. Prison would be hell for an ex-detective, but Sally suspected that losing his son was the greater punishment.

Clarke continued, "We have no evidence to prove Scott assaulted Stacy. We're closing the case. I'm sorry."

Sally looked out of the hotel's wall-to-ceiling window, beyond the busy street and the high-rise buildings, and up at the moon. Scott was going to get away with it.

"This can't be happening." Sally could feel her anger rising. She turned her eyes to the detective. "Walt Jackson must have known what Scott was doing to Stacy."

"He claims he knows nothing about it."

"What about the YMCA?" Paul said, pulling his bow tie loose. "Someone must have noticed Dad doing creepy things."

"Anna didn't see Scott do anything wrong. Tazeen is traumatized and hasn't spoken a word since her rescue. The other girls who attended the teens club only have good things to say about him."

Paul undid the top button of his dress shirt. "But the fake suicide note? Walt told Mom that Scott wrote it."

"Walt denies everything. Anyway, a fake suicide note doesn't prove that Scott's a rapist. And Nikki stands by her original statement that Zelda *was* bullied by Caroline."

Sally ground her teeth. The Jacksons had circled their wagons.

"You can't let Scott get away with it. He'll do it again."

Clarke stood wearily. "Sally, I have no proof."

"Then I'll get you proof," she said.

Clarke stared at her for a long moment. "I urge you both to move on. Forget about Scott. Good night."

They watched Clarke leave the hotel and disappear into the night.

"You mean it?" Paul asked. "You'll keep searching?"

"Oh yeah. I won't let Scott get away with it."

A LETTER FROM L.A. LARKIN

Thank you so much for reading *Next Girl Missing* and I really hope you enjoyed it. If you did, and you would like to keep up to date with my latest releases, please sign up at the following link. Your email address will never be shared, and you can unsubscribe at any time.

www.bookouture.com/l-a-larkin

Next Girl Missing is the first in a new series featuring Sally Fairburn, ex-cop and former victim support advocate, who becomes a private investigator when she's grieving for the loss of her daughter and trying to move past a toxic marriage in which she was gaslighted.

I had heard the term "gaslighting" before, but I knew little about it. Then one day an acquaintance revealed to me that her sister, who we will call Mrs. A, was being gaslighted by her husband and how devastated she and her family were. The husband had poisoned Mrs. A's view of reality, making her doubt herself and totally dependent on him. He turned her against family and friends in an attempt to isolate her from people who might help her. The sister told me how charming and loving the man appears in public and how manipulative he is in private. I began reading books on gaslighting, including *The Covert Passive-Aggressive Narcissist* by Debbie Mirza and *The Gaslight Effect* by Dr. Robin Stern. I thought about this for a while and then decided to create a PI series in which the main character not only solves crimes but must also go on a personal journey to find her true self again after being gaslighted by her husband. She will grow stronger and more confident throughout the series as she emerges from the fog of her gaslighting experience.

This novel is set in the imaginary town of Franklin, although it is loosely located in Washington state. It was great fun creating a totally new world for my series in which Sally will tackle new cases and new dangers.

Authors love book reviews, and if you can spare a moment to do a review, I would be so grateful. And please stay in touch with me via my social media. Thank you so much for your support!

Until next time,

L.A. Larkin

www.lalarkin.com

facebook.com/LALarkinAuthor

twitter.com/lalarkinauthor

instagram.com/la_larkin_author

ACKNOWLEDGMENTS

I want to thank you so very much for reading this book. I love receiving your comments and reading your reviews, and I am so grateful for your support. Book bloggers—thank you! You are the backbone of the book publishing industry and I'm so grateful to you all for giving *Next Girl Missing* such lovely feedback. I am so looking forward to taking you on an exciting journey in books two and three and beyond, following the trials and tribulations, the successes and setbacks, of an ordinary woman who wants to do good.

My publisher, Helen Jenner, is my guiding light, and her structural edit is always so insightful and encouraging. Thank you, Helen, for helping me to make this book really zing!

I also want to thank the wonderful editors, designers, proofreaders, and publicity experts at Bookouture, including Laura Kincaid, Dushi Horti, Kelsie Marsden, Noelle Holten, Kim Nash, Peta Nightingale, Melanie Price, and Alexandra Holmes. My literary agent, Phil Patterson, is a true friend, and he has guided me so superbly throughout my writing career. Even in the midst of the pandemic, when Phil was in isolation at home with Covid, he insisted we had a scheduled Zoom meeting to discuss next steps. He truly is dedicated to his authors, and I feel very privileged to be among them.

My beta readers, David Gaylor, Su Biela, Anna Wallace—thank you so much. Your feedback is invaluable, and I'd be lost without you!

I have dedicated this book to my beloved Golden Retriever,

Pickles, who passed away recently. I miss his companionship and love. Writing is a solitary occupation, but I never felt alone because he was always at my side.

My biggest thanks of all goes to my husband, Michael. Thank you for your patience and for understanding why I become a hermit when a deadline approaches. Love you lots!

Printed in Great Britain
by Amazon